I0763595

Draft Knight

Copyright

Written by: Willie S.

Before you read, you should know:

This book contains instances that mention and may or may not speak about cigarettes and/or smoking. The following is included as a warning to prevent smoking cigarettes and to warn against smoking.

SURGEON GENERAL'S WARNINGS:

Smoking Causes Lung Cancer, Heart Disease, Emphysema, and May Complicate Pregnancy.

Smoking By Pregnant Women May Result in Fetal Injury, Premature Birth, and Low Birth Weight.

The World Health Organization states:

Nicotine contained in tobacco is highly addictive and tobacco use is a major risk factor for cardiovascular and respiratory diseases, over 20 different types or subtypes of cancer, and many other debilitating health conditions. Every year, more than 8 million people die from tobacco use.

Dedication

To the unsung heroes of investigative journalism, those who tirelessly pursue truth in the face of danger, and to the memory of those who paid the ultimate price in their quest for justice. This book is a testament to your courage, resilience, and unwavering commitment to exposing the darkness that lurks beneath the surface of our world. Your dedication inspires us all to fight for a better tomorrow, even when the odds seem insurmountable. Your stories, though often untold, remain etched in the annals of history, a reminder of the power of truth and the enduring human spirit. This work is dedicated to you, the silent guardians of truth, who often work in the shadows, sacrificing personal safety and comfort to shine a light on the hidden evils within our society. Your bravery is not lost on us. You are the real-life counterparts to the characters within these pages; you are the ones who make the world a slightly less dangerous place, one thoroughly researched story at a time. This is for you, for your sacrifices, and for the continued fight against injustice, wherever it may hide. May this narrative serve as a small tribute to your tireless efforts and a reminder that even in the darkest corners, there is always hope for light.

Preface

The world of organized crime is a shadowy realm, shrouded in secrecy and deception. Its tendrils extend far beyond the headlines, reaching the highest echelons of power and influence. For years, I've navigated the treacherous waters of investigative journalism, uncovering the hidden truths behind carefully constructed facades. My experiences have provided me with a unique perspective on the intricate workings of these criminal enterprises, the ruthless efficiency of their operatives, and the devastating impact they have on innocent lives. This book delves into the heart of that darkness, presenting a fictional narrative inspired by real-world events and individuals. While the characters and specific scenarios are creations of imagination, the underlying themes of power, betrayal, and the relentless pursuit of justice are deeply rooted in the realities of organized crime. It is a world where morality is fluid, loyalty is a commodity, and survival often depends on the ability to anticipate and outmaneuver your adversaries. Through meticulous research and years spent immersed in the study of criminal behavior, I have sought to craft a story that is both compelling and authentic, offering a glimpse into a world rarely seen. This fictional narrative aims to showcase the lengths some will go to seize control and the complexities facing those who seek to fight back. The hope is to bring a unique perspective and entertainment value to this world, all while highlighting the real dangers and the dedication of those who oppose such criminal activities. Let this serve as a reminder that even in fiction, the fight for justice continues.

Introduction

This story unfolds through the intertwined perspectives of two men: Jake Harroll, a seasoned radio reporter grappling with the moral ambiguities of his profession, and Jason Reen, a ghost in the machine, a master assassin operating in the shadows. Their paths converge during a seemingly ordinary interview, a meeting that will irrevocably alter the course of their lives. Jason’s account of his thoroughly planned mission – eliminating Gomin Guill, the head of a vast criminal empire – is both chilling and captivating. It's a testament to his skill, his cold efficiency, and his unwavering commitment to the task. However, Jason's success is only the beginning. His actions unearth a conspiracy far greater than anyone could have imagined, a web of deceit and betrayal that reaches into the highest echelons of power. The narrative moves swiftly, shifting between Jason's first-person recollections of his globe-trotting pursuit and Jake's third-person perspective, providing a layered and suspenseful account. As the story progresses, the line between protagonist and antagonist blurs, forcing the reader to question their own assumptions about morality and justice. Jake, initially an observer, finds himself drawn into the vortex of this deadly game, compelled to uncover the truth and confront the powerful forces arrayed against him. The reader is invited to engage in a thrilling chase, experiencing the intricate details of assassination techniques, the tension of near misses, and the chilling realization that the world of organized crime is more intricate and pervasive than one might expect. This is not merely a tale of a lone assassin; it is a story about the seductive power of control, the devastating consequences of unchecked ambition, and the enduring human struggle for truth and justice in a world where the lines between right and wrong are constantly blurred. Prepare to be drawn into a world of shadows, where the price of truth is measured in lives, and the fight for justice is a relentless, dangerous game.

Table of Contents

First Encounter

Jake Harroll sat at a cold, chipped table in a nearly empty café, nervously tapping his fingers as rain hammered the windows. The city outside blared with sirens and horns—a fitting backdrop for what might be the biggest interview of his career. Three minutes remained until Jason Reen, the mysterious figure rumored to have dismantled Gomin Guill's criminal empire, was due to arrive.

Jake's notebook was filled with months of research and questions, but self-doubt lingered. The evidence pointed to Reen as the cause of Guill's disappearance, though the idea of a lone assassin seemed far-fetched. The café, chosen at Reen's cryptic request, was a place for secrets, and Jake felt the weight of danger in the air.

He had interviewed many criminals before, but this meeting felt different—tense, almost unreal. Reen was legendary, his identity buried in speculation and rumor, with nothing concrete except the burner phone and the instructions for this obscure rendezvous.

At 7:58 PM, the door chimed. A tall, lean figure entered, his presence instantly altering the atmosphere. Jake felt raw fear as Reen approached, every movement radiating quiet menace. Reen addressed Jake by name, then sat opposite him, his calm exterior belying a sense of coiled potential. Jake realized he might be uncovering not just answers, but new dangers. The interview had begun, and the stakes were higher than he'd ever imagined.

....

The café door chimed, slicing through the quiet. Jake's heart pounded—no amount of preparation could have steeled him for the reality of Jason Reen's arrival. Unlike the fearsome assassin Jake expected, Reen's presence was quiet but commanding, shifting the very atmosphere. He moved with a controlled, effortless confidence, his features shadowed and weary beneath a wide-brimmed hat. He seemed to carry the weight of dark experience, more ghost than man, making Jake's anxiety spike.

Without a word, Reen took a seat opposite Jake. His stillness was unsettling, his hands calmly folded, radiating a sense of restrained power. Jake nervously greeted him, acutely aware of the danger before him.

Reen's eyes finally met Jake's, intense and unreadable. "I understand you have questions," he said, his tone even and detached. Jake pressed on, asking about Gomin Guill, the infamous crime lord. At the name, a faint, fleeting smile crossed Reen's lips before he responded. "A man who thought he was untouchable. He was wrong."

Jason described Guill as a master manipulator, his criminal empire built on fear, deception, and a web of loyal accomplices. He explained how he dismantled Guill's organization piece by piece, exploiting weaknesses, turning allies into informants, and staying always a step ahead in the shadows.

He recounted his methods with clinical precision—surveillance, infiltration, and carefully orchestrated operations. There was no bravado, just the cold, hard facts of a relentless pursuit for justice, or something resembling it.

As rain pounded the windows, Jake scribbled notes, realizing he was hearing more than just tales of Guill's downfall. The interview was pulling him into a deeper, darker conspiracy—one that threatened to engulf him, too.

....

"Gomin Guill," Jason began, his voice a low murmur that barely carried above the café's hushed ambience. He leaned forward, his gaze intense, unwavering. "He wasn't just a kingpin. He was the architect. The puppet master. Everything he touched, everything he controlled, was shrouded in an almost supernatural level of secrecy."

He paused, taking a slow sip of his lukewarm coffee, the silence stretching between them, thick and heavy. Jake watched him, his notepad resting forgotten on the table, completely captivated by the chilling narrative unfolding before him. The rain outside had subsided, but the city still seemed to hum with a restless wave of energy, a reflection of the storm brewing within Jason's words.

"His empire wasn't built on bricks and mortar," Jason continued, "but on connections, on whispers, on the insidious power of fear. He operated through layers upon layers of intermediaries, each one knowing only their small part in the grand scheme. Think of it like an onion, Jake – peel back one layer, and you find another, and another, each more treacherous than the last. Getting to the heart, to Guill himself, was like navigating a labyrinth in perpetual twilight."

Jason described Guill’s empire with chilling precision. He spoke of vast offshore accounts, thoroughly laundered through a complex web of shell corporations and dummy companies spread across continents. He detailed the intricate network of informants, spies, and enforcers who ensured Guill's continued reign of terror. These weren't just street thugs; these were professionals, often former military or intelligence operatives, each a specialist in their own field – from cyber warfare and data manipulation to sophisticated assassination techniques and the brutal enforcement of Guill's will.

He spoke of Guill's lavish lifestyle – private jets, yachts the size of small cruise ships, villas in exotic locations that would make even the most powerful heads of state envious. Yet, despite this extravagant display of wealth, Jason insisted that Guill remained elusive, a ghost who rarely showed his face in public. His appearances were thoroughly orchestrated, fleeting moments captured on grainy security footage or whispered about in hushed tones within the underworld.

"He lived in the shadows," Jason said, his voice hardening. "He preferred to pull the strings from afar, letting his puppets dance to his tune. He was a master manipulator, a puppeteer who controlled lives with the flick of a wrist. He didn't get his hands dirty; he employed others to do the dirty work, those who were expendable, the ones he could sacrifice without a second thought."

Jake scribbled furiously, trying to keep up with the flood of information. The enormity of Guill's empire, the sheer scale of his operation, was staggering. This wasn't just organized crime; this was a sophisticated, globally networked organization with tendrils reaching into every dark corner of the world.

Jason described the meticulous planning that went into his mission. Months of surveillance, painstakingly piecing together Guill's routines, his movements, his weaknesses. He spoke of infiltrating inner circles, gaining the trust of Guill's closest associates, using cunning deception and manipulation to gather intelligence, weaving his way through a treacherous web of betrayals and double-crosses.

He spoke of his informants, a shadowy network of contacts spread across the globe – former police officers, disgruntled employees, disgruntled ex-lovers, hackers, and even corrupt government officials, each providing a piece of the puzzle. He'd assembled them not through brute force or intimidation but through a delicate blend of trust, blackmail, and carefully placed favors. It was a delicate dance, a high-stakes game of trust and betrayal, where one wrong move could cost him everything.

"Guill was a fortress," Jason explained, his voice laced with grim satisfaction. "But fortresses have weak points. My job was to find them, exploit them, and strike with precision."

Jason detailed the various targets he eliminated along the way – lesser figures in Guill's organization, individuals who posed a threat to his operation or held vital pieces of information. He described these hits not with relish, but with the detached efficiency of a surgeon performing a complex operation. Each kill was a precise, calculated move, leaving no trace, no witnesses. He spoke of his techniques, his tools – his preferred method being silent and utterly undetectable, a preference that spoke volumes about his commitment to staying unseen.

He described the elaborate precautions he had taken, the layers of security he employed to ensure his own anonymity. He spoke of fake identities, burner phones, encrypted communications, and secure locations, all thoroughly planned and executed with chilling precision. He was a master of disguise, a chameleon who could blend into any environment, appearing and disappearing without a trace, a ghost in the machine.

"It wasn't about the thrill of the kill," Jason clarified, seemingly reading Jake's unspoken thoughts. "It was about the objective. About dismantling the organization, piece by piece. About taking down Guill and crippling his empire." He paused, his eyes distant, lost in the memory of his mission. "It was a war, Jake, a war fought in the shadows, a war without rules or mercy. And I was the only soldier on the battlefield."

He described the final confrontation with Guill, a chilling account of a carefully orchestrated encounter in a remote, secluded location – a high-stakes game of cat and mouse played out against a backdrop of breathtaking landscapes and deadly silence. He revealed details of Guill's last moments, a swift, decisive strike, a silent execution that left no witnesses, no trace, only a chilling confirmation of his success.

As Jason spoke, Jake's apprehension grew. The details were thoroughly chilling, showing not just a master assassin but a strategist of terrifying competence. The level of planning, the flawless execution, the almost supernatural ability to remain unseen – it was all breathtaking in its horrifying efficiency. And yet, there was something else, a subtle undercurrent of something deeper than mere professionalism; a burning sense of justice, however dark and twisted, that fueled his actions.

The interview continued late into the night, the café emptying around them, leaving them alone in the soft glow of the lamps. The rain had long since stopped, but a damp chill clung to the air, mirroring the growing unease in

Jake's heart. As dawn approached, painting the sky with the pale hues of a new day, Jason finished his account of Gomin Guill's downfall. But the silence that followed wasn't the silence of closure; it was the heavy silence of a secret still yet to be fully uncovered. The seeds of a larger conspiracy, a far more terrifying network than he could have ever imagined, had been sown, and Jake knew, with a growing sense of dread, that his involvement in this dangerous game had only just begun. He had a story, but it was far from over. The true scope of Guill's organization, the identity of those who pulled the strings behind him, remained a mystery, a dangerous secret that threatened to draw him into the very heart of darkness he had just glimpsed. And with the rising sun, a new and far more perilous chapter was about to begin.

....

The pale morning light filtered through the café window, illuminating dust motes dancing in the air. Jason, his face etched with the fatigue of a long night's confession, took a slow sip of his lukewarm coffee. The intensity in his eyes, however, hadn't dimmed. He seemed to have stepped away from the harrowing narrative, and now looked at Jake with a detached, almost clinical focus. "Before I go into the actual takedown," he said, his voice quieter than before, a gravelly whisper, "let me explain the meticulous preparation that went into it. It wasn't just a matter of showing up and shooting. It was a symphony of planning, an intricate dance of meticulous detail."

Jake, still reeling from the revelations of the previous night, leaned forward, his notepad ready. He'd spent years chasing stories, interviewing sources, but nothing had prepared him for the sheer precision and cold efficiency that Jason described. This wasn't the impulsive, reckless act of a hired gun; it was the calculated operation of a master strategist.

Jason began by explaining his initial intelligence gathering. "Gomin Guill," he stated, "was a fortress surrounded by a moat of loyalists and spies. Getting close required more than brute force; it required intelligence, patience, and a thorough understanding of his operations. I started with open sources, sifting through news articles, financial records, anything that could offer a glimpse into his world." He paused, a subtle flicker of a smile playing on his lips, a stark contrast to the gravity of the subject matter. “Believe me, the internet is a treasure trove of information, if you know where to look.”

He detailed his methods, describing how he thoroughly analyzed social media posts, online forums, and even seemingly innocuous online shopping records to identify patterns and potential weaknesses in Guill’s security. He spoke of utilizing advanced search engines and data mining techniques, not merely for superficial information, but to uncover subtle connections and hidden relationships. The painstaking detail he presented was both captivating and chilling. It was a demonstration of the power of information in the digital age, a power Jason wielded with chilling expertise.

“Then there’s the human element,” Jason continued, his voice dropping to a near-inaudible murmur. "Guill surrounded himself with a network of informants, bodyguards, and loyalists. Penetrating that circle was crucial. I built relationships, cultivated trust, using both my own network and my considerable skills of observation. I spent months identifying potential weaknesses within his inner circle, individuals susceptible to coercion, bribery, or simply a change of allegiance. It wasn't about force, but about understanding the human psyche, and exploiting vulnerabilities."

He then moved onto his equipment. It wasn't just a matter of picking up the nearest weapon. He explained his selection process with an engineer's precision, describing different firearm models and their respective advantages and disadvantages based on specific scenarios and operational requirements. He detailed the intricacies of each piece of equipment: the custom-made silencers, the specialized optics, the high-tech communication systems, and the elaborate counter-surveillance measures. He spoke of researching ballistics, learning the subtle nuances of trajectories, and even the environmental factors that could affect the effectiveness of his weaponry. He demonstrated an intimate knowledge of each piece of his arsenal, explaining how he modified and maintained them with obsessive attention to detail.

"And the escape routes," he added, a hint of a grim satisfaction in his tone. "Those were just as thoroughly planned as the attack. Every possible contingency, every conceivable scenario had to be considered. I had several escape routes mapped out, each with alternative escape routes planned for each scenario. Failure wasn't an option."

He described how he spent weeks studying maps, satellite imagery, and traffic patterns, identifying blind spots and escape routes. He even considered weather patterns, using meteorological data to predict potential obstacles.

“Logistics were vital,” Jason continued, his gaze unwavering. “The timing, the location, even the weather. Everything had to be perfect. I didn't just pick a random day or a random location. I thoroughly analyzed Guill’s schedule, his patterns, his routines. I studied his habits, his preferences, even his personal quirks. The target’s security detail and routine were broken down into a complex matrix of potential variables, analyzed and accounted for. It wasn’t just about eliminating Gomin Guill, it was about doing it without leaving a single trace. It was about making it look like an accident, a natural cause of death, and leaving no way of tracking me.”

He thoroughly described his use of burner phones, encrypted communication channels, and the techniques he employed to disguise his identity and movements. He highlighted his mastery of blending into crowds, losing tails, and leaving no digital footprint. He thoroughly described the use of various disguises, the alteration of his appearance, and the techniques used to create false identities. He explained his use of secure messaging apps, encrypted email accounts, and the methods he employed to maintain anonymity online. His knowledge of the underground networks was extensive, a testament to years of immersion in the shadows. He highlighted his ability to utilize both open-source and clandestine intelligence channels, showing a familiarity with data mining, network analysis, and sophisticated surveillance techniques.

Jake found himself mesmerized, his pen scratching furiously across his notepad. It was a masterclass in operational efficiency, a chilling testament to Jason's skill and dedication. The level of detail, the obsessive planning, the absolute focus on precision – it was something out of a spy novel, yet here it was, unflinchingly recounted by the man who had executed it. It was more than just taking a life; it was a carefully crafted work of art, a thoroughly planned and executed masterpiece of lethal choreography.

He paused, his eyes locked on Jake's. "The preparations," he said softly, "were as important, if not more important, than the act itself. It wasn't about the guns or the gadgets, but about the forethought, the meticulous attention to detail, the anticipation of every possibility." He took another sip of his coffee, his gaze distant, lost in the memory of those long weeks of preparation. "It was a game of chess, Jake. And I had to anticipate every move my opponent would make, before he even knew what game we were playing."

The unspoken weight of that statement hung heavy in the air. It wasn't just about eliminating Gomin Guill. It was about outsmarting him, anticipating his every move, and staying one step ahead. It was about control, precision, and an absolute mastery of the game. And as Jason's detailed narrative wound down, Jake realized he was now entangled in a game far more intricate and dangerous than he had ever imagined, a game where the stakes were incredibly high, and his own life might well be the ultimate price to pay. The sun had fully risen now, casting long shadows across the café. The interview was over, but the game had only just begun. The larger conspiracy, the threads weaving through the darkness, were still unraveling, and Jake was, inextricably, part of the story now.

....

Jason, unfazed by his cold coffee, leaned back in his chair, his gaze fixed beyond Jake. "Tracking Gomin wasn’t about luck," he said quietly. "It was a matter of patience, resources, and a global network." He explained that his contacts weren't loyal allies but a mix of informants and disgruntled employees, each motivated by self-interest. Sofia, a fearful accountant in Bucharest, provided key financial details in exchange for safety, using encrypted messages and anonymous payments. Marco in Milan, a former security consultant, verified Sofia’s leads and filled in surveillance gaps, using technology to track Gomin’s movements and expose security weaknesses.

Gomin, always cautious, had one blind spot—his nephew Ricardo, whose gambling debts made him vulnerable. Through intermediaries, Jason convinced Ricardo to share details about Gomin’s upcoming travel in exchange for a fresh start. With this intel, Jason mapped out Gomin’s movements, scrutinized satellite images, and timed his approach perfectly, exploiting a brief lapse in security. He described using silent weapons and specialized tools, emphasizing that precision and leaving no trace were paramount.

As the sun set, Jake realized the gravity of Jason’s story. This was more than an assassination; it was a glimpse into a world of shadows and control, where every move was calculated and survival meant staying ahead in a dangerous game. The conspiracy ran deeper than Jake had imagined, and his involvement was only beginning.

27

A Minor Player

The rain hammered against the corrugated iron roof of the warehouse, a relentless percussion accompanying the frantic rhythm of Jason's heart. He wasn't nervous, not in the conventional sense. He felt a cold, clinical detachment, a professional absorption in the task at hand. This wasn't personal; it was business. Efficient, precise, and utterly devoid of sentiment. His target, a mid-level accountant named Borislav Petrov, was a small cog in Gomin Guill's vast criminal machine, but a cog nonetheless. Eliminating him wouldn't cripple the organization, but it would send a message. A ripple in the still waters, a warning to those who might consider stepping out of line.

Borislav, Jason had learned, was a creature of habit. He adhered to a rigid routine, leaving his small, nondescript apartment in the grimy industrial district of Sofia every morning at precisely 7:15, arriving at his office by 7:45. His lunch break was predictable, a hurried affair at a nearby café, followed by a return to his desk, where he remained until 6 pm sharp. He walked home, a solitary figure lost in the twilight gloom of the city's backstreets. Jason had spent three days observing him, thoroughly charting his movements, noting every detail, every slight deviation from the norm. He'd learned his favorite brand of cigarettes – Sobranie – the type of car he drove – a battered Lada Niva– even the precise number of steps he took from the curb to his apartment door.

The information was the key. Precision was paramount. A sloppy operation risked exposure, jeopardizing the entire mission. Jason favored simplicity, a clean, swift execution, leaving no trace, no witnesses. His tools were chosen with the same meticulous care as his targets. A silenced pistol, modified for pinpoint accuracy, a lightweight, easily concealed weapon. He'd even accounted for the wind speed and direction, ensuring that the trajectory of his bullet would not be affected by gusts of wind.

Tonight, Borislav's routine would be his undoing. Jason had chosen a location close to Petrov's apartment, a dimly lit alleyway, narrow and secluded, perfect for a quick in-and-out operation. He'd already secured a position, perched atop a nearby building, overlooking the alleyway. From here, the Lada's headlights would illuminate Borislav as he walked home, providing the perfect opportunity. The distance, approximately thirty meters, was within his effective range, even with the added challenge of poor lighting. He had practiced this shot a hundred times in his training, honing his skills until his movements were instinctive, fluid, almost graceful.

The air hung heavy with the scent of damp earth and exhaust fumes. The city sounds were muted, muffled by the rain, creating a strange, unsettling silence. Jason checked his watch – 6:02 pm. He adjusted the scope of his rifle, his breath slow and controlled. He focused on the alleyway, his eyes scanning for any sign of movement. The anticipation was not tension, but a focused, almost meditative state. A hunter awaiting his prey.

At 6:10 pm, the familiar rumble of a Lada’s engine echoed down the street. Jason’s heart rate remained steady. He was ready. A moment later, Borislav emerged from the darkness, a hunched figure hurrying towards his apartment, cigarette dangling from his lips. He lit a match, the brief flicker illuminating his face. The features were unremarkable, undistinguished, just another face in the bustling city. Yet, to Jason, he was a target. A necessary sacrifice.

The shot was instantaneous. A barely audible click, followed by the sharp, metallic thwack of a bullet striking its mark. Borislav stumbled, a choked gasp escaping his lips before he crumpled to the ground, his cigarette falling from his lifeless fingers. The entire operation took less than three seconds. The silence returned, heavier this time, broken only by the rhythmic drumming of the rain.

Jason waited for a full five minutes, ensuring there were no witnesses, no stray sounds to attract attention. He then descended from his vantage point, moving through the backstreets with the silent grace of a phantom. His movements were deliberate, yet swift, each step calculated, each turn precise. He left no trace of his presence, no fingerprints, no fibers, nothing to connect him to the scene. He was a ghost in the city's underbelly, a whisper in the shadows.

He disposed of the evidence, burning the cigarette packet and the empty shell casing in a secluded bin behind a deserted cafe. He then melted into the city, becoming just another face in the endless stream of humanity, a man without a past, a man without a future, existing solely in the present moment. He was an assassin, a shadow, a specter of death. And for Borislav Petrov, this night marked the beginning and the end of his life, all within the space of a few fleeting seconds.

Jason knew this was just the beginning. Eliminating Borislav was a small step, a preliminary move in a much larger game. The hunt for Gomin Guill would be far more complex, far more dangerous. It would demand all his skills, all his resources, and all his cunning. But he was ready. He had accepted the task, embraced the life, and he wouldn't rest until Gomin Guill was dead.

Back in the dimly lit cafe, Jake Harroll listened to Jason's recounting of the assassination, a chill creeping down his spine. Jason's calm, almost clinical description of the event was unnerving, chilling in its stark efficiency. He'd thoroughly documented every detail of the event, from the choice of location to the disposal of evidence. The precision was terrifyingly impressive. Yet, he had left no forensic evidence, no eyewitness accounts, only a body left lying in the street and the quiet acceptance of his grim profession.

The description had no emotional outbursts, no signs of remorse or self-doubt. It was purely a factual account, a report detailing the completion of an assignment. This was what made the story so disturbing. The coldness of Jason's demeanor, the sheer professionalism of his approach—it was as if he was describing the assembly of a piece of furniture, not the taking of a human life. It spoke volumes of the life he had led and the character he had become. This was not a man driven by vengeance or emotion; this was a man operating on a different level entirely. A master of his craft, devoid of any semblance of morality.

Jake felt a knot of unease tightening in his stomach. He found himself questioning the morality of it all, his journalistic instincts screaming for evidence, for corroboration. But Jason's tale, while horrifying, was strangely compelling, weaving a hypnotic spell of intrigue and danger. He was hooked, caught in the undertow of a story that was both fascinating and terrifying.

The account of Borislav's elimination felt almost too perfect. Jake, despite his initial skepticism, was beginning to believe that Jason was indeed capable of such precision and efficiency. But his journalist's mind still demanded proof. He needed more than just Jason's words. He needed tangible evidence, concrete proof that this man was who he claimed to be. He needed to verify Jason's claims, to ascertain the truth behind this intricate and dangerous tale. He knew, deep down, that this was only the beginning of a long and perilous journey into the heart of a vast criminal conspiracy. A journey that would put him and Jason squarely in the crosshairs. The investigation into Borislav's death had not only revealed Jason's lethal precision, but it also highlighted the complexity of Gomin Guill's organization, a far-reaching network of corruption extending beyond the borders of any single country. The sheer scale of it all was overwhelming. The implication was clear; this wasn't a simple gang; this was something far more insidious, far more dangerous. And Jake Harroll, the radio reporter, was now unexpectedly embroiled in it. The game had just begun.

Expanding the Net

The rain in Hong Kong hammered against the corrugated iron roof of the Kowloon tenement, a relentless percussion accompanying Jason's narrative. He leaned back in the plastic chair, the cheap fabric creaking under his weight. His voice, low and gravelly, was a counterpoint to the storm outside. Each word carefully chosen; precision with each syllable. He wasn't just recounting events; he was painting a picture, a thoroughly crafted portrait of deception and betrayal.

"Gomin wasn't a lone wolf," Jason said, his gaze drifting towards the neon glow bleeding through the grimy windowpanes. "He had layers, like an onion. Each layer, a different faction, vying for power, all bound by greed and fear." He tapped a long, slender finger against the chipped Formica tabletop. "To reach him, I had to peel back those layers, one by one."

His first infiltration point was surprisingly mundane: a seemingly innocuous charity gala hosted by one of Gomin's alleged philanthropic fronts. The event, a lavish affair brimming with Hong Kong's elite, was actually a thoroughly orchestrated gathering of key players within the organization. Jason, disguised as a wealthy art collector, blended seamlessly into the opulent setting, his expensive suit and cultivated charm effortlessly masking his lethal intent.

He described the gala in vivid detail – the clinking of champagne flutes, the hushed conversations, the glittering jewelry, the subtle displays of power – all masking a deadly game of intrigue beneath the surface. He observed, he listened, he learned. He identified key individuals, understanding their roles, their weaknesses, their connections to Gomin. He’d spent weeks researching, studying their habits, their routines, even their social media. A simple like on a yacht picture could lead to an address, an address could lead to a connection, a connection could unravel a network.

His charm wasn't merely superficial; it was a weapon, as sharp and deadly as any blade. He cultivated relationships, subtly manipulating conversations, gleaning information with practiced ease. He used intimidation sparingly, but when necessary, it was devastatingly effective. A single, cold stare, a pointed remark, a subtle threat conveyed volumes without uttering a word.

Infiltration wasn't always a smooth process. He recounted a harrowing encounter at a clandestine meeting in a hidden gambling den nestled within the labyrinthine streets of Macau. The atmosphere was thick with smoke, the air heavy with the scent of desperation and danger. He described the tense standoff, the sudden shift in the room's energy as he was unexpectedly recognized. He'd managed to deflect suspicion with a display of both lethal skill and unexpected wit, turning a potential confrontation into a fortuitous alliance with a disgruntled underling.

That alliance, born from necessity and mutual self-preservation, proved invaluable. The disgruntled underling, a low-level accountant named Lee, possessed access to Gomin's thoroughly kept financial records. Lee, motivated by a desire for vengeance and a hefty sum of money, provided Jason with the crucial information he needed to uncover the intricate web of offshore accounts, shell corporations, and hidden transactions that masked Gomin's illicit empire.

The information Lee provided painted a far more complex picture than Jason initially anticipated. It revealed a network far beyond Hong Kong, extending into the shadowy corners of Southeast Asia, reaching even into the heart of Europe. It revealed connections to powerful politicians, corrupt officials, and influential businessmen, all intertwined in a tangled web of money laundering, arms dealing, and human trafficking.

The journey wasn't without its setbacks. He spoke of navigating treacherous landscapes, evading surveillance, and outwitting his enemies. He detailed close calls – a near-miss in a crowded Bangkok market, a tense car chase through the winding streets of Rome, a deadly game of cat and mouse in a deserted warehouse in the Netherlands – each encounter a testament to his skills and his unwavering resolve. He painted these scenarios with brutal honesty, sparing no detail.

His account was punctuated by Jake's intermittent questions, his own skepticism battling with a growing sense of fascination. Jake, a seasoned journalist, pressed for details, his questions sharper, more incisive as Jason's story unfolded. He probed Jason's motivations, questioned his methods, challenged his assertions. He challenged the lack of tangible evidence, the absence of witnesses, the impossibly clean escapes.

Jason answered each question with unnerving calm, his answers precise, his explanations meticulous. He never flinched, never hesitated, never wavered. His confidence, bordering on arrogance, was unsettling, yet strangely compelling. His cold pragmatism, his detachment from emotion, added to the chilling aura he projected. He operated in a morally gray area, making choices that were ruthless, yet necessary. He viewed the world as a chessboard, where every move was calculated, every sacrifice justified.

The deeper Jason delved into Gomin's organization, the more dangerous the situation became. He faced betrayals from unexpected sources – allies who turned against him, information that was deliberately false, double-crosses designed to lead him into traps. The closer he got to Gomin, the more ruthless his enemies became.

As Jason's narrative progressed, Jake found himself increasingly drawn into the web of deceit. The thoroughly detailed account of Jason's assassinations, the complex network of criminal connections, the global reach of the organization— it was all too compelling to ignore. His initial skepticism faded, replaced by a gripping sense of intrigue and a deep-seated determination to verify Jason's claims.

The story was a tapestry woven with threads of betrayal, manipulation, and violence, each strand intricately connected to the others. Jason painted a world where trust was a dangerous commodity, where loyalty was fleeting, and where survival depended on one's ability to anticipate and adapt. He showed how a thoroughly planned operation could be undermined by a single unforeseen event. It was a brutal world, yet he moved through it with an almost supernatural grace.

The story culminated in a nail-biting description of a high-stakes meeting, a clandestine gathering in a secluded villa overlooking the Mediterranean Sea. The air was thick with tension, the players maneuvering for position, alliances shifting as quickly as the shadows. It was a scene worthy of a classic spy thriller, replete with betrayal, double-crosses, and a deadly climax.

And as Jason concluded his chilling tale, leaving Jake reeling from the enormity of what he'd heard, the rain outside finally began to subside. The storm had passed, but the tempest of his investigation had only just begun. The truth, it seemed, was far more dangerous and complex than Jake had ever imagined. The evidence suggested a much larger game was afoot, one that extended far beyond Gomin

Guill and threatened to engulf Jake in its deadly embrace. The assassin's tale was not just a story of one man's mission; it was a window into a world far more sinister and complex than he could have possibly imagined. And that world, it seemed, now encompassed him.

....

The silence that followed Jason’s confession was thick, heavy with the unspoken weight of the revelations. Jake, usually quick-witted and articulate, found himself speechless, the enormity of the situation pressing down on him like the humid Hong Kong air. He stared out at the now-calm harbor, the city lights twinkling like malevolent eyes in the darkness. The rain had stopped, but a storm raged within him.

"So," Jake finally managed, his voice raspy, "Gomin was just a pawn."

Jason nodded, his gaze distant, lost in the labyrinthine corridors of his past. "A very effective one, though. He kept the smaller factions in check, preventing a full-blown war. His death… it's destabilized everything."

"And who's pulling the strings?" Jake asked, his voice low, a tremor of unease in its depths. The simple question felt monumental, fraught with danger. He was no longer just a reporter pursuing a story; he was wading into the murky waters of a global criminal network, a world of shadows and secrets.

Jason shifted in his chair, the plastic creaking again. "That's the part I couldn't uncover. Gomin guarded his superiors jealously. His inner circle was small, tightly knit. I believe there's a council, or perhaps a single, shadowy figure directing everything. Their identities are carefully concealed, buried under layers of shell corporations and offshore accounts."

"So, you eliminated the visible head, and now the whole body is reacting?" Jake mused, piecing together the fragments of Jason's account. It was a terrifying prospect, a hydra with many heads. Taking down one only seemed to multiply the threat.

“Precisely,” Jason confirmed. “The organization is far more vast, far more entrenched, than anyone imagined. Gomin’s death… it was a trigger. A catalyst.”

Days turned into weeks as Jake delved deeper into the investigation. He painstakingly pieced together the scattered fragments of information Jason had provided, cross-referencing it with public records, leaked documents obtained from a wary informant he'd cultivated over the years, and the whisper network of contacts in his professional sphere. He was tracing the invisible threads of a complex web, each thread leading to a new dead end, a new unexpected complication.

One such complication emerged in the form of a rival organization, a shadowy group known only as "The Serpent's Fang." They were operating in the same sphere as Gomin’s organization, but their methods were even more brutal, their reach even wider. They had begun aggressively seizing control of Gomin's former territories, triggering a violent power vacuum. Jason’s actions, meant to eliminate a single threat, had unleashed a far greater one. The situation was spiraling rapidly out of control.

Another unforeseen challenge was the sheer scale of the organization's influence. It wasn't just confined to the criminal underworld; it had infiltrated legitimate businesses, political institutions, and even law enforcement agencies. Jake discovered evidence of bribery, blackmail, and intimidation on a massive scale, proving how deeply entrenched the tentacles of this criminal conspiracy truly were. He felt a chill run down his spine, realizing that he was dealing with a monster of unprecedented size and power.

His investigation led him down a rabbit hole of shell corporations, hidden bank accounts in tax havens, and offshore trusts that masked the true ownership of assets worth billions. He was a single man against a hydra, navigating a treacherous maze of deceit and subterfuge, each step fraught with danger. The organization was like an octopus, its tentacles reaching far and wide, its grip incredibly strong. Jake felt completely alone against this massive enterprise.

Then came the threats. At first subtle, almost imperceptible – a mysterious package left on his doorstep, a menacing phone call in the dead of night, a car following him at a distance. As his investigation progressed, the threats became more overt, more brazen. He discovered a thoroughly documented hit list, his name prominently featured among the targets. His name and address were being tracked across the dark corners of the internet and by the encrypted servers that the organized crime world used.

He realized he was no longer just investigating a crime; he was becoming a target. The organization wasn't just trying to stop his investigation; they were trying to silence him permanently.

The weight of it all crashed down on Jake, the suffocating pressure of his newfound role as a marked man. He was walking a tightrope, one wrong step away from a fatal fall. His usual investigative tools felt inadequate, his journalistic instincts failing him in the face of such overwhelming power and ruthlessness.

He found himself turning to Jason again, reluctantly acknowledging that the assassin's expertise was more valuable than he had ever imagined. Jason, however, remained enigmatic, his past shrouded in a fog of secrets he wasn't entirely comfortable revealing. While he agreed to aid Jake, his help came with conditions—conditions that tested Jake's journalistic ethics and his very sense of morality.

Jason warned him about the dangers inherent in such an operation, explaining the elaborate precautions needed to survive against an organization that could anticipate his moves. He needed to completely abandon his life as a journalist if he intended to pursue the case, at least for now. Jake was at a crossroads: continue his investigation and potentially pay the ultimate price, or back down and live with the knowledge that he had failed to expose a far-reaching conspiracy that could unravel society.

The next few days were a whirlwind of clandestine meetings, coded messages, and perilous maneuvers. Jake learned the cold, hard truth about the organization's tactics: their willingness to use extreme violence, their extensive reach into governments and institutions, and their capacity for deception at every level. He was thrown into a world of betrayals, shifting allegiances, and double-crosses, where trust was a luxury he could no longer afford.

One such betrayal came from within his own circle. A supposed ally, someone he had trusted implicitly, turned out to be a mole working for the organization. Jake narrowly escaped a carefully planned ambush, the near-death experience leaving him shaken but resolute. This experience showed him the true nature of the enemy he was up against. The organization was meticulous and resourceful and could strike from the most unexpected of sources.

In the aftermath of the ambush, Jason revealed yet another layer of complexity – an unexpected connection between the Serpent's Fang and the organization that had initially hired him. The two rival groups weren't just fighting for territory; they were both puppets in a larger game, manipulated by an unseen hand.

The revelation was a seismic shock, shaking the very foundation of Jake's understanding of the situation. The seemingly straightforward assassination had opened up a Pandora’s Box of complexities, revealing an intricate web of deceit and betrayal that extended far beyond his initial assumptions. The struggle to uncover the truth now seemed a monumental task, one far greater than any single individual could handle.

Jake, a reporter, used to uncovering stories, felt profoundly outmatched. He had underestimated the adversary, underestimated the depth and reach of the organization, and most importantly, underestimated the cost of this investigation. This was far more than a story anymore. It was a fight for survival, and the odds were stacked against him. The storm had passed in Hong Kong, but the tempest of his investigation was far from over. The darkness had only just begun to truly reveal its terrifying form.

....

The humid Hong Kong air hung heavy, clinging to Jake like a second skin. He'd spent hours staring at the cityscape, the glittering towers a stark contrast to the chilling revelations Jason Reen had laid bare. Gomin Guill wasn't the mastermind; he was a pawn, a high-ranking one, yes, but still a pawn in a far larger game. And Jason, the seemingly ruthless assassin, wasn't just eliminating targets; he was dismantling a carefully constructed web, a web that now seemed to be reaching out, its tendrils wrapping around Jake himself.

Jason's confession hadn't ended with the death of Guill. It had only scratched the surface, revealing a network of informants, double agents, and shadowy figures operating in the deepest recesses of global power. He spoke of individuals he called "assets," people who owed him debts, who held information vital to unraveling the organization's true structure. These weren't loyalists; they were opportunists, mercenaries motivated by self-preservation and profit. Their loyalty was fluid, transactional, as fickle as the tides.

One such asset, a former high-ranking member of Guill's inner circle named Tanya Relova, now lived in a self-imposed exile in Prague. Jason described her as a woman of formidable intelligence and even more formidable ruthlessness, someone who'd grown disillusioned with the organization's brutality. She'd escaped with a trove of incriminating data, data that could potentially bring the entire operation crashing down. But she was wary, haunted by the organization's long reach and the fear of retribution.

"She won't trust me," Jason had said, his voice low and gravelly. "She wouldn't trust anyone easily. But she'll trust someone who can prove their value. Someone who can offer her protection, and more importantly, leverage."

That leverage, it turned out, was Jake.

Jason's plan was audacious, bordering on reckless. He intended to use Jake's journalistic integrity – his reputation for uncovering the truth – as a bargaining chip. Tanya Relova, Jason reasoned, would see Jake as someone capable of exposing the organization's secrets to the world, a credible threat that could force the organization to leave her alone. It was a dangerous game, relying on Jake's willingness to become a player in a deadly game he hadn't even known he'd entered.

The first step was reaching Tanya. Jason provided Jake with a heavily encrypted email address, a digital ghost in the cyberworld. The message was simple: "The story continues. Your involvement is now unavoidable." He'd explained the risks, the potential danger, the possibility of becoming a target himself. Jake had felt a surge of adrenaline, a strange mixture of fear and exhilaration. The reporter in him, the one who craved the scoop, was battling with the human being who valued his life.

The response arrived days later, encrypted and untraceable. Tanya was guarded, suspicious, her words laced with an undercurrent of cynicism. She laid out her conditions, her demands stark and precise. She needed absolute anonymity; she needed guarantees of her safety; and she needed assurance that her information would be used to dismantle the organization, not to further enrich someone else's pockets.

Jason had anticipated these demands. He'd already begun to establish a network of support, a shadow team comprised of his former associates, individuals operating outside the law, but with impeccable skills. One was a master of disguise and infiltration, another a technological expert capable of creating impenetrable security systems. These weren't friends, not really; they were mercenaries, hired guns with their own motivations and agendas. But for now, their agendas aligned with Jason's, and consequently, with Jake's.

Jake found himself meeting these individuals in clandestine locations – abandoned warehouses, dimly lit cafes in foreign cities, anonymous hotel rooms. The meetings were tense, filled with unspoken threats and mutual distrust. He learned about the organization's intricate structure, its global reach, its chilling efficiency. He learned about its methods, its brutality, its willingness to eliminate anyone who threatened its existence. He saw the dark side of the world, a world Jason had inhabited for years, a world that was now threatening to consume him.

Tanya's information confirmed Jason's revelations and added terrifying detail. She revealed the names of key players, the locations of hidden accounts, the methods used to launder money and evade authorities. The organization wasn't just a criminal enterprise; it was a sophisticated, well-oiled machine, infiltrating governments, manipulating markets, and controlling vast swaths of the global economy. Its tentacles stretched far beyond Gomin Guill; Guill was merely a figurehead, a replaceable component in a vast and complex system.

The task ahead seemed impossible. Taking down this organization was like trying to slay a hydra – for every head cut off, two more grew back. But with Tanya's help and Jason's network, Jake found a strange, uneasy sense of purpose. He was no longer just a reporter chasing a story; he was a soldier in an unseen war, fighting against an enemy far more powerful and ruthless than anything he'd ever encountered.

The alliance between Jake, Jason, and Tanya was precarious, built on mistrust and mutual need. It was a pact forged in the shadows, a dance with death where one wrong step could mean annihilation. Yet, in the face of overwhelming odds, they forged ahead, fueled by a shared desire to expose the truth and dismantle the organization that threatened to engulf them all. They were a strange, unlikely team; a journalist, an assassin, and a former insider, united by circumstance and a shared enemy, bound together by a web of deceit far more intricate than the one they sought to unravel. The journey ahead promised to be perilous, filled with betrayal, double-crosses, and unforeseen dangers. But for now, they had found a fragile foothold in this dangerous game, a fragile alliance against a powerful foe, each holding a piece of the puzzle, each playing a crucial, and possibly deadly, role. The fight for survival, for justice, for truth, had only just begun. The darkness was closing in, and they were ready. Or at least, they had to be. The fate of the world, or at least the fate of a few unsuspecting individuals, hung precariously in the balance. And Jake, once just a reporter chasing a story, now found himself at the heart of it all, a pawn in a far larger and deadly game, but possibly, just possibly, with a chance to become a player.

....

The neon signs of Kowloon bled crimson and turquoise onto the rain-slicked streets. Inside a dimly lit bar, Tanya, her face etched with a weariness that belied her youthful appearance, nervously stirred her drink. Across from her, Jason, his usual impassivity slightly fractured, watched her with a hawk-like intensity. The air crackled with unspoken tension, the silence punctuated only by the clinking of ice and the low murmur of Cantonese conversation from nearby tables.

“He’s compromised,” Tanya finally said, her voice low and strained. "Gomin wasn’t the only one. There are others, higher up, pulling the strings. And they know we’re onto them.”

Jason nodded with his gaze unwavering. “I suspected as much. The level of security around Guill… it was overkill. A smokescreen.” He leaned forward, his voice dropping to a near whisper. “They knew someone was digging. They were waiting for us to stumble into their trap.”

Jake, seated at a nearby table, subtly observing the exchange, felt a chill crawl down his spine. The casual elegance of Jason’s demeanor concealed a cold, calculating mind. Tanya, once a seemingly loyal operative within the organization, now appeared shaken, haunted by the ghosts of her past. The fragile alliance they had forged felt increasingly tenuous, threatened by shadows they couldn't quite grasp.

"Who?" Jake finally asked, his voice barely audible above the background noise. "Who's pulling the strings?"

Tanya hesitated, her eyes darting around the bar. "A name… I only know a code name. 'The Serpent.' He orchestrates everything from the shadows. I never met him, but his influence permeated every level of the organization."

Jason's eyes narrowed. "The Serpent… an appropriate moniker. He's elusive, a master of disguise. He operates through intermediaries, layers upon layers of deception. Tracking him will be like chasing smoke."

The next few days were a blur of clandestine meetings, coded messages, and frantic searches through encrypted databases. Tanya, leveraging her former connections within the organization, provided crucial information, but the information was always incomplete, a piece of a larger puzzle deliberately withheld. She had been, it became clear, a pawn in this grand game, used and discarded like a worn-out tool. Her betrayal, or perhaps more accurately, her self-preservation, had led her to them, yet a lingering doubt remained, a question hanging heavy in the air: how much of what she was telling them was truth, how much carefully constructed deceit?

Jason, meanwhile, employed his extensive network of contacts, each interaction fraught with risk. He moved through the shadowy underbelly of Hong Kong with the practiced ease of a phantom, disappearing and reappearing at will. His methods were brutal, efficient, leaving only whispers and a trail of carefully orchestrated chaos in his wake. But even Jason, with his seemingly superhuman skills, was not immune to the undercurrents of betrayal that swirled around them. The lines between ally and enemy became increasingly blurred. Even those trusted at one point could be revealed to be working in the interest of the Serpent, their loyalty bought or coerced.

One evening, during a tense meeting in a secluded warehouse, Jake discovered a hidden microphone. The chilling realization hung in the air – they were being monitored, their every move watched, their plans anticipated. The betrayal cut deep, its sting almost as sharp as the blade of Jason's hidden knife. The sense of paranoia escalated, making every interaction, every alliance, incredibly difficult to trust.

Their investigation led them to a hidden offshore bank, its accounts holding evidence of money laundering on a scale that dwarfed even Gomin Guill's operations. The Serpent’s reach extended far beyond Hong Kong, into a global network of corruption and influence. As they delved deeper, they uncovered a series of shell corporations, each thoroughly designed to obscure the flow of money, its origins and destinations deliberately obscured. The complexity of the scheme was staggering, a labyrinthine web of deceit designed to confound even the most skilled investigators.

Tanya revealed another piece of critical information - a hidden meeting between a known associate of The Serpent and a high-ranking official within the Hong Kong government. The implication was staggering: the conspiracy extended into the highest echelons of power, protected by those sworn to uphold the law. This was no longer a simple criminal enterprise; it was a sophisticated network of power, its tendrils wrapped tightly around the heart of the city, choking its lifeblood.

Jason, using his unique skills, managed to infiltrate the meeting, witnessing firsthand the level of corruption and the chilling ruthlessness of The Serpent's operatives.

He gathered evidence but almost didn't escape alive; a near-death experience during which a trusted contact was silenced forever, revealing the deadly lengths to which The Serpent went to protect his secrets.

The betrayal wasn't confined to external forces. Internal conflicts began to brew, fueled by mistrust and the mounting pressure. Each member of their team, Jake, Jason and Tanya, wrestled with their own doubts and fears, questioning the loyalty and motives of their supposed allies. Tanya's past, her ties to The Serpent's organization, remained a source of suspicion; her revelations, though valuable, were tainted by the possibility of manipulation.

Jake, grappling with the ethical implications of his involvement, questioned whether he could trust Jason, a man whose profession was violence and deceit. Was he truly committed to exposing the truth, or was he just playing his own dangerous game? The line between justice and vengeance began to blur, as the ethical considerations he once held dear seemed trivial in the face of overwhelming danger and the necessity of survival.

The culmination of their investigation led to a confrontation in a deserted dockyard. They were ambushed. The air filled with the sharp crack of gunfire, the metallic clang of steel on steel. Jason, displaying his unparalleled combat skills, fought with a ferocity that bordered on savage, protecting Jake and Tanya while simultaneously dismantling the Serpent's security team. The fight was brutal, a chaotic ballet of death, with each side aiming for total annihilation. But it was a brutal, desperate fight that left several dead and Jake injured.

In the aftermath of chaos, amidst the shattered remains of cars and fallen bodies, Tanya made a final, devastating revelation. She confessed her involvement in the Serpent's plan: to frame Jason. He was, in fact, The Serpent's pawn. The Serpent had been manipulating them all, using them as weapons in his own intricate game. She revealed she had only joined forces with them to ensure her own survival but had betrayed their trust from the very beginning. The Serpent had been testing their loyalty to determine whether Jake would be a suitable asset. This shocking revelation highlighted that despite the dangerous nature of their alliance, the Serpent had been the true puppeteer behind it all, orchestrating the entire situation for his own nefarious ends.

The events of that night left Jake reeling, his trust shattered, his world turned upside down. He was left with a simple truth: the world he thought he knew was a carefully constructed illusion, a vast web of deceit woven from lies and betrayal. The fight was far from over; a new phase of this deadly game had just begun, one even more treacherous and uncertain than before. The survival of Jake, now aware of the far-reaching plot to overthrow justice and establish The Serpent's control, hangs on a thread. He is a man on a mission now, but one that is fraught with peril, deceit, and more betrayal than he could ever have imagined.

....

The hum of the city faded into a dull roar as Jake stared out his apartment window, the rain mirroring the tempest brewing inside him. Tanya's words echoed in his mind – whispered confessions of betrayal, of a network far deeper and more insidious than even Jason had hinted at. Gomin Guill hadn't been the kingpin; he'd been a pawn, a carefully placed piece in a much larger, more sinister game. The implications were staggering. His initial interview, intended as a sensational scoop, had inadvertently plunged him into the heart of a conspiracy that threatened to unravel everything he thought he knew.

He'd spent the last few days poring over Jason's thoroughly kept journals, a testament to the assassin's methodical nature and chilling efficiency. Each entry was a chilling snapshot of a thoroughly planned operation, a cold, clinical account of executions carried out with surgical precision. Yet, interwoven between the stark descriptions of violence were cryptic references to a shadowy organization known only as "The Serpent," a name that sent a shiver down Jake's spine. The organization's reach extended far beyond the drug trade and money laundering, its tendrils snaking into the highest echelons of power, twisting political landscapes and corrupting institutions.

He'd contacted his editor, a gruff but supportive man named Bernard, to inform him about the turn of events. Bernard, initially skeptical, listened intently as Jake recounted his story – the enigmatic assassin, the global conspiracy, the looming threat of The Serpent. He'd initially wanted to run it as a series of articles. Jake, however, already sensed the massive undertaking this would turn out to be. He felt a growing need to investigate the entire situation personally. He didn't want just a scoop; he craved the truth, even if it meant venturing into dangerous territory.

The more Jake delved into Jason's story, the more complex the puzzle became. The assassin's accounts were laced with subtle hints, encrypted messages hidden within seemingly innocuous details. He found himself spending hours in the library, researching obscure historical events, decoding cryptic symbols, and piecing together fragments of information like a meticulous craftsman assembling a fragile mosaic.

One recurring element in Jason's writings was a recurring symbol: a stylized serpent coiled around a skull. He found similar symbols in various unrelated places – ancient texts, obscure religious iconography, even graffiti in the back alleys of Kowloon. It was a recurring motif; the same symbol that Tanya had mentioned as the organization's calling card. Each instance seemed to confirm the organization's power.

Jake's investigation took him from dusty archives in Oxford to the bustling souks of Marrakech, each location offering a new piece of the puzzle. He interviewed former intelligence officers, disgruntled politicians, and even a former associate of Gomin Guill – each encounter painting a more complete, albeit terrifying, picture of The Serpent's global reach and influence.

In Marrakech, he met Omar, a wizened old man who had once been Gomin Guill's right-hand man. Initially reluctant, Omar eventually opened up after Jake showed him the serpent symbol. His eyes, filled with a mixture of fear and regret, told a tale of decades spent serving an organization he now understood to be pure evil. Omar spoke of backroom deals, political assassinations, and the ruthless efficiency with which The Serpent eliminated any threat to its power. He spoke of a figure known only as "The Eye," the organization's shadowy leader, a person who pulled the strings from behind the scenes, their identity remaining shrouded in mystery.

The information Omar provided gave Jake a new direction. He learned of a series of encrypted messages exchanged between Gomin Guill and The Eye, messages hidden within seemingly innocuous financial transactions. Deciphering these messages would be crucial to understanding the organization's structure and upcoming plans.

His investigation led him to a Swiss bank, where he spent weeks combing through financial records, deciphering coded transactions, and painstakingly reconstructing the organization's financial web. He worked late into the night, the cold fluorescent lights casting long shadows over his hunched figure. The sheer scale of the conspiracy was overwhelming; the amount of money involved dwarfed anything he'd ever encountered.

As he dug deeper, Jake realized that The Serpent wasn't merely a criminal organization; it was a sophisticated network operating on a global scale, infiltrating every aspect of society. Its tentacles reached into politics, finance, and even the media, creating a carefully constructed illusion of normalcy while pulling the strings of power from the shadows. The realization sent a chill down his spine; he was dealing with a force, far more powerful; far more dangerous than he’d ever imagined.

He began to understand the significance of Jason's mission. Gomin Guill's elimination had been more than just a contract killing; it had been a calculated move, a carefully orchestrated event designed to destabilize The Serpent from within. Jason's actions had disrupted the organization's carefully constructed balance of power, exposed its vulnerabilities and drew attention to its existence.

But Jason's actions had also placed a target on his back. Jake knew that The Serpent would stop at nothing to silence him, and he too was now in immense danger. He was no longer just a reporter chasing a story; he was a player in a deadly game, a pawn in a conflict far beyond his comprehension. The weight of the situation bore down on him, a crushing pressure that threatened to overwhelm him.

He felt a growing sense of dread, a constant awareness of being watched, of being followed. The city that had once felt vibrant and alive now felt suffocating, a labyrinth of shadows and secrets. He found himself constantly scanning his surroundings, his senses heightened, his reflexes sharpened. He had changed from a mere reporter to a man hunted.

He knew he needed help, but who could he trust? The authorities were likely compromised, their ranks infiltrated by The Serpent's agents. He couldn't involve Bernard either, the risk to his editor was too high. He was alone, adrift in a sea of deceit, with the weight of a global conspiracy resting on his shoulders. The only person he could possibly turn to was Tanya, a woman haunted by her past and burdened by a knowledge that could either save or destroy him. But finding her, and convincing her to trust him, would prove more difficult than he imagined. The realization that he might have to rely on a woman who was herself implicated, fueled by a burning desire for revenge, left him both anxious and excited. He felt the chill of anticipation run down his spine. The game, he knew, had just begun.

Closing In

The Parisian rain hammered against the corrugated iron roof of the abandoned warehouse, a relentless percussion accompanying the frantic beat of Jason's heart. He crouched low, the chill seeping into his bones, his breath misting in the frigid air. The scent of diesel and decay hung heavy, a fitting aroma for the den of iniquity he was about to infiltrate. His target, Dimitri Voldi, a lieutenant in Gomin Guill's organization, was inside. Voldi, known for his brutality and penchant for elaborate torture methods, was a significant player, his network of informants stretching across Eastern Europe. Eliminating him would be a considerable blow to Guill's operation, but it wouldn't be easy.

Jason checked his gear one last time: the custom-modified Heckler & Koch silenced pistol, a small but deadly tool, felt reassuringly heavy in his hand. He had three spare magazines, each holding fifteen rounds – enough, he hoped. He also had his Glock 19 as backup, a reliable sidearm always ready. A small, almost invisible earpiece was nestled in his ear, a connection to his network of contacts, feeding him real-time information. The pressure was immense. This wasn't just another contract; it was a crucial step in his mission to dismantle Gomin's empire. Failure wasn’t an option.

The intel was precise: Voldi was meeting with a known arms dealer, negotiating a shipment of high-powered weaponry. The rendezvous point was this abandoned warehouse, a desolate location perfectly suited for clandestine meetings and equally perfect for Jason's purposes. He had been tailing Voldi for three days, studying his patterns, thoroughly mapping his movements. He’d identified several escape routes, accounted for potential security, and mapped the warehouse's interior layout from aerial photographs and satellite imagery. Preparation was everything, and Jason was a master of preparation.

His breath hitched as he heard voices from inside. He pressed himself harder against the cold, damp wall, listening intently. Voldi’s distinctive, gravelly voice cut through the murmur of the conversation. The arms dealer, a notorious figure known only as “Seraph,” was haggling over the price, his voice sharp and insistent. Jason waited, patience, a virtue he'd honed over years of deadly precision.

The warehouse was a labyrinthine mess of stacked crates, discarded machinery, and shadowed corners. Jason navigated through the darkness, utilizing the faint moonlight filtering through cracks in the walls to guide his way. His senses were heightened, every creak and groan amplified in the echoing silence. He moved like a phantom, a ghost gliding through the debris, his presence imperceptible to the unsuspecting occupants.

He located Voldi and Seraph in a makeshift office, a dimly lit space cluttered with paperwork and weapons. Voldi, a hulking figure with a shaved head and a cruel scar across his cheek, was examining a sample of weaponry, while Seraph, a lean man with sharp features, barked orders to a trio of armed guards stationed near the entrance. Jason assessed the situation. Three guards, a clear path to Voldi, and a back exit already identified. It was a risky move, but he had to seize this opportunity.

He chose his moment, moving with lethal efficiency. A swift, silent move, a precise shot, and one of the guards fell without a sound. The other two, startled by the sudden noise, turned to investigate. Jason moved like a shadow, two more shots, two more bodies slumping to the cold concrete floor. Voldi and Seraph were now fully focused on Jason, their eyes wide with fear and disbelief. Voldi lunged for the pistol in his belt, but it was too late.

Jason moved faster, his shot clean, precise, aimed directly at Voldi's heart.

Voldi hit the ground, his life draining away as Jason swiftly moved to Seraph, who made a desperate attempt to flee, his hands reaching for the pistol at his waist. Jason disabled him with a quick, expertly delivered strike, using his training in hand-to-hand combat to subdue him without making a sound. This was a display of both precision and ruthlessness. He knew his efficiency saved lives and further ensured his escape.

The cleanup was methodical and swift. Jason used his knowledge of the building and his years of experience to erase all traces of his presence. He disarmed the fallen guards, wiping down every surface that might have his fingerprints. He destroyed the paperwork which had incriminating data, ensuring no trace of his presence could be found. He even used the warehouse's inherent decay to his advantage. The very nature of the dilapidated structure made it impossible to find anything out of place. He ensured not even the scent of his presence could linger.

As he slipped out into the rain-soaked alley, the sounds of the city washing away the echoes of his violence, he felt the weight of the world still upon his shoulders. He had removed one piece of the puzzle, but the larger image remained shrouded in mystery. He knew, deep down, that this was only the beginning of a much larger, more perilous game. Gomin Guill was still out there, and Jason's work was far from over. The pressure to succeed, to continue dismantling the organization was heavier than ever. The stakes were incredibly high; this was his life's work. His mission was far from complete, and the shadows still held many unanswered questions.

Jake, meanwhile, sat hunched over his transcription of Jason's account, the chilling details painting a vivid picture of a world he never knew existed. The audio recordings, enhanced and thoroughly analyzed, corroborated Jason’s every claim. He had been skeptical at first, even cynical, but the evidence was overwhelming. He was staring into the heart of a vast, shadowy organization, an entity far more intricate and dangerous than he could have ever imagined. He felt a knot of fear tightening in his stomach, a chilling realization that he was now much more deeply involved than he ever intended to be. The information Jason had provided, though horrifying, was invaluable, providing leads that could unravel the entire operation.

He realized that he was no longer just a reporter pursuing a story; he was now a player, a pawn in a deadly game of international intrigue. He considered his next move, the weight of responsibility suddenly heavy on his shoulders. He had a moral obligation – to bring the truth to light, even if it meant risking his own life. The implications of his investigation were far-reaching; this wasn't just about a criminal syndicate; it was about uncovering a web of deceit that touched the highest levels of power. He had to proceed cautiously, thoroughly, but he had to proceed. His journalistic integrity, his own sense of justice, demanded it. He picked up the phone, his fingers trembling slightly, ready to make the call that would send ripples throughout the world. The pursuit of truth often leads to dangerous paths. He was ready to walk down that path, despite the danger.

....

The warehouse's cavernous space echoed with the drip, drip, drip of water, a counterpoint to the rhythmic thump of Jason's own pulse. He'd positioned himself in the shadows, the damp concrete cold against his cheek. Euragar Voldi, a mountain of a man with eyes like chips of ice, sat at a scarred wooden table, a half-empty bottle of vodka sweating in the gloom. Two heavily armed guards flanked him, their boredom barely concealing the simmering violence beneath.

Jason's plan was intricate, a choreography of movement and distraction. He'd studied Voldi for weeks, piecing together his routines, his habits, his weaknesses. He knew the layout of the warehouse like the back of his hand, having infiltrated it several times under the cover of darkness. This was more than just eliminating a target; it was a surgical strike, designed to minimize collateral damage and maximize impact.

The first move was subtle. A carefully placed pebble, dislodged from the crumbling wall, skittered across the concrete floor. One of the guards, lulled into complacency, shifted his weight to investigate. That split-second distraction was all Jason needed. He moved like a phantom, a whisper of motion in the darkness. A specially modified dart, tipped with a fast-acting paralytic, found its mark in the guard's neck. The man crumpled silently to the ground, his weapon clattering uselessly.

The second guard, startled by the sudden fall, spun around, his hand instinctively reaching for his weapon. Jason was faster. A swift, precise strike to the pressure point behind the ear rendered him unconscious before he could even react. The whole sequence played out in a matter of seconds; a deadly ballet performed in the shadows.

Voldi, finally realizing something was amiss, let out a guttural roar. He lunged for the pistol holstered at his hip, but Jason was already on him. The fight was brutal, a clash of steel and muscle. Voldi's size and strength were undeniable, but Jason's training, honed over years of lethal combat, gave him an edge. He moved with a deadly grace, anticipating Voldi's every move, deflecting blows, countering with precision strikes.

The air crackled with tension. The warehouse seemed to hold its breath as the two men grappled, a whirlwind of fists and feet, the metallic clang of Voldi's pistol hitting the floor a sharp punctuation to the savage dance. Jason used Voldi's own momentum against him, leveraging his bulk to send him crashing into a stack of rusty barrels. The impact was deafening, the sound swallowed by the vastness of the warehouse.

Jason didn't waste the opportunity. As Voldi staggered to his feet, disoriented and winded, Jason moved in for the kill. It wasn't a messy, brutal execution. It was swift, clean, and efficient. A single, precise strike to the carotid artery silenced Voldi permanently. He collapsed without a sound, his eyes wide with disbelief.

Jason surveyed the scene. Three bodies lay scattered across the floor, testament to his deadly efficiency. He thoroughly wiped down the surfaces he'd touched, leaving no trace of his presence. He didn't linger, didn't savor the victory. His mission was complete, but the larger game was far from over.

As he slipped back into the Parisian night, the rain continuing its relentless assault, Jason knew he was walking a tightrope. Each successful mission brought him closer to the heart of the conspiracy, but also closer to the inevitable reckoning. The organization was vast, its tentacles reaching every corner of the globe. Gomin Guill might be gone, but the network he built, the intricate web of corruption and violence, remained.

Meanwhile, Jake Harroll, fueled by adrenaline and a growing sense of dread, was piecing together the fragments of information Jason had provided. The Parisian police had found Voldi's body, a scene that was initially baffling, then chillingly clear to those who understood the signature of a ghost. The details Jason had shared – the precise location, the method of killing, the lack of forensic evidence – all pointed to one inescapable conclusion: a professional, an assassin of extraordinary skill.

Jake's journalistic instincts screamed at him to follow the trail, but the risks were immense. He had witnessed firsthand the organization's reach, their capacity for violence. He knew they were watching him, sensing the shift in the balance of power. He wasn't just chasing a story anymore; he was in the crosshairs.

The next call came unexpectedly. A heavily disguised figure, his voice distorted beyond recognition, contacted Jake through a secure line. "You know too much, Mr. Harroll," the voice hissed. "We appreciate your… curiosity. But your investigation ends here."

The line went dead, leaving Jake in an icy silence. The threat was explicit, unmistakable. He knew he was playing a deadly game, and the stakes were higher than ever before. He had to move fast, find allies, gather more evidence, before they silenced him permanently. His initial pursuit of truth had led him into a world of shadows, a world where survival was a daily battle and trust was a luxury he could no longer afford. The revelation of Gomin Guill's death had ignited a firestorm, a power vacuum that threatened to consume him.

The evidence, gleaned from Jason's accounts and his own investigation, pointed to a global network far larger than he could have ever imagined. Banks, politicians, even powerful international corporations – all seemed to be intertwined in a web of corruption and deceit. The trail led to offshore accounts, hidden trusts, and shell companies that obscured the flow of money and power. Jake felt a growing sense of unease, a visceral certainty that he was close to discovering something truly terrifying.

He spent sleepless nights poring over documents, cross-referencing information, connecting the dots. The organization's influence extended far beyond mere criminal activity. It seemed to be involved in manipulating political processes, influencing elections, and even orchestrating international conflicts to advance their own nefarious agenda. The implications were staggering.

The pressure mounted with each passing hour. He knew he was being watched, followed. He could feel the eyes on him, the weight of their scrutiny, the chilling realization that he was fighting against a force far more powerful than any single individual. He had to find a way to expose them, to break their power, but he knew he couldn't do it alone.

His search for allies began a perilous journey through the murky underworld of informants, whistleblowers, and disillusioned insiders. He encountered individuals who had once served the organization, people who had witnessed its brutality firsthand and were now seeking redemption. These were dangerous contacts, operating in the shadows, their loyalty tested by desperation and self-preservation.

With each new contact, the picture grew clearer, more terrifying. The organization wasn't just about money and power; it was about control, about manipulating the world on a global scale. And at the very heart of it all lay a mystery – the identity of the true mastermind. Who was pulling the strings? Who was orchestrating this vast network of corruption and violence?

Jake’s investigation had taken on a life of its own, leading him down a rabbit hole of conspiracy and intrigue. He had to tread carefully, cautiously, every step fraught with danger. He was playing a game of cat and mouse, and the cat was a predator of immense power and reach. The fight for truth, he realized, was far from over. And the stakes were far higher than he could ever have imagined. He was in deep, dangerously deep, with no guarantee of ever finding his way back. The relentless pursuit of justice had turned into a desperate struggle for survival.

....

Dimitri Voldi slammed his fist on the table, the sound jarring in the oppressive silence. The vodka bottle teetered precariously before settling back down, its contents sloshing ominously. "This is unacceptable!" he roared, his voice thick with a Slavic accent that grated on Jason's nerves. "Gomin's dead, and we're left with nothing but a mess."

One of the guards shifted, the metallic clang of his weapon a stark reminder of the lethality of the situation. Jason held his breath, his senses on high alert. He was a ghost in the shadows, a silent observer to this unfolding drama, but his mission was far from over. Gomin's death, while a success in itself, had only scratched the surface of a deeper, more insidious conspiracy.

Dimitri's tirade continued, punctuated by furious gestures and muttered curses. He spoke of betrayals, of double-cross, of a network of informants far more extensive than he'd ever imagined. Names were dropped – names Jason recognized from his own investigations, names that linked to seemingly unrelated crimes across continents. The puzzle pieces were slowly, agonizingly, coming together, revealing a pattern far more intricate and dangerous than he'd initially anticipated.

This wasn't just about Gomin; it was about a vast, shadowy organization that stretched its tendrils everywhere, its influence far-reaching and devastating. Gomin had been a pawn, a powerful one, certainly, but ultimately expendable. The real power resided elsewhere, hidden in the labyrinthine corridors of international finance and clandestine operations. The implications chilled Jason to the bone.

Suddenly, the warehouse door creaked open, revealing a figure silhouetted against the faint light filtering in from outside. Dimitri fell silent, his eyes narrowing as the figure stepped into the room. It was a woman, tall and elegant, dressed in impeccably tailored clothing that seemed out of place in the grimy warehouse. She carried herself with an air of quiet authority that commanded attention.

"Elena," Dimitri breathed, a hint of something akin to respect in his voice, a stark contrast to his previous fury. "What brings you here?"

Elena smiled, a slow, deliberate curve of her lips that didn’t reach her eyes. "I believe we need to have a discussion about the future of our… endeavors," she said, her voice low and melodious, a deceptive counterpoint to the chilling implication in her words. "Gomin's death has created… complications."

The conversation that followed was a masterclass in veiled threats and carefully chosen words. Jason listened, unseen, absorbing every detail. He learned that Elena was a powerful player in her own right, a woman with connections to governments and corporations that dwarfed even Gomin's reach. She was a figure of immense power, a puppet master pulling strings from the shadows. And, to Jason's utter surprise, she seemed to have a vested interest in ensuring that the truth about Gomin's death, and the larger conspiracy it uncovered, remained buried.

The unexpected twist lay in her motive. Elena wasn't simply trying to protect the organization; she was actively working to manipulate events to her own advantage. She was using the chaos caused by Gomin's demise to consolidate her own power, eliminating rivals and solidifying her position at the top. Gomin's death was not just a setback; it was an opportunity.

This revelation changed everything. Jason's mission had expanded beyond eliminating a single criminal. He was now hunting a phantom, a shadow figure whose reach extended far beyond the criminal underworld. He had underestimated the depth of the conspiracy, the power and influence of the players involved. The fight had just gotten a whole lot more dangerous.

As Elena and Dimitri finalized their plans – plans that involved silencing anyone who might uncover the truth – Jason began to reassess his situation. He had to get out, and he had to get out quickly. The shadows offered little protection now; he was no longer a silent observer, but a target. He moved with the grace of a phantom, his movements fluid and silent, slipping away unnoticed amidst the hushed whispers and shadowy figures.

Meanwhile, Jake Harroll, back in his office, was piecing together the fragments of information he'd gathered. He was far removed from the shadowy warehouse, yet the weight of the unfolding conspiracy pressed down on him. He'd been investigating Gomin, a ruthless criminal mastermind, but the truth, as it always seemed to do, extended far beyond the initial scope of his investigation. The sheer scale of the network he was uncovering was staggering, reaching into the highest echelons of power and influence.

He reviewed the notes from his interview with Jason, the chilling account of a meticulous assassin, a man driven by a sense of justice as twisted as the organization he was fighting against. He'd initially seen Jason as a hired gun, a tool in a larger game. But now, with the information from the warehouse – the overheard conversations, the hints of a far larger conspiracy – Jake began to realize that

Jason might be something more, a rogue element in a world ruled by ruthless pragmatism.

The more Jake investigated, the more he realized that he was playing a dangerous game. He was treading on thin ice, walking a tightrope between exposure and discovery. He wasn't just investigating a crime; he was uncovering a web of deception that snaked its way through governments, corporations, and criminal enterprises. He was dealing with people who would stop at nothing to protect their secrets, people who would kill to ensure their continued power.

The information that he had uncovered was explosive. It implicated politicians, business tycoons, and even some members of law enforcement. He knew that releasing this information would not only cause chaos but also put his own life at risk. But he also knew that he couldn't ignore the truth. He had a responsibility to expose this organization, to bring them down.

He looked at the photographs, the documents, and the recordings he'd painstakingly gathered. The evidence was overwhelming. He had to find a way to make this information public, but he needed to do it carefully. He needed to ensure his own safety, and, if possible, he needed to find a way to collaborate with Jason, the assassin who had inadvertently stumbled upon the same truth. He was, unknowingly, now an integral part of the same desperate game for survival.

The chase intensified, not just for Jason, but for Jake as well. They were both caught in a whirlwind of danger, each playing their own part in a dangerous game of cat and mouse, a game where the stakes were life and death. The unexpected alliance, the hidden connections, the sheer scale of the conspiracy – it all added a new layer of complexity and suspense to the story, a chilling reminder of the hidden depths of power and corruption.

Jake knew that he was in over his head. He was a journalist, not a spy, not a soldier. He didn't have the skills or training to handle this situation. But he was determined to continue his investigation. He had a responsibility to the truth, to the victims of this organization. He had to find a way to expose them, no matter the price.

He decided to contact a trusted source, a former FBI agent who specialized in organized crime. The agent, a man named Marcus, had a reputation for being incorruptible. He was a man who wouldn't flinch in the face of danger, a man who would do whatever it took to bring down the bad guys.

Marcus listened intently as Jake laid out the details of his investigation, the shocking revelations about the vast criminal organization, and its unexpected alliances. He listened without interruption, his expression unreadable.

When Jake finished, Marcus leaned back in his chair, his eyes narrowed. "This is bigger than we thought," he said quietly. "Much bigger." He paused, then added, "We need to tread carefully. This organization has deep roots, and they are not afraid to use violence."

Marcus agreed to help. Together, they would devise a plan to expose the organization, a plan that would be both meticulous and dangerous. They knew that they were up against a powerful enemy, an enemy that was willing to do anything to protect its secrets. But they were also determined to bring them down. The chase was on, a dangerous game of cat and mouse, where the stakes were higher than ever before.

The clock was ticking, and the consequences of failure were dire. The lives of countless individuals, and perhaps even the fate of nations, hung in the balance. The hunt was far from over, and the true extent of the conspiracy remained shrouded in secrecy, a chilling enigma waiting to be unraveled. The unexpected twist, the hidden connections, had only deepened the mystery, intensified the chase and raised the stakes to an unprecedented level. The game had begun, and the fight for truth was just beginning. The relentless pursuit of justice had transformed into a desperate struggle for survival against a force far more powerful and far more insidious than either Jake or Jason could have possibly imagined.

....

The Parisian rain hammered against the taxi window, blurring the already chaotic cityscape into a watercolor wash of gray. Jason gripped the worn leather seat, his knuckles white. Each drop felt like a tiny hammer blow against his tense composure, mirroring the frantic rhythm of his own pulse. Dimitri's words echoed in his ears: "Nothing but a mess." A mess that Jason was now tasked with cleaning up, a task far more complex than eliminating a single, albeit powerful, man.

The information Dimitri had reluctantly spilled – a cryptic mention of "The Velvet Circle," a shadowy cabal operating in the shadows of Gomin’s empire – sent a jolt of icy dread through Jason. Gomin had been a pawn, a highly expendable one at that, in a far larger game. The implications were staggering; eliminating Gomin hadn't ended the threat; it had only scratched the surface. Now, the true architects of this criminal enterprise remained hidden, their identities obscured by layers of deceit and an intricate web of international connections.

He glanced at the file clutched in his hand, the thin paper damp with the city's relentless downpour. It contained the last known location of one Lucian Moretti, a name that whispered through the underbelly of the criminal world like a venomous snake. Moretti, Dimitri had implied, was Gomin's right-hand man, the keeper of secrets, the man who held the key to unlocking the mystery of the Velvet Circle. Finding Moretti was paramount; he was the key to understanding the organization's structure, its funding, and its ultimate goals.

The taxi screeched to a halt outside a nondescript building nestled in a labyrinthine alleyway. The air hung heavy with the scent of stale cigarettes and desperation. Jason paid the driver, a surly man who cast a wary eye over him, and stepped into the oppressive darkness. The building, a dilapidated former warehouse, exuded a palpable sense of decay and danger. He knew that Moretti was somewhere within these crumbling walls, playing a deadly game of cat and mouse.

His senses sharpened, every nerve ending tingling with adrenaline. The faint sounds of muffled voices and the distant clang of metal punctuated the suffocating silence. He moved with the practiced grace of a phantom, his footsteps barely disturbing the dust that coated the floor. He navigated the maze-like corridors, each turn revealing a new chamber of shadows. The air grew colder, the atmosphere more sinister, as he neared his target.

He found Moretti in a dimly lit room, surrounded by heavily armed men. Moretti himself was a picture of nervous energy, pacing back and forth like a caged animal. He was clearly aware that his time was running out. Jason assessed the situation; a direct confrontation would be suicidal. He needed a strategy, a plan to extract information from Moretti without raising the alarm. He silently moved to a vantage point, observing the room and its occupants.

He noticed a subtle detail – a small, almost imperceptible tremor in Moretti's hands. It betrayed his anxiety, a chink in his otherwise composed exterior. Jason saw an opportunity. He used his skills to disrupt the security system, triggering a momentary lapse in attention among the guards. It was a fleeting window of opportunity, but it was all he needed.

He slipped into the room, his movements fluid and precise. He moved with the silent efficiency of a predator, his presence unnoticed until it was too late. Before Moretti could react, Jason had him pinned to the wall, a cold, hard barrel pressed against his temple. The room fell silent, the only sound the ragged breathing of Moretti and the rhythmic thumping of Jason's heart.

"Tell me about the Velvet Circle," Jason hissed, his voice a low growl. "Tell me everything."

Moretti, his eyes wide with terror, began to spill his secrets. He spoke of a network spanning continents, an organization fueled by greed and ambition, its tentacles wrapped around the world's financial systems and political landscapes. He spoke of coded messages, hidden bank accounts, and clandestine meetings in the most remote corners of the globe. The information was a torrent, a deluge of names, dates, and locations, painting a terrifying picture of the organization's true power and reach.

The details were chilling; each revelation unveiled a deeper layer of corruption. Moretti spoke of assassinations, extortion, and money laundering on an unprecedented scale. The Velvet Circle wasn't just a criminal organization; it was a global shadow government, pulling the strings from the darkness, manipulating events on the world stage. Jason listened intently, absorbing every word, piecing together the fragments of this elaborate puzzle.

As Moretti spoke, Jason felt a growing sense of dread. He realized that he was facing something far larger, far more powerful, than he could have ever imagined. Eliminating Gomin had been a significant step, but it was only the beginning of a far greater battle. He understood now the true magnitude of the threat; this wasn't about a single criminal mastermind; it was about a vast, insidious network that controlled governments, manipulated markets, and held the world hostage. The stakes were impossibly high.

He extracted the information he needed, a detailed account of the Velvet Circle’s operations and its key players. He left Moretti alive, a walking, talking testament to his power, a man who would eventually lead authorities to the heart of the organization. Jason knew that the risks were immense, that he was walking a tightrope above an abyss. But he also knew that he couldn’t stop. The weight of responsibility pressed down on him, a crushing burden he was determined to bear.

The rain continued to fall, washing away the grime and the blood, but not the darkness that clung to the city. As Jason slipped back into the Parisian night, he felt a chilling sense of urgency. He knew that time was his greatest enemy, a relentless force that threatened to swallow him whole. The chase had intensified, becoming a frantic race against a clock that was ticking down toward a catastrophic climax. He had uncovered a monstrous conspiracy, one that threatened to engulf the world in its shadow. And Jason, armed with this newfound knowledge, was now the only one who could stop it.

He knew that he couldn't do this alone. He needed Jake, the radio reporter who had originally drawn him into this world. Jake possessed the journalistic skills and the network of contacts necessary to bring the truth to light, to expose the Velvet Circle to the world. He pulled out his phone, his fingers clumsy and hesitant as he dialed Jake’s number. The connection was immediate, a lifeline in the suffocating darkness.

"Jake," he said, his voice strained, "we have a problem. A much bigger problem than we ever imagined."

He relayed the details, the shocking revelations about the Velvet Circle. He could hear Jake's breathing on the other end of the line, the silence punctuated by the rapid click of keys on a keyboard. The urgency in his voice was palpable.

"I'm on my way," Jake said, his voice tight with a mixture of fear and determination. "This is bigger than us, Jason. Much bigger. But we'll face it together."

The line went dead. Jason hung up, a grim smile playing on his lips. The race against time had begun, a desperate struggle against a formidable enemy. The fate of the world hung precariously in the balance, and Jason, the assassin, now a reluctant hero, was determined to win. The fight had only just begun. The hunt for the truth had turned into a fight for survival, a relentless pursuit of justice against a force far more powerful and insidious than either of them could have ever imagined. The consequences of failure were unthinkable. And the stakes? They were the fate of the world.

....

The Parisian rain continued its relentless assault, a drumming counterpoint to the frantic beat of Jake’s heart. He stared at the crumpled photograph in his hand – a grainy image of Gomin Guill, his face contorted in a rictus of pain, death’s final curtain call. Jason’s confession, delivered in hushed tones amidst the city’s cacophony, had shattered Jake’s carefully constructed world. He’d interviewed countless criminals, delved into the murky underbelly of society, but this…this was different. This wasn't just a story; it was a bomb ticking away, threatening to consume him whole.

He rubbed his tired eyes, the city lights blurring into indistinct streaks. The initial adrenaline rush had faded, replaced by a chilling wave of self-doubt. He’d initially approached the story as a typical investigative piece, a compelling tale of a ruthless assassin and his equally ruthless target. But Jason’s final words, the implication of a far-reaching conspiracy, had irrevocably altered the narrative. He wasn’t just reporting a crime; he was potentially stepping into the crosshairs of a powerful, shadowy organization.

The ethical dilemma gnawed at him. He was a journalist, a chronicler of events, not an action hero. His weapon was a microphone, not a gun. But the information he possessed, the truth he'd uncovered, was too dangerous to ignore. To bury it would be a betrayal, not just of Jason's trust, but of his own journalistic integrity. Yet, to pursue it meant risking everything – his career, his safety, perhaps even his life.

He thought back to his initial interview with Jason. The assassin's cold precision, his chilling detachment, had been captivating. Yet, beneath the veneer of professional killer, Jake sensed a flicker of something else, a hint of moral ambiguity. Jason hadn't celebrated his success; he'd seemed burdened by it, haunted by the weight of his actions. His reticence about the larger conspiracy, the deliberate omission of certain details, had hinted at a deeper game at play, a web of deceit far beyond his initial understanding.

The information Jason had revealed – fragmented, incomplete, yet undeniably significant – pointed towards a vast network operating beyond the reach of any known law enforcement agency. They weren't mere criminals; they were puppeteers, pulling strings from the shadows, manipulating governments and economies with ruthless efficiency. And Jake, armed with these fragments of truth, had become an unwitting pawn in their dangerous game.

He replayed the conversation in his mind, each word, each pause heavy with unspoken meaning. Jason had mentioned coded messages, hidden symbols, encrypted communications – a language only the initiated could understand. He'd spoken of a "cleaner," someone responsible for eliminating loose ends, ensuring the organization's secrecy remained intact. The thought sent a shiver down Jake's spine. Was he now a loose end? Was he being watched?

The taxi pulled up to his apartment building, the sudden stillness jarring after the chaotic energy of the city streets. He paid the driver, his mind still racing, the weight of his predicament pressing down on him. He entered his apartment, a small, sparsely furnished space, a stark contrast to the opulent world he'd glimpsed through Jason's stories. He felt exposed, vulnerable, the walls seeming to close in on him.

He switched on his laptop, the glowing screen a beacon in the otherwise dimly lit room. He opened his notes, re-reading Jason's account, searching for clues, for anything that might shed light on the organization's structure, its motives, its reach. Each sentence, each detail, seemed to hold a hidden significance, a subtle clue to a larger puzzle.

Hours passed in a blur of research, his fingers flying across the keyboard, his eyes scanning countless documents and online forums. He discovered cryptic messages, coded references, and fragmented information – pieces of a jigsaw puzzle he was desperately trying to assemble. He found connections to seemingly unrelated events, global incidents that had initially been dismissed as isolated occurrences. Now, piecing them together, he saw a pattern, a sinister thread connecting them all – the same shadowy organization.

As the night deepened, the weight of his discovery pressed down on him. This wasn't just a story anymore. It was a fight for survival, a desperate race against time. He was no longer a detached observer; he was an active participant, a potential target. The line between journalist and investigative subject had blurred, becoming indistinguishable. He was no longer simply reporting the news; he was becoming the news.

He thought about his family, his friends, the life he had carefully constructed. The thought of putting them in danger filled him with a cold dread. But he knew he couldn't back down. The information he had was too important to ignore. To do so would be a failure of his conscience, a betrayal of his commitment to truth.

He continued his research, digging deeper, pushing past the boundaries of his comfort zone. He felt like he was walking a tightrope, one wrong step away from a catastrophic fall. The organization's reach was far greater than he had initially imagined, its tentacles extending into every corner of the globe. He felt a wave of nausea, the realization of the enormity of his undertaking washing over him. He was facing a force that was far more powerful, far more dangerous, than anything he could have ever anticipated. This wasn't just a story; it was a war, and he was fighting it alone.

The morning light found him slumping over his laptop, his eyes bloodshot, his mind reeling. He'd contacted a few sources, cautiously probing, testing the waters. The responses were cryptic, evasive, yet undeniably confirming his suspicions. The organization existed, and it was far more powerful and insidious than anyone had ever dared to imagine. He felt a sense of grim determination hardening his resolve. He had to continue, had to find a way to expose them, to bring them down. His life was now on the line, but so was the fate of the world, or at least a significant portion of it. He knew he couldn’t fail. The chase had only just begun, and the stakes were higher than ever before. His dilemma wasn't just moral; it was a matter of survival, a battle against a force that operated in the shadows, a force that had already claimed countless victims and showed no sign of stopping. Jake Harroll, the radio reporter, had become something else entirely – a reluctant warrior in a war he never asked for, but one he could no longer afford to ignore. The world, unknowingly, held its breath.

The Showdown

The air hung thick with the scent of ozone and fear. Gomin Guill, his face a mask of controlled fury, stood silhouetted against the panoramic window of his penthouse apartment, overlooking the glittering cityscape of Monaco. Rain lashed against the glass, mirroring the storm brewing inside. Jason Reen, his silhouette equally stark against the darkened doorway, held his breath, the weight of the mission pressing down on him like a physical burden. He'd spent months thoroughly tracking Guill, weaving through a labyrinthine web of deceit, betrayal, and murder. This was the culmination, the final act in a thoroughly orchestrated play.

The penthouse was a stark contrast to the opulent opulence one might expect. The minimalist décor, almost spartan in its austerity, hinted at a man who valued function over frivolous display, a man who preferred the shadows to the spotlight. But the strategic placement of security cameras, subtly concealed within the architecture, revealed a deep-seated paranoia, a constant awareness of potential threats. Jason had accounted for them all, or so he thought.

He moved with the grace of a phantom, a whisper of motion in the darkened space. The only sounds were the relentless drumming of the rain and the barely audible hum of the sophisticated security system. Guill, however, remained unmoved, his eyes – cold, calculating, and unnervingly perceptive – fixed on Jason. He knew he was coming. The air crackled with unspoken tension, the silence a palpable entity between them.

"You're a persistent one, Reen," Guill finally said, his voice a low, smooth baritone, devoid of any discernible emotion. "I admire your tenacity, even if I despise your methods."

Jason remained silent with his gaze unwavering. He didn't need to speak; his presence spoke volumes. Years of training, honed to a razor's edge, had prepared him for this moment. Every muscle in his body was coiled tight, ready to spring into action.

"You've come a long way to kill me," Guill continued, a hint of amusement creeping into his tone. "And for what? A pittance compared to the wealth and power I command?"

"You underestimated me," Jason responded, his voice barely a whisper, yet carrying an authority that silenced the room. “You underestimated the people you wronged.”

The words hung in the air, a prelude to the inevitable violence. Guill’s amusement vanished, replaced by a chilling determination. He made a subtle gesture, and two hulking figures emerged from the shadows, their hands instinctively reaching for the weapons concealed beneath their jackets. The carefully orchestrated dance of death was about to begin.

The ensuing confrontation was a brutal ballet of death, a whirlwind of motion and violence. Jason moved with lethal efficiency, his movements precise and economical. He disarmed one of Guill's guards with a swift, almost effortless maneuver, his hand snapping out to strike a nerve cluster in the man's neck, leaving him incapacitated but alive. The other guard lunged, but Jason anticipated the attack, deflecting the blow and countering with a swift kick that sent the man sprawling. The fight spilled across the room, shattering glass and scattering debris.

Guill, however, was no ordinary target. He was a cunning strategist, a master manipulator who had anticipated some degree of resistance. He wasn’t armed, but he was prepared. He moved with surprising agility for a man of his age and build, his movements calculated and deliberate. He knew the layout of his penthouse intimately, using the furniture and décor as shields, turning the opulent surroundings into a deadly obstacle course.

Jason was forced to adapt, improvising as he went, utilizing his environment with the same deadly precision as his opponent. He disarmed the second guard using only his own body weight as leverage, causing him to fall before he could respond. The fight became a test of wills and a battle of attrition. Each blow landed with the force of a sledgehammer while each parry was executed with flawless timing.

The clash between them was a study of contrasts. Guill, the calculating mastermind, relying on strategy and deception. Jason, the silent assassin, relying on instinct and brute force. But beneath the surface of their deadly dance, a deeper game was being played. A game of deception, betrayal, and hidden agendas.

As the fight raged, Jason noticed something out of place. A small, almost invisible camera, embedded in the baseboard near the fireplace. It was a subtle detail, easy to overlook, yet it spoke volumes. This wasn't simply a private residence; it was a command center, thoroughly monitored, protected. The camera was a piece of the bigger puzzle that he was trying to solve.

He grabbed the camera, knowing this small piece of technology could unravel far more than just this room. This was evidence he needed to prove the depths of this organization's far-reaching corruption. The sudden shift in focus gave Guill the opening he needed. He lunged, delivering a swift, brutal blow that sent Jason reeling.

Jason, dazed but not defeated, rolled away from the blow, creating enough distance to draw a small, specialized knife. He had known going into the encounter that this one could not be a clean, precise kill. He was not attempting to erase any traces of his presence. He needed Guill to talk. The next few seconds would determine the fate of not just Guill but also the larger organization.

....

The silence stretched, taut and unbearable, broken only by the rhythmic drumming of the rain against the glass. Gomin Guill, his composure finally cracking, let out a harsh laugh, a sound devoid of mirth. "You think this is over, Reen? You think eliminating me is some kind of victory?" He gestured with a disdainful sweep of his hand towards the panoramic view, the city lights twinkling like fallen stars in the storm. "You've only scratched the surface."

Jason remained motionless, his hand resting lightly on the custom-made Beretta tucked into his waistband. He'd anticipated resistance, expected a fight, but Guill's words were a different kind of weapon, a chilling revelation that sent a shiver down his spine. Months of meticulous planning, countless sleepless nights, the lives he'd taken – all of it seemed to shrink in significance against the enormity of what Guill implied.

"What do you mean?" Jason's voice was low, a controlled tremor betraying the unease churning within him.

Guill took a slow, deliberate step towards him, the glint of manic energy in his eyes. "Gomin Guill," he said, his voice dripping with venom, "was a pawn. A useful one, admittedly, but just a pawn, nonetheless. You eliminated a player, Reen, but you haven't touched the game."

He produced a small, worn leather-bound notebook from an inner pocket of his tailored suit. He tossed it casually towards Jason. “That notebook,” Guill rasped, his voice strained, “contains the names. The names of the true players. The architects of this… empire.”

Jason caught the notebook, its weight surprisingly heavy in his hand. The leather felt cool and smooth against his fingers, but the contents promised to be anything but. He flipped it open, his eyes scanning the thoroughly handwritten entries. Names – names he recognized from hushed conversations, coded messages intercepted during his surveillance, whispers in the underbelly of the criminal world. Names that represented power, wealth, and influence on a scale he hadn’t imagined.

Among the names, he noticed several prominent figures: politicians, CEOs of multinational corporations, even a high-ranking official within the international banking system. They weren’t merely connected to Guill; they were the architects of his operation, the puppet masters pulling the strings from behind a veil of respectability and legitimacy. The organization was far more vast, far more insidious than he’d ever conceived.

A wave of nausea washed over him. This wasn't just an assassination; it concealed a more sinister plot. Guill's death, Jason realized, was a deliberate act, a sacrifice designed to distract from the true power brokers. His success had only inadvertently exposed the tip of a much larger iceberg.

"They'll be coming for you now, Reen," Guill said, a strange sense of satisfaction in his voice. "They'll be coming for everyone who knows."

The implication hung heavily in the air, a silent threat that echoed the storm raging outside. Jason knew Guill was right. His elimination of Guill wouldn't go unnoticed. The true players would see him as a loose end, a threat to be neutralized.

As the police sirens wailed in the distance, a sudden realization struck Jason. Jake Harroll. He'd been entrusted with the truth, and now he was a potential target as well. The notebook in his hand, filled with the names of the powerful and influential, was a death sentence, not just for him, but for anyone who held the information.

The rain intensified, the wind howling like a tormented beast, mirroring the chaos brewing within him. He had to get the information to someone safe, someone who could expose this conspiracy without becoming another victim. The notebook was more than just a list of names; it was a map to a treacherous underworld, a blueprint for a vast criminal enterprise that operated in the shadows, pulling the strings of power from behind the scenes.

He glanced at Guill, his face contorted in a grimace of pain and defeat. The man's eyes, though filled with hatred, held a hint of something else – a perverse sense of triumph. He had played his role perfectly, a sacrificial lamb whose death had opened a Pandora's box of revelations.

Jason slipped the notebook into his jacket, his heart pounding a frantic rhythm against his ribs. He had to act fast, before the storm of vengeance descended upon him. He knew that simply escaping wouldn't be enough. He needed a plan, a strategy to expose the truth and survive the inevitable retaliation. He needed to find a way to turn the tables on those who controlled the game.

He looked out at the rain-lashed cityscape. The lights, once mesmerizing, now appeared cold and menacing, a symbol of the vast network of corruption he’d stumbled upon. The hunt for Gomin Guill was over, but the game, far from being over, had just entered a terrifyingly new phase.

As he slipped out of the penthouse, leaving behind the body of Gomin Guill and the echoing silence of the rain-swept city, Jason knew the next phase would be the most dangerous yet. He wasn't just facing a criminal organization anymore; he was facing a vast and powerful conspiracy that stretched into the highest echelons of society, a conspiracy that had woven its tendrils into the very fabric of the world. He was a lone wolf, hunting in the densest jungle, and he knew that one wrong step could be his last.

His mission had changed. He was no longer just an assassin; he was a whistleblower, a man armed with the truth, fighting a battle against an enemy far more formidable than any individual. His journey had taken a sharp, unexpected turn, and as he disappeared into the anonymity of the Monaco night, he knew that his fight for survival had just begun. The revelation had raised the stakes exponentially; it was no longer about eliminating a single criminal mastermind but exposing a sprawling network of corruption that threatened to destabilize the world's order.

The notebook felt heavy in his pocket, a burden of knowledge and danger. The names within were not just names; they were ticking time bombs, each representing a potential point of catastrophic failure within the system. He thought of Jake Harroll, the journalist who had initially sought him out. Jake was now a critical part of this puzzle, a potential ally, but also a potential target. He had to reach him.

He needed to inform someone he could trust, someone who could help to unravel the intricate web of deceit and power that had ensnared him and possibly the entire world. The immediate concern was safety; he needed to evade capture, to disappear into the labyrinthine alleys of Monaco, shedding his past as efficiently as he had eliminated Gomin Guill. The meticulous planning and precision that had characterized his previous missions now needed to be channeled into self-preservation and the creation of a viable strategy for exposing the truth. He had to consider all angles; he was not just fighting against a criminal organization; he was facing a conspiracy that permeated every level of society. He needed to carefully analyze his next move, anticipate his enemies' reactions and strategize his path to exposure.

The escape was a dance of shadows, a calculated maneuver through dimly lit streets, each step echoing with the weight of his newfound knowledge. His every move was a gamble, a calculated risk that could determine his survival and the unraveling of this massive conspiracy. The night was his ally, concealing him from prying eyes, offering a momentary reprieve from the imminent threat. Yet, the ever-present sense of danger hung in the air, a palpable reminder of the deadly game he was playing.

He knew that reaching Jake Harroll was his top priority. Harroll was a seasoned journalist, someone with the connections and resources needed to navigate this complex and dangerous world. But contacting Harroll was fraught with peril; he had to choose his method of contact with extreme care, as any slip could expose them both. He needed a secure and untraceable means of communication, a way to share the sensitive information contained in the notebook without alerting his pursuers.

The adrenaline coursed through his veins, a potent cocktail of fear and determination. He was a man on the run, hunted by an enemy he barely understood. Yet, a steely resolve had settled within him. The revelation hadn't broken him; it had galvanized him. The fight was far from over; it was just beginning. He had a story to tell, a truth to reveal, and he would not rest until the puppet masters were exposed, their reign of terror brought to an end. He was no longer just an assassin; he was a soldier of truth, fighting a battle against the shadows, and in the darkness of the Monaco night, he knew his next move. The game had changed, and the stakes had never been higher.

....

The rain hammered against the windows of the Monaco penthouse, mirroring the chaotic storm raging inside Jason Reen. Gomin Guill, the seemingly untouchable kingpin, lay sprawled on the Persian rug, a crimson stain blooming across his expensive Italian suit. Yet, the victory felt hollow, a fleeting moment of triumph in a much larger, far more sinister game. Gomin's last words echoed in Jason's ears, a chilling prophecy: "You've only scratched the surface."

Jason had thoroughly planned Gomin's demise, a symphony of calculated movements and flawlessly executed maneuvers. He'd infiltrated Gomin's inner circle, exploiting weaknesses, turning loyalty, and weaving a web of deceit that ensnared the criminal mastermind. He'd anticipated Gomin's security, his escape routes, his every habit. But the reality of Gomin's death only served to amplify the lurking shadows, the whispers of a vast conspiracy that stretched far beyond one man's reach.

He knelt beside the body, his gloved hands carefully searching for anything that might offer a clue, a breadcrumb leading him towards the puppeteers pulling the strings. Gomin’s death wasn't a simple assassination; it was a thoroughly crafted act designed to expose the layers of this intricate criminal organization. He found nothing overtly incriminating – no hidden files, no coded messages, just the usual paraphernalia of a wealthy and powerful man. But the absence of obvious evidence only deepened the mystery. It suggested an organization operating with an almost supernatural level of secrecy and sophistication.

He contacted his handler, a shadowy figure known only as "The Curator," a woman whose voice was as cold and precise as a surgeon's scalpel. Their conversations were always brief, encrypted, and conducted through a series of untraceable channels. He relayed the events of the night, the details of Gomin’s final moments, the unsettling sense of incompleteness that clung to the air like a persistent fog.

The Curator’s response was as expected – concise and chillingly pragmatic.

"Gomin was a pawn, Reen," her voice hissed through the encrypted line. "His death was merely a prelude. The true enemy remains unseen."

The Curator's words confirmed Jason’s suspicions. Gomin had been a powerful figure, but he hadn't been at the top of the pyramid. He'd been a key player, no doubt, but merely a highly visible component in a much larger machine. The organization's reach extended far beyond Monaco's glittering casinos and opulent hotels. He had been eliminating the symptoms, not the disease.

The next few days were a blur of frantic activity. Jason thoroughly cleaned the penthouse, erasing every trace of his presence, a ritual he had perfected over years of clandestine operations. He left no fingerprints, no DNA, no witnesses. He was a ghost, a whisper in the wind. Then, he vanished, melting into the anonymity of the city, leaving behind only a chilling void where a powerful crime lord once reigned.

He flew to Zurich, a city known for its discreet wealth management and complex financial networks. He had a hunch that the trail would lead to the labyrinthine world of offshore accounts and shell corporations. He spent weeks poring over financial records, tracking money flows, deciphering coded transactions, all the while maintaining a low profile, avoiding detection by the unseen eyes that constantly watched him. He navigated the shadowy world of international finance, a world where money laundered through a network of shell companies and offshore accounts, obscuring the origins of funds and the identities of its benefactors.

The trail eventually led him to a series of encrypted emails, hinting at a global network of arms dealers, corrupt politicians, and influential businessmen – individuals who were all connected, their actions carefully coordinated. These emails spoke of a far-reaching plan, a clandestine operation involving the smuggling of illegal weapons, the manipulation of global markets, and the clandestine funding of terrorist organizations. The scale of the conspiracy was staggering, reaching into the highest echelons of power and influence.

He started to see a pattern, a sinister web of interconnectedness. The organization wasn't just involved in crime; it was manipulating events on a global scale, pulling the strings from the shadows, profiting from chaos and instability. Gomin had been a valuable asset, but he was also expendable – a sacrificial lamb offered up to deflect attention from the true masterminds. Jason now understood the depth of the conspiracy, the scale of the threat, and his own perilous position within it.

He reached out to Jake Harroll, the radio reporter, the only person he could trust. He had a story to tell, a story that could shake the foundations of the world. The risk was enormous – exposing this organization could have deadly consequences. But Jason had crossed a point of no return. He was no longer just an assassin; he was a whistleblower, a crusader against a global conspiracy that threatened the very fabric of society. He knew that his life was on the line, but the stakes were far too high to back down.

The meeting with Jake was clandestine, taking place in a deserted warehouse on the outskirts of Berlin. Jason handed Jake a flash drive containing all the information he had gathered. It contained the encrypted emails, financial records, a list of names, and a roadmap leading towards the heart of the conspiracy. The weight of the information, the potential consequences of exposure, felt almost tangible in the air between them.

Jake, a seasoned journalist who had covered numerous stories of corruption and organized crime, was stunned by the scale of the conspiracy, the sophistication of the operation, and the sheer audacity of the players involved. He understood the immense danger, the risks involved in pursuing this story, but he also recognized the importance of exposing the truth, no matter the cost.

“This could change everything, Jason,” Jake said, his voice a low, gravelly whisper. "This is bigger than any story I've ever covered."

Jason knew the risks, the potential for deadly retaliation. But he also knew that silence was complicity. He had eliminated Gomin, but he had also opened Pandora's Box. The fight was far from over; it had just reached a new, more dangerous level. He handed Jake a burner phone, a secure encrypted line used to communicate with The Curator. It was a lifeline, a last resort, a connection to a network of allies as secretive and dangerous as the enemy they were facing. The game was afoot, and this time, the stakes were not just his life, but the fate of the world. He knew the next chapter would be filled with more danger, more betrayal, and more ruthless adversaries. But he was prepared, and he wouldn't falter.

The hunt was on; the fight for truth had just begun. The shadows were deep, but the fight for justice, no matter the cost, was worth it. He wouldn't rest until the puppet masters were brought to light, their reign of terror ended, and the world was made safe from their evil machines.

....

The Monaco rain, a relentless assault on the glass, mirrored the frantic rhythm of Jason's heartbeat. He'd killed Gomin Guill, but the victory tasted like ash in his mouth. The penthouse, moments ago a scene of brutal efficiency, was now a chaotic mess. He needed out, and he needed out now. Gomin's final words – "You've only scratched the surface" – gnawed at him, a chilling premonition of the storm to come.

His escape wasn't a Hollywood-style sprint; it was a calculated, brutal ballet of evasion. He moved with the practiced grace of a phantom, a shadow slipping through the cracks of the opulent apartment. He'd disabled the security cameras – a simple task for someone with his skills – but he knew the building's staff, the neighbors, even the city's surveillance systems, would soon be alerted. The penthouse, a symbol of Gomin's power, was now a death trap.

He'd secured the encrypted burner phone Jake had given him, tucking it deep within his jacket. It was his lifeline, a connection to the shadowy network known only as The Curator. The Curator was a legend, a whisper in the dark, a facilitator of justice in a world where justice was a luxury. They were his only hope for navigating the treacherous waters ahead.

His escape route had been thoughtfully planned, a labyrinth of fire escapes, service tunnels, and back alleys. It was a route he'd studied in the days leading up to the confrontation, anticipating precisely this scenario. But even the best-laid plans could unravel. As he navigated the narrow fire escape, a sudden jolt sent a searing pain through his left shoulder. He'd underestimated the guard stationed on the lower floor. A bullet had grazed him, a near miss that felt like a kiss of death. The pain was intense, a burning fire spreading through his arm, but he couldn't afford to slow down. He pressed his hand against the wound, his adrenaline masking the searing agony.

He descended the fire escape, each metal rung, a testament to his determination. His breath came in ragged gasps, the city's cacophony a relentless percussion accompanying his desperate flight. Below, the streets of Monaco teemed with life, oblivious to the violent drama unfolding above. He reached the ground floor, his body screaming in protest, each step a victory against the encroaching pain.

The service tunnels were a maze of damp concrete and echoing shadows. He moved through them with the silent efficiency of a predator, his senses heightened, his every nerve on edge. He could hear the sirens wailing in the distance, a mournful symphony announcing his impending doom. He pressed on, pushing his body beyond its limits, propelled by a primal fear and an unwavering resolve.

The escape felt surreal, an extended hallucination sparked by blood loss and adrenaline. The world seemed to warp and blur, colors bleeding together, sounds blending into a disorienting symphony of sirens, footfalls, and the rhythmic pounding of his own heart. He emerged from the tunnels into the back alleys, a labyrinth of shadows and forgotten corners. The rain continued its relentless assault, washing away the traces of his passage.

He found refuge in a small, dimly lit bar, tucked away in a forgotten corner of the city. The bar was nearly deserted, the only occupants, a grizzled bartender, and a lone, melancholic patron. He slumped onto a stool, the dampness of his clothes clinging to him like a shroud. The pain in his shoulder throbbed with a sickening rhythm. He needed medical attention, seeking it would mean risking capture. His face, pale and streaked with rain and blood, reflected the harsh, unforgiving light of the bar.

The bartender, a wizened man with eyes that had seen too much, silently placed a glass of amber liquid before him. It was strong, potent, a fiery elixir that burned its way down, temporarily numbing the pain. He drank it slowly, savoring the temporary oblivion. The silence was punctuated only by the rhythmic tick-tock of a clock, a relentless reminder of the ticking time bomb inside him. He pulled out the burner phone, its cold metal a reassuring weight in his hand. He needed to contact The Curator. He needed to disappear. He needed to survive.

He pressed the call button, the connection snapping into place after several tense rings. A voice, low and measured, answered at the other end. It was a voice devoid of emotion, a voice that spoke volumes about the power and danger it represented. "Curator," he whispered, his voice hoarse from blood loss and exhaustion.

The voice at the other end responded, its tone devoid of warmth but laced with a sharp intelligence. "Reen. I anticipated this. We have an extraction team on standby. They will contact you shortly. Remain calm. Remain hidden."

Jason hung up, a surge of relief coursing through him. He wasn't alone. He had allies. He had a chance. But even as relief washed over him, the chilling words of Gomin Guill echoed in his mind. "You've only scratched the surface." The escape was just the beginning. The real fight, the battle for truth, was yet to come. He took another slow sip of his drink, his eyes fixed on the relentless rain hammering against the bar window. He knew the storm was far from over. It was merely intensifying.

The extraction team arrived an hour later, discreet and professional. They moved like shadows, appearing from the darkness and disappearing into it, their faces hidden behind tactical gear. They whisked him away from the bar, seamlessly blending into the anonymity of the night. They provided him with basic first aid, attending to his bleeding shoulder while simultaneously driving him through the twisting streets of Monaco. The car, a nondescript sedan, was a mobile sanctuary, a temporary shield against the storm.

The drive was tense, every corner a potential ambush, every siren a reminder of the danger they were all in. Jason felt the comforting weight of the burner phone in his pocket. It was more than just a means of communication; it was a symbol of hope, a connection to a world beyond the reach of Gomin's organization, a world where truth could still prevail, however improbable it might seem. He closed his eyes, allowing himself a brief moment of rest, but even in sleep, the ghost of Gomin's last words haunted him. The escape was temporary. The fight was far from over. The hunt for the puppet masters, the shadowy figures who had orchestrated Gomin’s reign of terror, had only just begun. And Jason Reen, despite his wounds, his exhaustion, and the gnawing fear that lived in the pit of his stomach, was ready. He was ready for the fight of his life. The fight for the world.

....

The aftermath was a whirlwind. The Monaco police, sirens wailing like banshees, arrived with the efficiency of a well-oiled machine, their flashing lights painting the opulent penthouse suite in a strobe-like display of chaos. Jake, still reeling from the sheer audacity of what he'd just witnessed – a professional hit carried out with chilling precision in the heart of Monte Carlo – found himself thrust into the maelstrom. He hadn't been expecting this. He'd gone to interview an assassin, not become an unwitting participant in an international crime scene.

The air was thick with the metallic tang of blood, the sharp scent of expensive cologne clashing jarringly with the cloying sweetness of spilled champagne. Gomin Guill lay sprawled across a Persian rug, a grotesque parody of his former power and influence. The police, initially dismissive of Jake's presence, were quickly overwhelmed by the sheer scale of the crime scene. They were used to petty theft and high-society squabbles, not an assassination of this magnitude. Their initial professionalism began to unravel as the reality sunk in: this was a major player, someone who pulled strings in the highest echelons of power.

Jake, however, wasn’t focused on the police. He was focused on the details. His journalist’s instincts kicked in, overriding his initial shock and fear. He started thoroughly documenting everything: the positions of the bodies, the trajectory of the bullets, the scattered documents, the subtle signs of a struggle. He had the presence of mind to discreetly pocket a small, intricately carved wooden box he'd spotted tucked under a velvet cushion – something that felt profoundly out of place in this opulent setting. Its weight felt unusual; it was heavier than it looked.

As the police secured the scene, their methodical work, a stark contrast to the chaotic aftermath, Jake noticed something else: a faint, almost imperceptible scent, a chemical residue, clinging to the air. It wasn't the smell of gunpowder, which he was familiar with from years of covering crime scenes. This was different – cleaner, more synthetic. He knew instinctively that it was significant, a clue hinting at a level of sophistication far beyond typical underworld dealings. He recognized the subtle metallic undertone from articles he’d read in specialist chemistry journals. A trace amount of a rare chemical compound, often used in advanced military weaponry.

Later, in the relative calm of his hotel room, the rain still drumming against the window, Jake began to examine his findings. The wooden box was surprisingly heavy, and its intricate carvings, while beautiful, were oddly utilitarian. It felt less like a decorative piece and more like a sophisticated mechanism. After careful examination, he discovered a small, almost invisible latch, releasing a hidden compartment containing a single microfiche.

He'd expected something dramatic, something easily deciphered, perhaps a list of names or a complex financial ledger. Instead, the microfiche contained a seemingly cryptic series of numbers and symbols. It looked like a cipher, a sophisticated code requiring deciphering. He had to find someone who could break it.

His mind raced. He knew he was out of his depth. This wasn't just a simple case of organized crime; this was something far more sinister, more complex, a conspiracy that reached far beyond Gomin Guill's control. The assassination wasn't just an end; it was a beginning. He recalled Jason Reen's words: "You've only scratched the surface." It seemed more prescient than ever.

He reached out to Dr. Evelyn Reed, a cryptographer he’d met at a journalism conference several years ago.

Evelyn was known for her expertise in decoding complex ciphers, and he had a gut feeling that she was his only chance. He explained the situation, carefully omitting the details of his involvement with Jason and the full extent of the Gomin Guill assassination. He framed it as a journalistic investigation into a powerful crime syndicate, a story that would take down a corrupt organization. The truth, he felt, would be too much for her to handle without context, and, he feared, could put her in danger.

Evelyn agreed to meet, her voice tinged with a hint of caution, a professional courtesy that masked her obvious concern. She was a woman who dealt with danger only through meticulous preparation and planning, a counterpoint to the chaotic reality he was now facing.

The meeting took place in a discreet café tucked away in a quiet corner of Geneva. Evelyn, with her sharp eyes and sharp intellect, was a picture of intellectual determination. She examined the microfiche, the faint image glowing under the lens of her magnifying glass. Silence filled the space as she thoroughly noted down the patterns, her concentration absolute.

Several hours later, her face illuminated by the soft glow of her laptop screen, she looked up. "It's a modified

Vigenère cipher," she said, her voice low and to the point. "Very sophisticated. Whoever created this knew what they were doing. They're not amateurs." She paused, her fingers flying across the keyboard. "I've broken it. This... this is not good."

The decoded message was brief, chillingly precise. It was a list of names, locations, and dates, an insidiously planned timeline of future assassinations. The targets were not just low-level criminals; they were politicians, influential businessmen, even a high-ranking official within Interpol. They were all connected, somehow, to the shadowy network that had used Gomin Guill as a pawn. It revealed a network of influence and power stretching across continents, a spider's web of corruption that threatened to destabilize global security.

This was bigger than Gomin Guill, bigger than anything Jake had ever imagined. This was a conspiracy reaching the highest echelons of power – a secret organization pulling the strings from the shadows, using violence and intimidation to maintain control. The implications were staggering, potentially threatening global security and stability. He realized now just how dangerous

Jason's mission had truly been, how much danger he'd been in.

Jake felt a chilling wave of fear. He'd walked into a seemingly straightforward interview and stumbled upon a global conspiracy that could topple governments. He was no longer just a reporter investigating a crime; he was a target. He looked at Evelyn, a flicker of uncertainty in her eyes. They both knew their lives were now on the line. Their investigation had just become exponentially more perilous. The hunt was far from over, and they were now fully embroiled in a dangerous game they never intended to play. They both knew that the world they thought they knew had just been irrevocably altered, and their fight for truth had become a fight for survival. The truth, once revealed, would have far-reaching consequences, and its pursuit was fraught with danger. The final confrontation had only just begun. The shadow organization would stop at nothing to protect its secrets.

Following the Clues

The acrid smell of gunpowder still clung to Jake's clothes, a phantom scent mirroring the lingering unease in his gut. Gomin Guill was dead, but the victory felt hollow, a fleeting moment of triumph in a vast, shadowy war. The final confrontation, a chaotic ballet of gunfire and shattered glass, had yielded more questions than answers. Gomin's last words, a whispered name barely audible above the sirens, had sent a chill down Jake's spine. It wasn't just Gomin's operation; it was something far larger, a conspiracy reaching the highest echelons of power.

The evidence, scattered amidst the debris of Gomin's opulent penthouse apartment, was cryptic, a puzzle composed of fragmented clues. A torn piece of paper, bearing the embossed crest of a Swiss bank, hinted at offshore accounts and laundered money. A seemingly innocuous USB drive, recovered from Gomin's shattered laptop, held the key – a complex encryption code protecting files that could potentially expose the entire operation. Jake felt a surge of adrenaline, a mix of excitement and fear. He was treading on dangerous ground, venturing into a world where the lines between right and wrong blurred, and survival depended on instinct and cunning.

His first stop was the office of Marcus Thorne, a veteran cybersecurity expert Jake had met through a shared contact, a grizzled former intelligence officer named Isabella Morai. Marcus, a wiry man with eyes that held the weariness of countless sleepless nights spent wrestling with digital demons, agreed to help, his skepticism tempered by a glint of professional curiosity. The encryption was sophisticated, military-grade, but Marcus, with his team of specialists working through the night, began to crack the code.

Days bled into nights as the team painstakingly deciphered the encrypted files. The information revealed a chilling network of global influence, stretching across continents and touching upon figures of immense political power. Gomin, it turned out, was merely a pawn, a ruthless enforcer in a much larger game orchestrated by a puppet master pulling strings from the shadows. The files contained coded messages, financial transactions, and a complex web of shell corporations used to funnel illicit funds. The scale of the operation was staggering, a sophisticated criminal enterprise that dwarfed anything Jake had ever encountered in his career.

One name kept recurring in the decoded files: Alex Voldi. The name evoked whispers, a phantom figure lurking in the darkest corners of the international underworld. Voldi’s influence, the files revealed, extended beyond organized crime; he had tentacles wrapped around governments, corporations, and even seemingly respectable charitable organizations. He operated from the shadows, using proxies and intermediaries to maintain his anonymity, a true master of deception.

The next step was to find someone who knew Voldi, someone that was willing to talk. Isabella Morai was his only lead. She had dealt with individuals on the fringe of the global criminal underworld for years, a shadowy network of informants and contacts built over decades of covert operations. She agreed to help, but only on her terms. She wouldn't compromise her network, and she wouldn't engage in any overt action. Her help would be limited to providing Jake with information, guiding him towards individuals who could possibly shed light on Voldi's operations.

Isabella's information led Jake to a small, dilapidated bar in a forgotten corner of Prague. It was a place where shadows lingered and secrets were whispered, a den of iniquity where informants, spies, and mercenaries traded information and favors. There, amidst the haze of cigarette smoke and the clinking of glasses, Jake met Dimitri, a grizzled former KGB agent, his face a roadmap of past betrayals and close calls. Dimitri, initially reluctant, eventually agreed to help. He knew Voldi, although only indirectly. He spoke of Voldi as a myth, a figure of immense power and ruthlessness, almost god-like in his ability to manipulate events from afar.

Dimitri revealed details about Voldi's operations, his methods of controlling and manipulating global markets, using his financial power to influence politicians and business leaders. Voldi was a master puppeteer, pulling the strings of global events for his own nefarious gains. Dimitri was careful, guarded, speaking in riddles and coded language. It took Jake several sessions, carefully piecing together the fragments of information Dimitri provided, before a clearer picture started to emerge. Voldi was not merely involved in organized crime; he was attempting to destabilize governments, manipulating global markets for personal profit, and creating chaos to consolidate his own power.

The information Dimitri provided, along with the data from the USB drive, painted a terrifying picture. Voldi's reach was vast, his influence pervasive. He was far more dangerous than Gomin ever was, a true criminal mastermind operating on a global scale. Jake felt the weight of the situation bearing down on him, the realization that he was facing a foe who was almost impossible to defeat. He was playing a dangerous game, a game where the stakes were life and death, a game that could very well cost him his life. But the thrill of the chase, the allure of uncovering the truth, kept him pushing forward.

His investigation led him to a series of offshore accounts, shell corporations, and complex financial transactions designed to obscure the trail. He started tracing the flow of money, following the digital breadcrumbs left by Voldi and his associates. The trail led him across continents, from the bustling markets of Hong Kong to the quiet, secluded villas of the French Riviera. He uncovered evidence of arms deals, bribery, and political corruption, a vast network of deceit designed to keep Voldi hidden from the prying eyes of the law.

The more Jake delved into Voldi's world, the more dangerous it became. He realized he was being watched, followed. The organization was aware of his investigation, and they were coming after him. He felt the icy grip of fear, a primal instinct to survive kicking in. He was no longer just a reporter; he was a target. His life was in danger. He had to be smarter, faster, more ruthless than his adversaries. The chase was on, and he had to stay one step ahead. He needed a strategy, and he needed it fast. The information he had was not enough. He needed allies. But who could he trust? In this world of spies, double agents, and backstabbing informants, loyalty was a rare and precious commodity, and trust was even rarer. The fight had just begun.

....

The flickering neon sign of the "Golden Dragon" cast a lurid glow on the rain-slicked street. Jake Harroll, his trench coat pulled tight against the chill November air, hesitated before entering. This wasn't the kind of place a seasoned investigative journalist usually frequented, but desperation had a way of blurring the lines between professional ethics and sheer survival. He needed allies, and whispers in the shadowed corners of the city had led him here – to a contact known only as "Seraphina."

Seraphina, a woman shrouded in mystery even within the city's murky underworld, was said to possess an unparalleled network of informants. Her price was steep, but Jake was willing to pay. He had been living on borrowed time ever since Gomin Guill's death, the organization's tendrils reaching out to snuff out any loose ends, including him. He needed to understand the conspiracy, not just survive it.

Inside, the air hung thick with the scent of stale cigarettes and something else, something acrid and unsettling that clung to the back of his throat. The dim light revealed a dimly lit space filled with a motley crew of characters: hardened criminals, nervous informants, and figures so obscure they seemed to melt into the shadows. Seraphina, when she finally appeared, was even more enigmatic than the rumors suggested. Tall and slender, with eyes that seemed to pierce through him, she was a predator in human form, effortlessly navigating the treacherous currents of the underworld.

Their meeting was terse, businesslike. Jake laid out his case, carefully omitting any detail that could compromise his sources or expose his vulnerability. Seraphina listened intently, her expression unreadable, and when he finished, she simply said, "You're digging in dangerous territory, Mr. Harroll. Very dangerous."

Her information, when it finally came, was a fragmented jigsaw puzzle. She confirmed his suspicions: Gomin Guill was just a pawn, a brutal enforcer for a far more extensive organization, one that stretched across continents and wielded influence far beyond the reach of law enforcement. She spoke of shadowy figures, names whispered in hushed tones, code words that sent shivers down Jake's spine. She mentioned a clandestine network of offshore accounts, shell corporations, and encrypted communications, all thoroughly designed to mask the organization’s true power. Most importantly, she provided a name: Viktor Voldi.

Voldi, she explained, was the puppet master, the unseen hand that controlled the strings. He operated from the shadows, leaving no trace, a phantom pulling the levers of power. He was more than just a crime boss; he was a master strategist, a manipulator of global events, pulling the strings of political leaders and corporate executives alike. Seraphina's network had traced Voldi's activities to a secluded compound nestled deep within the Swiss Alps, a fortress of impenetrable security, a place where Voldi supposedly conducted his operations, planning his next moves.

Leaving the Golden Dragon, Jake felt a renewed sense of purpose, tempered with a growing awareness of the mortal danger he faced. He knew he couldn't do this alone. He needed more allies, and a crucial link emerged from Seraphina's briefing: a former operative within Voldi's organization, a man named Dimitri. Dimitri, Seraphina explained, had grown disillusioned with Voldi's ruthlessness and was seeking a way out, a chance to atone for his past actions.

Finding Dimitri proved to be a different challenge entirely. It required navigating a treacherous labyrinth of coded messages, encrypted emails, and clandestine meetings in dimly lit back alleys. The process was slow, painstaking, testing Jake's patience and resilience. Each step brought him closer to the truth, but also closer to the organization's wrath. He felt their eyes on him constantly –

in crowded streets, in empty parking lots, even in his own apartment. Paranoia was becoming a constant companion.

Finally, after days of tireless effort, Jake located Dimitri in a rundown apartment building in a forgotten corner of the city. Dimitri was a broken man, haunted by the ghosts of his past, his eyes reflecting the weight of his actions. He was wary, skeptical, but Jake's persistence and the shared desperation in their circumstances forged an uneasy alliance.

Dimitri's knowledge was invaluable. He provided insights into the organization's structure, its methods, and its intricate network of connections. He revealed the intricate layers of deception that masked Voldi's true identity, detailing the various shell companies and offshore accounts that were used to launder money and fund the organization's operations. He described the elaborate security measures in place at the Swiss compound, making it clear that a direct assault would be suicide.

He also revealed the extent of Voldi's ambition: not just criminal empire building, but something far more sinister. Voldi, Dimitri claimed, was planning a major terrorist attack, an act that would destabilize the world's financial markets and plunge the world into chaos. This attack, unlike past operations, wouldn't simply target wealth and power; it aimed at changing the very balance of global influence, plunging the world into a state of protracted conflict. The scale of Voldi's ambition was terrifying.

Jake realized that what began as a simple investigation into Gomin Guill's assassination had spiraled into something far bigger, far more dangerous than he could have ever imagined. He was no longer just a reporter chasing a story; he was a soldier in an invisible war, fighting against a powerful, ruthless enemy. The information Dimitri provided, coupled with Seraphina's network, painted a disturbing picture of an organization far more deeply entrenched than he could have ever anticipated.

Armed with this new information, Jake began to formulate a plan, a strategy to expose Voldi and dismantle his organization. He knew it was a long shot, a dangerous gamble, but he had no choice. He had to try. The fate of countless innocent people depended on it, and his own survival hung precariously in the balance. He wasn't just protecting himself anymore; he was protecting the world. He felt the weight of this realization, the daunting task ahead, but the fight within him, born of a deep-seated sense of justice, burned bright. He had found unlikely allies, but the true battle had just begun. The journey to expose Voldi was a path paved with risk and uncertainty, yet Jake, fueled by the urgency of the situation and the grim determination to survive, was ready to face whatever lay ahead.

....

Seraphina, a woman whose age was as enigmatic as her past, sipped her tea, the delicate china rattling slightly in her gloved hand. The Golden Dragon, despite its outwardly glamorous façade, hummed with a low thrum of danger, a palpable tension that prickled Jake's skin. He'd learned to read these subtle cues over years spent navigating the murky underbelly of the city. He'd expected answers from Seraphina, perhaps a lead, a name, something tangible to help him unravel the conspiracy that had ensnared him. Instead, she offered him something far more unsettling: a name whispered like a curse.

"Voldi," she'd said, her voice, barely a breath, "He's the one who orchestrated everything. Gomin was merely a pawn, a disposable piece in a much larger game."

Voldi. The name resonated with a chilling emptiness, a void that suggested vast power and complete ruthlessness. Jake had never heard of him, and yet, the way Seraphina spoke, the way her eyes flickered with a mixture of fear and awe, told him this man was a force of nature. A force far more dangerous than Gomin Guill ever could have been.

Leaving the Golden Dragon, the city lights seemed dimmer, the shadows deeper, knowing that he was now chasing a ghost, a phantom pulling strings from a distance he couldn't yet comprehend. The information Seraphina provided was scant, but it was enough to ignite a new fire within him. He knew he had to find out more about this Voldi, understand his motivations, his reach, his methods. This wasn't just about exposing a criminal organization anymore; it was about taking down a kingpin, a puppet master who operated from the shadows, manipulating events from a distance, unseen, unheard.

Jake's investigation led him down a rabbit hole of encrypted communications, offshore accounts, and shell corporations—a complex web woven by someone with immense resources and an army of skilled operatives. He spent weeks poring over financial records, tracing money laundering schemes that snaked across continents, all leading back to a single, elusive point: Voldi. He discovered Voldi's influence extended far beyond the criminal underworld; it reached the highest echelons of power, subtly manipulating political landscapes and shaping global events. This was a man who played chess on a global scale, moving nations and individuals as if they were mere pawns.

The deeper Jake delved, the more he realized the extent of Voldi's reach. He wasn't simply a drug lord or arms dealer; he was a master manipulator, a strategist of unparalleled skill. His empire wasn't built on brute force but on intricate networks of deception and control. He wielded influence through intimidation, bribery, and blackmail, silencing anyone who dared to cross his path. His methods were so refined, so thoroughly planned, that his presence was felt only in the devastating consequences of his actions.

One lead led him to a former associate of Voldi's, a man named Dmitri, now living under a false identity in a remote village in the Carpathian Mountains. Tracking him down required weeks of relentless pursuit, navigating treacherous terrain and dodging surveillance, but eventually, he found Dmitri, a broken man haunted by his past. Dmitri, initially hesitant and fearful, agreed to speak, his eyes reflecting the trauma he had endured.

Dmitri revealed Voldi's origins, tracing his ascent from a ruthless street thug in the Soviet era to the global power broker he had become. He spoke of Voldi's unwavering ambition, his ruthless efficiency, and his uncanny ability to anticipate and exploit weaknesses. He described Voldi's chilling detachment, his lack of empathy, a man who saw humanity as a resource to be manipulated and discarded. He recounted tales of Voldi's ruthlessness, his willingness to eliminate anyone who posed a threat, no matter how small. The stories painted a picture of a man operating outside the boundaries of morality, someone who viewed the world as a game, and human lives as mere pieces.

Dmitri provided Jake with invaluable information, including details about Voldi's inner circle, his methods of operation, and his hidden assets. He revealed the existence of a secret vault, hidden deep within a seemingly innocuous building in Zurich, containing evidence of Voldi's extensive criminal activities. This was the key, Jake realized. This vault held the proof, the smoking gun that could bring Voldi's empire crashing down. But accessing it would be extremely dangerous. It was heavily guarded, protected by layers of security, and surrounded by Voldi's most loyal and lethal operatives.

The journey to Zurich was fraught with peril. Jake relied on his instincts, his years of investigative experience, and a network of contacts to navigate the treacherous landscape of international espionage. He faced close calls, narrowly evading surveillance, outsmarting Voldi's agents, and relying on his wits and resourcefulness to stay alive. Every step he took was a gamble, a calculated risk that could cost him his life. He was operating outside the law, a lone wolf fighting against a formidable foe. But the stakes were too high to back down.

The vault itself was located within a seemingly ordinary office building, tucked away on a quiet street. Jake, using his contacts, gained access to the building's blueprints and discovered a secret passage leading to the vault. The infiltration was risky; he had to navigate laser grids, pressure plates, and armed guards. He used a combination of stealth, technical skills, and brute force to overcome the obstacles, his heart pounding in his chest with every step. The tension was palpable, the air, thick with the scent of danger.

Finally, he reached the vault, a massive steel door that seemed impervious to any attack. He used a combination of technological expertise and old-fashioned lock-picking skills to open the vault. Inside, the evidence was overwhelming: incriminating documents, financial records, and encrypted communications, all thoroughly organized, irrefutable proof of Voldi's criminal empire. This was the smoking gun.

But just as he was about to secure the evidence, alarms blared, shattering the silence. Voldi’s men were alerted. He was trapped, surrounded, and now he had to find a way to escape, not just with his life, but with the evidence that could bring down the most powerful and dangerous man in the world. He knew his chances of survival were slim, the odds heavily stacked against him. But Jake Harroll wasn’t one to back down from a challenge, no matter how daunting. He had come too far, risked too much, to let Voldi escape justice. The fight, far from over, had entered its most dangerous phase. The game was on, and the stakes were higher than ever. He had the evidence, but escaping with it alive was another story. The battle for survival had begun. The true extent of Voldi's reach and the danger he posed was yet to be fully revealed. But Jake, armed with the incriminating evidence from the vault, was ready to face whatever lay ahead.

....

The flickering neon sign of the Golden Dragon cast long shadows as Jake scrambled through the back alley, the stolen data stick burning a hole in his pocket. The adrenaline coursing through his veins was a potent cocktail of fear and exhilaration. He'd escaped Voldi's men, but the victory felt hollow, a temporary reprieve in a war he’d only just begun to understand. Seraphina’s cryptic warning echoed in his mind: "The Dragon has many teeth." He'd underestimated the scope of Voldi's operation, the insidious tendrils reaching into every corner of the city, even into places he’d once considered safe.

His escape route led him to a dilapidated warehouse district, the air thick with the stench of decay and desperation. The rhythmic clang of metal on metal from a nearby scrapyard was the only sound besides the frantic pounding of his own heart. He needed time, a safe space to analyze the data. He checked his phone—no signal. He was truly alone.

The data itself was a labyrinthine web of financial transactions, coded messages, and encrypted files, each piece a crucial link in a chain leading to the true puppet master pulling Voldi's strings. Hours melted into a blur as Jake deciphered the complex code, his concentration broken only by the occasional rustle of rats in the shadows. The information painted a picture far more intricate and disturbing than he could have imagined. Voldi, it turned out, was merely a high-ranking lieutenant, a ruthless enforcer for a syndicate far older and more powerful than anyone had ever suspected.

The connections were chilling in their breadth. He uncovered links to seemingly legitimate businesses: a prominent shipping company, a seemingly charitable foundation, even a prestigious university. Each entity served as a crucial cog in the machine, laundering money, transporting goods, and providing cover for the syndicate's illicit activities. It was a sophisticated operation, a complex network of interwoven deceit that had been operating for decades, its tentacles wrapped tightly around the city's arteries.

One name surfaced repeatedly in the data: Tanya Relova. The file described her as a "key facilitator," a woman who skillfully navigated the treacherous world of international finance, expertly masking the flow of illegal funds through a series of shell corporations and offshore accounts. Her wealth was staggering, her influence pervasive. Yet, publicly, Tanya Relova was a philanthropist, a respected member of the city's elite, her name synonymous with charitable donations and community support. The deception was breathtaking in its audacity.

Jake's research led him down a rabbit hole of offshore accounts, encrypted emails, and coded messages. He unearthed evidence suggesting a deep connection between Tanya Relova and a shadowy organization known only as "The Velvet Circle." Their activities were shrouded in secrecy, their methods ruthless. They seemed to operate above the law, manipulating political figures, corrupting law enforcement, and controlling vast sums of money. Their reach extended far beyond the city limits; their influence felt across continents.

The data revealed that The Velvet Circle was not merely a criminal syndicate. It was a sophisticated network of power brokers, using their wealth and influence to manipulate global events, creating instability and chaos to further their own nefarious ends. They were a hidden hand, pulling the strings of governments and corporations, shaping the world's narrative to their advantage.

As Jake dug deeper, he realized that the assassination of Gomin Guill, the mission that had initially brought him into this dangerous world, was merely a pawn in a much larger game. Gomin had apparently stumbled onto a secret that threatened The Velvet Circle, a secret so dangerous that his elimination was deemed necessary. Gomin had been a loose end, a threat that had to be neutralized.

Jake's heart pounded in his chest as he realized the sheer scope of the conspiracy. He was no longer dealing with a simple crime syndicate; he was up against a global network of power, an organization so powerful and well-connected that bringing them down seemed an impossible task. The odds were overwhelmingly against him, but he couldn't back down. He had to expose The Velvet Circle, regardless of the personal risks involved.

He decided to focus on Tanya Relova. She was the key, the linchpin that connected all the loose ends. He needed to find a way to expose her, to unravel the web of deceit that protected her. But how? Tanya Relova was a ghost, her movements shrouded in secrecy, her actions carefully planned and executed. Getting close to her, let alone gathering evidence against her, seemed like an impossible feat.

His investigation led him to a series of high-stakes poker games, the kind where millions of dollars changed hands in a single night. These were not the casual games of chance; they were carefully orchestrated events, used as clandestine meetings by the city's elite and the criminal underworld. He knew that Tanya Relova frequented these games, using them as a cover for her dealings with The Velvet Circle.

Jake, armed with a forged ID and his journalistic instincts, infiltrated one such game, blending seamlessly with the crowd of wealthy gamblers and shadowy figures. The air was thick with cigarette smoke, the scent of expensive perfume, and the palpable tension of high-stakes gambling. He observed Tanya Relova from across the room, her elegance masking a steely determination in her eyes. She moved with grace and confidence, her every move precise and calculated. He saw her engage in hushed conversations with several men, exchanging cryptic messages and coded hand signals.

He spent weeks thoroughly documenting her movements, gathering clues and piecing together the puzzle. He discovered that she used a complex network of encrypted communication channels, making it nearly impossible to trace her activities. She was cautious, aware of his presence, but Jake remained elusive.

One night, he witnessed a heated exchange between Tanya and a notoriously ruthless member of The Velvet Circle. During their argument, Tanya dropped a small, intricately carved jade pendant. It was seemingly innocuous, but Jake recognized its significance. He'd seen a similar pendant in one of the encrypted files; it was a symbol used by The Velvet Circle, a sign of membership. This was the break he'd been waiting for.

Jake thoroughly documented everything, carefully storing each piece of information. He knew his life was on the line, every step a calculated risk. But he was closer than ever to unraveling the conspiracy, to exposing the true power behind the shadowy organization that controlled the city, and perhaps, the world. The fight was far from over, but now, armed with this piece of tangible evidence, he had a real chance. The game was afoot, and the stakes were higher than ever before. The path to justice would be fraught with danger and deception, but Jake Harroll was prepared to follow it to its end.

....

The stolen data stick felt heavy in Jake's pocket, a tangible representation of the danger he'd inadvertently invited into his life. He'd thought he was playing a dangerous game, a high-stakes investigation, but the reality was far more sinister. The information wasn't just about Gomin Guill; it was a roadmap to a sprawling network of corruption that extended far beyond the city limits. It was a web woven from deceit, violence, and political influence, a tapestry of power so vast it made his initial investigation seem like child's play.

He'd managed to extract the data from Voldi's heavily secured server room – a feat he still couldn't quite believe he'd accomplished – but escaping wasn't the end of his problems; it was just the beginning. The adrenaline rush that had sustained him through the escape was fading, replaced by a cold, hard dread. He was no longer just a reporter chasing a story; he was a target.

The Golden Dragon's neon glow seemed to mock him, a sinister reminder of the power he was up against. He'd barely managed to decipher a fraction of the data, enough to understand the sheer scale of the conspiracy, but also enough to know he was woefully unprepared for the fight ahead. The names, dates, and locations contained within the data were chillingly familiar – names whispered in hushed tones in backroom deals, dates coinciding with unexplained accidents and suspicious deaths, locations that were seemingly innocuous but held deep, dark secrets.

His apartment felt less like a sanctuary and more like a cage. Every shadow seemed to conceal a threat, every creak of the floorboards a potential intrusion. He spent the next few days in a state of heightened anxiety, constantly looking over his shoulder, convinced that Voldi's men – or worse, someone far more powerful – were watching him, waiting for the right moment to strike.

Sleep, a luxury he could ill afford. The data files filled his laptop screen, a labyrinthine network of interconnected individuals and corporations, all linked by a common thread: Gomin Guill and the vast criminal empire he'd only scratched the surface of. He spent hours tracing the connections, piecing together the puzzle, feeling the growing weight of the responsibility he'd shouldered.

He contacted Seraphina, the only person he felt he could trust, but even she seemed hesitant. Her voice, usually so calm and collected, was tight with worry. "Jake, you've dug yourself into a hole deeper than you realize," she'd warned, her words laced with a chilling foreboding. "They're not going to let this go. You need to get out, disappear."

But disappearing wasn't an option. The data contained evidence of crimes against humanity, of political corruption on an unimaginable scale. He couldn't simply walk away; he had a responsibility to expose the truth, to bring these criminals to justice. He owed it to Gomin Guill, to the victims of this massive conspiracy, to the city, and maybe even to the world.

His journalistic instincts, honed over years of investigating crime and corruption, screamed at him to proceed with caution, to thoroughly document every step, every lead, every contact. He started compiling a detailed report, backing up the data on multiple encrypted drives, and employing various techniques to safeguard his work, anticipating the inevitable attempt to silence him.

The threat wasn't just physical; it was psychological. He felt constant pressure, a sense of being watched, of being manipulated. He second-guessed every move, every phone call, every online interaction. Paranoia had become his unwelcome companion, a constant reminder of his precarious position.

He started noticing subtle things – a black car parked across the street, a figure lingering in the shadows, a phone call that seemed oddly timed and too perfect to be coincidental. He knew that they were probing, testing his resolve, trying to gauge his next move. The game of cat and mouse had begun, and he was the mouse.

His network of contacts, usually so reliable, were suddenly tight-lipped, evasive. Those who previously offered information readily now clammed up, suddenly preoccupied or unavailable. He understood; the organization's reach was extensive, and fear was a powerful weapon.

Days bled into nights, fueled by coffee and a growing sense of urgency. The deeper he delved into the data, the more terrifying the implications became. The organization wasn't just involved in drug trafficking and arms dealing; they had infiltrated every level of government, from local officials to high-ranking politicians. They were pulling the strings, manipulating events, and controlling the narrative, making sure no one ever suspected the true extent of their power.

He learned of clandestine meetings in secluded locations, coded messages exchanged in encrypted channels, and shell corporations used to launder billions of dollars. The trail of evidence led him down a rabbit hole of deceit and subterfuge, a world where truth was a commodity and betrayal was a necessity.

He discovered that Gomin Guill wasn't the mastermind, but merely a powerful pawn in a much larger game. The organization's leader remained shrouded in mystery, a ghost orchestrating events from the shadows, pulling the strings of power with an unseen hand. The true extent of their influence was only now becoming clear, a chilling reminder of how fragile democracy truly was.

The danger was growing exponentially. He wasn't just dealing with thugs and gangsters; he was facing an organization with resources and reach to eliminate him without a trace. He needed a plan, a way to expose them without becoming another victim, another statistic in their long list of silenced witnesses. The weight of the world, or at least a significant portion of the city's underworld, was resting on his shoulders, and he knew that every breath he took brought him closer to the precipice of a deadly confrontation. The fight wasn't just for his own survival; it was for the sake of justice, for the sake of truth, and for the sake of a city teetering on the brink of collapse. The game was on, and this time, the stakes were everything.

The Informant

The humid air hung heavy in the cramped, dimly lit backroom of a Vietnamese pho restaurant. The aroma of simmering broth and star anise did little to mask the underlying scent of fear that clung to the peeling paint and worn vinyl booths. Across the scarred Formica tabletop from Jake sat a woman, her face obscured by a wide-brimmed straw hat, her hands clasped tightly in her lap. He'd been led here by a circuitous route, a series of cryptic messages and dead drops, each step closer to this clandestine meeting increasing his apprehension. This was it – his potential key to unlocking the vast, shadowy conspiracy that had nearly swallowed him whole.

"They call me Mai," the woman said, her voice a low, husky whisper, barely audible above the clatter of dishes and hushed conversations from the main dining area. She didn't look up, her gaze fixed on the chipped ceramic coaster beneath her trembling hands. The hat cast deep shadows, rendering her features almost entirely indistinct. Even her age was uncertain; she could have been anywhere between thirty and fifty.

Jake leaned forward, his voice a careful counterpoint to hers. "Mai. I understand you have information about the organization – about the people behind Gomin Guill."

A slight nod, barely perceptible beneath the hat. "I know things. Things Gomin didn't want known. Things that would shake the very foundations of…everything." She paused, taking a shaky breath. The silence stretched, thick and suffocating. The only sound was the rhythmic clinking of chopsticks from the nearby tables.

Jake had spent the last few weeks piecing together fragments of information, like shards of a broken mirror reflecting a distorted image of the truth. Gomin Guill's death had been a significant blow, but it had only scratched the surface of the vast, intricate web of corruption he'd uncovered. Gomin was a pawn, a high-ranking one, certainly, but a pawn nonetheless. The real players, the puppet masters, remained hidden, their faces obscured by a veil of secrecy and power.

Mai's information, Jake knew instinctively, could be the missing piece of the puzzle. But informants were a dangerous commodity. They were often unreliable, prone to exaggeration or outright fabrication. And in this world, betrayal was a constant threat.

“Tell me what you know,” Jake urged gently, his tone reassuring, yet firm. He needed to establish trust, to make her understand that he was different, that he wasn't one of them .

Mai hesitated, as if weighing the risks. "Gomin was a cleaner," she finally whispered, her voice barely a breath. "He eliminated loose ends, inconvenient witnesses. But he wasn't the mastermind. He was…disposable."

"Disposable?" Jake echoed, his mind racing. The implications were staggering. If Gomin was merely a disposable asset, then the true orchestrators of this vast conspiracy were far more powerful, more sophisticated, and far more dangerous than he had ever imagined.

"The organization is much larger than you think," Mai continued, her voice regaining a sliver of strength. "It spans continents, its tentacles reaching into every level of power, from the highest echelons of government to the lowest levels of the underworld. They control everything from arms trafficking to international finance, from politics to media."

Jake felt a chill crawl down his spine. He'd suspected a vast operation, but the sheer scale of Mai's revelation was breathtaking. This wasn't just organized crime; it was a global shadow government, operating in plain sight, controlling the strings of power.

"Who are they?" Jake pressed, his voice low and urgent. "Who's pulling the strings?"

Mai leaned closer, her voice dropping to a near-inaudible murmur. “The Serpent’s Coil,” she whispered, the name hissing like venom. “They call themselves that. And they are everywhere."

She then began to detail the organization's structure, describing a hierarchical system, with layers of command and control designed to ensure operational security. There were regional bosses, financial controllers, tech specialists, and an army of enforcers – all working in concert towards a single, unknown purpose.

She spoke of encrypted communications, offshore accounts, and a complex network of shell corporations designed to launder billions of dollars in illicit funds. She described the use of advanced surveillance technology, sophisticated encryption methods, and a ruthless approach to eliminating threats. She detailed the organization's use of political influence to shield itself from law enforcement scrutiny. She even spoke of coded messages embedded within seemingly innocent media articles, a form of internal communication beyond the reach of conventional surveillance.

As the hours ticked by, Mai unraveled more and more of the organization's intricate operations. Her account was punctuated by moments of profound fear, her voice trembling as she recounted instances of violence, intimidation, and betrayal. She spoke of colleagues who had disappeared without a trace, and of the constant threat of exposure. She described the paranoia that permeated the organization, the ever-present suspicion that even close allies could not be trusted.

Jake listened intently, his notepad filled with a chaotic jumble of notes, numbers, names, and locations. He recognized some of the names; some of the locations seemed vaguely familiar, appearing in other unrelated news articles he'd encountered during his investigation. He made connections, drew inferences, his understanding of the Serpent's Coil expanding with every revelation.

As the night deepened, a new layer of complexity emerged. Mai revealed that the Serpent's Coil wasn't just a criminal enterprise, but something far more sinister. They were actively manipulating global events, using their vast resources to influence elections, destabilize governments, and create chaos, all in pursuit of an unknown, long-term goal.

“They are building something,” Mai whispered, her voice barely above a breath. "Something big. Something terrifying. And I don't know what it is."

The revelation sent a shiver down Jake's spine. He had faced dangerous criminals before, but this was on a different scale entirely. This wasn't just about greed or power; this was about something far more insidious, something that threatened the very fabric of society.

He looked at Mai, her face still hidden beneath the hat, and understood that he was no longer just a reporter investigating a crime. He was embroiled in a dangerous game of cat and mouse, a desperate race against time to expose a global conspiracy that could change the world. And he was just a pawn in this game, too, perhaps even more vulnerable than he ever realized, now knowing that the Serpent’s Coil were likely already aware of their meeting. He had to get out, and fast. But more importantly, he had to figure out how to use Mai's information before the organization did.

....

The woman, Mai, finally spoke, her voice a low, husky whisper that barely carried over the clatter of dishes from the main dining area. "They know," she said, her words precise, each syllable carrying the weight of years spent navigating the treacherous currents of the underworld. "The Serpent's Coil. They know you're here."

A cold dread gripped Jake. He'd suspected it, of course. His every move since uncovering the evidence implicating a power far greater than Gomin Guill felt like a tightrope walk over a chasm of uncertainty. But hearing it confirmed, spoken in that hushed, conspiratorial tone, solidified the imminent danger.

"How?" Jake asked, his voice barely above a breath. He glanced at the entrance, half-expecting to see figures emerge from the shadows, their faces obscured by darkness and malice.

Mai shifted slightly, her hat momentarily tilting, revealing a flash of sharp, intelligent eyes. "They have eyes everywhere, Mr. Harroll," she said, her gaze piercing. "Informants, collaborators...even those who believe they are working against them, are often just pieces on their board."

She leaned closer, her voice dropping to a near-inaudible murmur. "Gomin Guill wasn't the head of the Serpent's Coil. He was a lieutenant, a pawn. The true power…it's far more insidious, more diffuse. Think of it as a hydra—cut off one head, and two more grow in its place."

Jake absorbed this chilling revelation, the pieces of the puzzle slowly clicking into place. Gomin's thoroughly crafted empire, his global network of illicit activities, had all been a smokescreen, a distraction from the true nature of the organization. He had been chasing shadows, chasing a ghost. And now, he was the one being hunted.

"Who is behind it, then?" Jake pressed, his voice betraying a hint of desperation. The weight of the situation pressed down on him, the realization of his own vulnerability, a heavy cloak. He was out of his depth, just a journalist thrust into a world of ruthless killers and shadowy conspiracies.

Mai hesitated, her eyes darting nervously towards the entrance. "There are whispers," she began, her voice barely a breath. "Whispers of a man known only as 'The Architect'. A puppet master, pulling strings from the shadows. He is the one who orchestrates everything, controlling the flow of information, the movement of money, the violence…everything."

"And this Architect…where do I find him?" Jake asked, his voice laced with a mixture of determination and trepidation. He needed answers, even if those answers led him into a deeper pit of danger.

"You won't find him easily," Mai replied, her voice laced with a chilling certainty. "He operates through intermediaries, through layers of deception and misdirection. Tracking him down is like chasing a phantom. But…" she paused, her eyes gleaming with a strange mixture of fear and excitement, "there is someone who might know more. Someone who could lead you to him."

The information felt like a lifeline, a fragile thread in a tangled web. But even as a sense of hope flickered within him, Jake felt a cold wave of apprehension wash over him. He sensed a trap, a deliberate setup, a subtle maneuver designed to lure him into a deeper, darker labyrinth.

Mai produced a small, crumpled piece of paper from beneath her hat, handing it to Jake. It contained a single name and a phone number.

"This is Kenji Tanaka," she whispered. "He was Gomin's right-hand man, but he's…disillusioned. He might be willing to talk, but approach with caution. He is capable of deception himself."

Jake looked at the paper, the name and number seeming to pulse with a dangerous energy. He knew instinctively that this was a double cross waiting to happen. Kenji Tanaka could be a crucial ally, or a deadly adversary. The choice, it seemed, was his.

He thanked Mai, a simple gesture that barely conveyed the depth of his gratitude. He slipped a wad of cash into her hand, enough to ensure her silence, her safety, her escape. Their meeting had been a calculated risk, a gamble on both their parts. He was unsure who had risked more.

As he slipped out of the restaurant, the humid night air felt heavy with unspoken threats. The city lights seemed to mock him, their brilliance a cruel contrast to the darkness that surrounded him. He knew he was playing a deadly game, a game with stakes far higher than he had ever imagined.

He found a payphone – a relic of a bygone era – and dialed the number. The phone rang, a jarring sound in the quiet night. A voice answered, clipped and formal.

"Tanaka," the voice said. It was exactly as Mai had described, devoid of warmth or emotion.

Jake introduced himself, keeping his tone carefully neutral. He explained that he was a journalist investigating Gomin Guill's death, that he possessed information that could implicate others. He baited the hook, offering a chance for Tanaka to escape the long shadow of the Serpent's Coil.

Tanaka listened silently. His silence was more chilling than any threat. Finally, he spoke. "Meet me," he said, his voice betraying a hint of weariness. "Tomorrow, at the docks. Sunset."

The location itself sent a shiver down Jake's spine. The docks were a place of shadows, of hidden corners and clandestine meetings. It was a place where secrets were born, and lives were extinguished.

The next day, Jake arrived at the appointed location, the setting sun casting long, ominous shadows across the dilapidated warehouses and rusting cranes. The air hung heavy with the smell of salt and decay, a fitting backdrop for the dangerous encounter that lay ahead.

He found Tanaka waiting, his figure silhouetted against the fiery hues of the sunset. Tanaka was exactly as he expected – sharp, calculating, and deeply suspicious. Their conversation was a dance of evasion and revelation, a delicate game of trust and betrayal.

Tanaka confirmed Mai's account. The Architect was real, a shadowy figure controlling a vast criminal empire. He confirmed the depth of the conspiracy, painting a picture of a global network of corruption, bribery, and violence.

But then, the double-cross began.

As Tanaka revealed crucial information, subtly shifting his weight, he also spun a web of deceit. He offered information about the Architect's operations, but he also planted disinformation, misleading Jake, leading him down blind alleys. Tanaka was playing his own game, using Jake's desperation to further his own agenda, whatever that may be.

The meeting ended with a sense of unease hanging in the air, the threat of betrayal palpable. Jake left the docks with more questions than answers, the information he had obtained was a dangerous cocktail of truth and lies. He was closer to the Architect, yet further away than ever before. The double-cross had succeeded, leaving Jake stranded, alone, and vulnerable in the heart of the Serpent's Coil's web. The game, he realized, was far from over. It had merely begun anew, with the stakes raised even higher. The hunt for the Architect would necessitate a more intricate strategy, a deeper understanding of the Serpent's Coil, and perhaps, an unexpected alliance. The question was, could he find a trustworthy ally amidst this sea of deceit? And more importantly, could he survive?

....

The humid Hong Kong air hung heavy, clinging to Jake like a second skin. He felt the city pulse around him, a chaotic symphony of honking taxis, chattering crowds, and the low hum of unseen machinery. Mai's warning echoed in his ears: They know . He wasn't just hunting the Architect; he was now being hunted. The Serpent's Coil, a hydra with countless heads, was tightening its grip.

His hotel room, a sterile, minimalist space overlooking the harbor, felt less like a sanctuary and more like a pressure cooker. He'd spent the last few hours poring over the data Mai had provided – fragments of encrypted communications, snippets of code, and digital breadcrumbs leading into a labyrinthine world of technological espionage. It was a war fought not with guns and knives, but with algorithms and satellites.

The Serpent's Coil wasn't just a criminal organization; it was a technologically advanced, highly sophisticated entity. Their reach extended far beyond the street-level thugs and enforcers. This was a network that leveraged cutting-edge surveillance technology, exploiting vulnerabilities in global communication networks, and employing a level of technological prowess that dwarfed anything Jake had ever encountered in his years as a reporter.

He traced the digital trails, his fingers dancing across the keyboard, the glow of the screen illuminating his increasingly haggard face. He found evidence of sophisticated deep packet inspection, allowing them to intercept and analyze vast quantities of internet traffic, identifying patterns and pinpointing individuals of interest. They weren't just passively monitoring; they were actively manipulating data streams, inserting false information, and sowing discord.

One particular data point caught his attention: a series of encrypted transactions linked to a shell corporation registered in the Cayman Islands. The amounts were staggering, dwarfing even the sums associated with Gomin Guill's operations. This resulted in a much larger, more powerful entity pulling the strings. The Architect, he suspected, wasn't just a figurehead; he was the conductor of an orchestra of technological spies, orchestrating a symphony of deception and control.

The Serpent's Coil's technological prowess extended beyond simple data interception. Jake unearthed evidence of sophisticated facial recognition software, capable of identifying individuals in crowded areas with astonishing accuracy. They had deployed a network of strategically placed cameras, integrated into seemingly innocuous infrastructure, creating a pervasive surveillance grid across major cities. He shivered, realizing that he was likely already being watched, his every movement tracked, his every conversation monitored.

He discovered evidence of their use of ghost servers, hidden deep within the dark web, acting as staging grounds for cyberattacks and data breaches. These servers were untraceable, constantly shifting locations, making them virtually impossible to shut down. The Serpent's Coil's ability to seamlessly move across borders and jurisdictions, utilizing the anonymity of the internet, highlighted their sophistication. It was a game of cat and mouse played on a global scale, with the Coil possessing superior technology and resources.

But Jake wasn't defenseless. He possessed skills of his own, honed through years of investigative work. He contacted a former colleague, a cybersecurity expert named

Tanya Deen, a woman who had spent years infiltrating various hacking groups, building up an intimate understanding of their techniques and motivations. She agreed to help, her voice laced with a mixture of apprehension and excitement. “This is bigger than we thought, Jake,” she warned. “They’re not just criminals; they’re a digital shadow government.”

Tanya helped him understand the complexities of the Serpent's Coil's network. She explained their use of quantum cryptography, a near-unbreakable encryption method. They were leveraging advances in quantum computing to secure their communications, making them virtually impenetrable to traditional decryption techniques. Their use of blockchain technology for financial transactions added another layer of complexity, making it incredibly difficult to trace their funds.

Together, they devised a strategy to counter the Coil's surveillance. Tanya provided Jake with encrypted communication tools and software to mask his digital footprint, making him harder to track. She also identified several vulnerabilities in the Coil’s system, potential points of entry that could allow them to disrupt their operations. It was a high-stakes game of digital chess, each move carrying the potential for devastating consequences.

The next few days were a blur of frantic activity. Jake worked tirelessly, thoroughly piecing together fragments of information, uncovering hidden connections, and gradually unraveling the Serpent's Coil's intricate web of deceit. He discovered that the organization was actively manipulating global markets, orchestrating financial crises to line their pockets. They were manipulating political narratives, using disinformation campaigns to sow chaos and influence elections. Their reach was far-reaching, their influence insidious.

Tanya's expertise proved invaluable. She identified a pattern in the Coil's communications, a subtle glitch in their encryption that could be exploited. This provided a way to potentially intercept their communications, providing crucial intelligence about their plans and operations. She also developed a counter-surveillance program designed to detect and disrupt the Coil's tracking systems.

But as they got closer to the truth, the danger escalated. Jake felt the Coil's surveillance intensifying, the feeling of being watched becoming almost palpable. He sensed their digital tendrils reaching out, probing his defenses, attempting to penetrate his security. He knew it was only a matter of time before they caught him.

The hunt for the Architect had become a war fought on multiple fronts – a physical chase through the labyrinthine streets of Hong Kong, punctuated by desperate digital skirmishes in the shadowy corners of the internet. The lines between the real world and the digital realm had blurred, transforming the hunt into a terrifying and exhilarating game of survival. The stakes were higher than ever before; failure wasn't just defeat; it was annihilation. The Serpent's Coil would stop at nothing to protect its secrets, and Jake knew he had to be one step ahead, always. The game, he realized, was far from over. It was just getting started.

....

The encrypted email arrived at 3:17 AM, the time stamp a mocking reminder of the relentless pursuit. It contained a single, chilling image: a satellite photograph of a sprawling compound nestled deep within the Amazon rainforest. Its perimeter shrouded in unnatural darkness. Beneath the image, there is a single word: "Iquitos." Jake knew, instinctively, that this wasn't just another piece of the puzzle; it was a tectonic shift in the game. The Serpent's Coil wasn't just a regional threat; it was a global behemoth.

His immediate thought was of Jason Reen. Had Jason uncovered this information before his own demise? Was this a trail Jason had laid for someone – for Jake? The possibility ignited a cold fire in his gut. He'd always been a reporter, not a soldier. But the information he was uncovering suggested that the lines between the two professions had been completely erased. This was no longer an investigative story; it was a fight for survival.

The email's metadata pointed to a server located in Switzerland, a neutral territory known for its stringent data protection laws. Tracing the origin proved fruitless; the digital trail vanished like smoke in the wind. He knew, however, that the photograph was more than just a picture;

it was a carefully calculated challenge, a taunt from an unseen enemy. Iquitos held the key.

The journey to Iquitos was a blur of frantic research, clandestine meetings, and sleepless nights. He contacted his old contacts – grizzled veterans of investigative journalism and former intelligence operatives – gathering whatever information they could provide. The picture of the Serpent's Coil began to sharpen into focus, revealing a network of staggering complexity. Their reach extended far beyond Asia and the Americas; evidence hinted at operations in Eastern Europe, Africa, and even the Middle East. They were moving illicit goods across borders, laundering money through shell corporations, influencing political power plays, and maintaining a global network of informants and enforcers. They were, in essence, a shadow government.

He unearthed a series of articles detailing suspicious land purchases in the Amazon basin, cleverly masked under the guise of environmental conservation projects. These acquisitions, traced to various shell companies, funneled millions of dollars into a labyrinthine network of offshore accounts. The scale was breathtaking, the complexity mind-boggling. The land wasn't merely being bought; it was being fortified. The compound in Iquitos was clearly more than just a remote base; it was a heavily guarded hub, a nerve center of this immense criminal enterprise.

His investigations uncovered whispers of a substance called "Aether," a new, highly addictive synthetic opioid, far more potent than anything on the market. Rumors suggested Aether was being manufactured in the Amazon compound, and its distribution was carefully orchestrated, feeding the growing global addiction crisis, while simultaneously amassing unimaginable wealth for the Serpent's Coil. This was their gold mine – a drug empire operating on a global scale.

The journey to Iquitos was harrowing. A chartered flight took him to a small, forgotten airstrip outside the city, where he was met by a local guide, a wiry man named Ricardo with eyes that seemed to hold the secrets of the rainforest itself. Ricardo, a former soldier with a reputation for knowing the jungle better than anyone, was Jake's only contact in Iquitos. He was quiet, his gaze constantly scanning the surroundings, as if anticipating danger around every bend.

The journey through the jungle was a perilous trek. The humidity was suffocating, the insects relentless, and the sheer scale of the rainforest oppressive. At times, the density of the foliage felt like a claustrophobic embrace. Ricardo moved with the quiet efficiency of a jungle cat, his knowledge of the terrain and his intuitive sense of danger proving invaluable. They moved by night, avoiding the oppressive heat and the prying eyes of those who might be watching. Sleep was a luxury they couldn't afford.

Finally, they arrived at the edge of the compound. It was larger than the satellite image suggested, a fortress hidden behind a wall of dense vegetation. High-tech surveillance equipment was evident, indicating a high level of security. Ricardo pointed out the laser grids and infrared sensors; bypassing this would require cunning and precision. This wasn't some secluded hideaway; this was a military-grade installation.

They spent days observing the compound, thoroughly mapping out its layout, identifying weak points, and assessing the security protocols. Ricardo's local knowledge and Jake's technical skills complemented each other, allowing them to formulate a plan. The risk was colossal; failure meant certain death.

Over the next few days, they discovered the compound was not just a production facility; it was a sophisticated training center. They observed groups of highly trained individuals undergoing intense combat drills, their movements precise and deadly. The Serpent's Coil wasn't just a criminal organization; they were a private army. Their power, Jake realized, was far greater than he could have imagined.

One night, they witnessed a clandestine airstrip within the compound. Several small planes landed and took off, their movements rapid and efficient, suggesting a vast logistical network. The scale of the operation was staggering. This wasn't just a regional drug operation; this was a global criminal empire, sophisticated, well-funded, and ruthlessly efficient.

They also noticed coded messages being transmitted from the compound, short bursts that suggested communication with other locations around the world, hinting at a network of operations spanning continents. The implications were terrifying. The organization’s reach was far more extensive than anything he’d ever encountered.

Jake’s original mission, the investigation into Gomin Guill's assassination, now seemed insignificant compared to the vast conspiracy he was unraveling. He had stumbled upon something far larger, far more dangerous, something that threatened global security. He was no longer investigating a crime; he was fighting a war against a shadow empire that controlled the levers of power from the shadows. The fight for survival had just begun, and the odds were stacked against him. The Serpent's Coil was vast, powerful, and relentless. And they knew he was coming.

....

The humid Iquitos air hung heavy, thick with the scent of decaying vegetation and something else, something metallic and faintly sickening. Jake stared at the satellite image again, the blurry outline of the compound a stark contrast to the vibrant green of the surrounding rainforest. "Iquitos," the word echoed in his mind, a silent accusation of his own naiveté. He'd thought he was dealing with a regional crime boss, a violent but ultimately contained threat. Now, staring at the sprawling complex, hidden deep within the Amazon’s emerald heart, he knew the truth: he'd underestimated the Serpent's Coil by a factor of a thousand.

He’d spent the last twenty-four hours lost in a maelstrom of research, his small apartment transformed into a makeshift command center. Maps plastered the walls, satellite images littered his desk, and the glow of his laptop screen painted his face in an ethereal light. He'd dug into Gomin Guill’s financial records, tracing the labyrinthine web of shell corporations and offshore accounts. The trail led not to a single source of funding, but to a constellation of seemingly disparate entities, all connected by an invisible thread of deceit and violence. These were not just criminals; they were puppeteers, pulling strings from the shadows, influencing governments and markets with the same ruthless efficiency they used to eliminate their enemies.

The initial shock had given way to a cold, hard determination. Fear was a luxury he couldn't afford. He was a journalist, not a soldier, but the line had blurred beyond recognition. He had a story to tell, a truth to uncover, and he wouldn't let fear, or the Serpent's Coil, silence him. This wasn't just about exposing a crime; it was about survival. He was fighting for his life, and the lives of countless others who were unknowingly caught in the Serpent's Coil's web.

His phone buzzed. It was Isabella Rossi, his contact in Interpol. Their previous interactions had been cautious, professional; now, their conversation was urgent, laced with a shared understanding of the looming danger.

"Jake, I've managed to corroborate some of your findings," Isabella's voice was strained, a stark contrast to her usual calm demeanor. "The financial trail you uncovered… it leads to several high-ranking officials in several South American governments. They're deeply entrenched, Jake. This is bigger than we thought."

"I'm aware," Jake replied, his voice tight with grim resolve. "It's a global operation. They're not just involved in drug trafficking and arms dealing; they're manipulating entire economies, controlling political landscapes. They're a shadow government."

"We need to be careful," Isabella warned. "They have eyes everywhere. Your investigation… it's attracted unwanted attention."

Jake knew she was right. The email, the satellite image, the cryptic message – it was a clear warning. They were watching him, tracking his every move. He could feel their eyes on him, even through the miles of ocean and rainforest that separated them.

He spent the next few days thoroughly preparing. He contacted old contacts, colleagues from his days as an investigative journalist. He reached out to specialists – cryptography experts, data analysts, military strategists. He needed intelligence, he needed resources, and he needed them fast. His network, once a collection of loose connections, solidified into a battle-ready team, united by a shared determination to expose the truth. Their combined skills – technical expertise, investigative prowess, and strategic planning – would be essential in navigating the treacherous terrain ahead.

His preparations weren't limited to information gathering. He underwent intense physical training, pushing his body to its limits. He knew he'd be facing a formidable opponent; survival wouldn't be about intellectual prowess alone. He had to be physically prepared for any contingency, for any scenario the Serpent's Coil might throw at him. He honed his skills with firearms, he learned hand-to-hand combat techniques, and he studied survival tactics, preparing for a potential confrontation deep within the unforgiving Amazon rainforest.

He knew he was walking a tightrope and one misstep could be fatal. The Serpent's Coil was ruthless, efficient, and possessed unlimited resources. They were masters of deception, able to manipulate situations to their advantage with ease. They'd already shown their willingness to eliminate anyone who posed a threat, no matter how insignificant they might seem. His own survival hinged on a delicate balance of meticulous planning, calculated risks, and a dash of sheer luck.

As he packed his bags, the weight of the impending mission settled on his shoulders. He wasn't just investigating a crime; he was confronting a vast, shadowy organization with global reach and influence. He felt the familiar adrenaline surge, the rush of excitement and terror that always accompanied the pursuit of truth. This was a David and Goliath scenario, but Jake Harroll wasn't just any David. He was armed with years of investigative experience, a network of trusted contacts, and an unwavering commitment to justice. He was ready to face the Serpent's Coil, even if it meant risking everything.

The journey to Iquitos was fraught with anxiety and anticipation. He flew commercially, avoiding private jets, aware that his every move was being monitored. The flight was a torturous blend of boredom and intense focus, each passing hour a step closer to the heart of the Serpent's

Coil's operations. He spent the flight reviewing his plans, thoroughly checking and rechecking his equipment. He ran through possible scenarios in his mind, anticipating their moves, preparing countermeasures.

The humid air hit him like a wall the moment he stepped off the plane. Iquitos was a chaotic blend of bustling markets, ancient architecture, and modern development, a testament to the city's rich history and its struggles to cope with its present reality. He booked into a small, unremarkable hotel, careful to avoid any lavish accommodations that could attract unwanted attention. He was in enemy territory, and he had to move like a ghost.

His initial reconnaissance efforts were shrouded in secrecy. He spent days observing the compound from a distance, relying on his contacts for information, carefully piecing together the puzzle. He discovered the compound was heavily fortified, guarded by layers of security personnel, equipped with advanced surveillance technology. It was a fortress, designed to repel any intrusion. He discovered that the outer perimeter was patrolled by armed guards, the inner sanctum protected by sophisticated electronic surveillance systems. Penetrating this level of security would require careful planning and a significant amount of luck.

The realization of the enormity of the task ahead didn’t deter him. Instead, it fueled his resolve. He was no longer just a reporter; he was a warrior, battling a shadowy enemy that threatened the stability of the world. His fight was not just for himself; it was for the people whose lives were impacted by the Serpent's Coil's actions, those who were unaware of the sinister forces controlling their lives from the shadows. He had a story to tell, a truth to reveal, and he would not rest until justice was served. His mission had evolved from an investigation into a murder to a battle against a global criminal empire. The fight had just begun. The odds were stacked against him, but Jake Harroll was ready.

Personal Sacrifice

The chipped paint on the windowsill felt rough against Jake's cheek as he stared out at the rain-slicked streets of Prague. He hadn't slept properly in weeks. The relentless pursuit of the truth, a truth that stretched far beyond the assassination of Gomin Guill, had consumed him. He'd traded comfortable nights in his apartment for cramped hotel rooms, traded familiar faces for the wary glances of informants and the ever-present shadow of danger. The gnawing anxiety was a constant companion, a cold knot in his stomach that tightened with every unanswered question. His usually meticulous grooming habits were neglected; his face was unshaven, his eyes bloodshot and shadowed with exhaustion.

He'd pushed his colleagues at the radio station to the limit, his relentless calls and demands for resources stretching their patience thin. He'd missed his daughter Lily's birthday; a missed call that still echoed with guilt. The voicemail message – a tiny, childish voice wishing him a happy birthday – played on repeat in his head, a constant reminder of the sacrifices he was making. He'd promised Lily a trip to the zoo, a promise now hanging limp and broken, a casualty in the war against this sprawling, insidious criminal organization. His relationship with Sarah, his girlfriend, had frayed under the strain. Their once vibrant connection had withered, replaced by tense silences and hurried goodbyes. He'd seen the hurt in her eyes, the unspoken question of how long this could go on, and he couldn't offer her an answer. He barely had one for himself.

The information gleaned from Jason Reen had opened Pandora's Box. Gomin Guill's death hadn't brought an end to the story; it had merely shifted the focus, revealed a deeper, more disturbing reality. The trail now led to individuals far more powerful, their reach extending into the highest echelons of power, protected by layers of secrecy and corruption. Jake felt the weight of this knowledge pressing down on him, the immense responsibility of uncovering a truth that could shatter the foundations of several nations.

His apartment, usually a sanctuary, now felt like a stranger's space. He rarely went there; a fear that someone might be waiting, monitoring his movements, kept him restless. He'd adopted a nomadic existence, moving from safe houses provided by his increasingly unreliable sources, each location a temporary haven before he moved on to the next. He'd learned to sleep with one eye open, to trust no one completely. Paranoia, a unwelcome companion, had become his constant shadow.

He missed the mundane routines of his life: the morning coffee with Sarah, the bedtime stories for Lily, the simple pleasures that now seemed like distant memories. His life had been torn apart, thoroughly disassembled like a precision watch by the relentless pursuit of this story. The cost was high, a price paid not just in lost sleep and neglected relationships, but in the erosion of his own identity. He was changing, morphing from a dedicated journalist into something harder, more cynical, his idealism chipped away by the harsh realities of the criminal underworld.

His latest lead had brought him to Prague. A cryptic message, delivered through a series of coded emails, had pointed him to a specific location: an abandoned warehouse on the outskirts of the city. The informant, a former associate of Gomin Guill who'd grown disillusioned, had promised evidence that could expose the entire conspiracy. But the informant had also warned of the risks involved, of the ruthless efficiency of the organization and its willingness to eliminate anyone who stood in its way.

The rain hammered against the window, mimicking the frantic beat of his heart. He checked his equipment: a small, high-powered recorder, a concealed microphone, a backup battery. He ran a hand through his already disheveled hair, checking the compact mirror hidden within his palm. He was alone, the isolation adding to the growing sense of dread. Yet, he felt a strange resolve hardening within him, a mixture of fear and determination. He couldn't turn back now, not when he was so close.

The warehouse loomed before him, a dark silhouette against the stormy sky. Each step towards it felt like a step into the abyss, a plunge into the unknown. He knew the risks; he'd faced them countless times before. But this was different. This felt like the culmination of everything, the point of no return. This was a gamble, a desperate roll of the dice, with his life, his career, and his relationships hanging in the balance. Yet, the thought of failing, of leaving the truth unexposed, was even more terrifying.

The heavy metal door creaked open, revealing a cavernous space filled with shadows. The air hung thick with the smell of damp earth and decay. The informant, a gaunt figure shrouded in darkness, emerged from the shadows, his face hidden by a hooded cloak. He held a small, worn briefcase. The meeting was quick, tense, conducted in hushed whispers. Jake received the data, a complex array of encrypted files that held the key to the entire conspiracy. As he copied it to his secure drive, he heard the tell-tale sound of approaching footsteps, the click of heels on the concrete floor. He glanced at the informant, a silent exchange passing between them.

The escape was a blur of adrenaline and instinct. He ran, the rain washing away the dust and grime of the warehouse, the sounds of pursuit echoing behind him. He weaved through the narrow streets of Prague, the city's labyrinthine alleys becoming his temporary sanctuary. He felt the weight of the briefcase pressing against his side, a physical manifestation of the responsibility he carried.

He reached his safe house, breathless and soaked to the bone. He collapsed onto a worn couch, his body trembling with exhaustion and fear. The data, his hard-earned prize, lay beside him, a testament to his sacrifices. The battle was far from over, but tonight, at least, he had survived. The cost had been high, perhaps even too high.

But as he finally closed his eyes, he found a strange sense of peace. He had come too far to turn back now. The truth, elusive and dangerous as it was, was within his grasp. And he would fight to protect it, no matter the cost. The price of truth, he realized, was everything. And he had paid it.

....

The flickering gaslight cast long, dancing shadows across the cramped Prague apartment. Jake ran a hand through his already disheveled hair, the faint scent of stale cigarettes clinging to his fingers. The data, a digital labyrinth of encrypted files and coded messages, sat on his laptop, a silent testament to weeks of relentless investigation. It painted a picture far more sinister than the assassination of Gomin Guill; it revealed a vast network of corruption, stretching across continents, implicating politicians, businessmen, and even elements within law enforcement. He'd risked everything – his career, his safety, even his sanity – to uncover this truth, but now, faced with the sheer scale of the conspiracy, doubt gnawed at him.

The first moral dilemma hit him like a physical blow. He had the evidence to expose the entire network, to bring down the powerful men who pulled the strings from the shadows. But the cost? He'd seen firsthand the brutal efficiency of Guill's organization, the lengths they would go to protect their secrets. Exposing them risked not only his own life but the lives of countless others, including the informants who had risked everything to help him. He was no superhero; he was a journalist, a man with a microphone and a notepad. Was he capable of handling the fallout? Could he even justify jeopardizing so many lives for the sake of a story, no matter how important?

He considered going to the authorities, the international bodies he knew would be interested. But trusting them felt like a gamble, a desperate roll of the dice. He'd seen how easily information could be twisted, how easily investigations could be buried, compromised by the very institutions designed to protect people. Was this just another layer of the corruption, a deeper web of deceit designed to trap and neutralize anyone who strayed too close to the truth? The thought was chilling, a cold hand squeezing his heart.

Then there was the matter of Jason Reen. The assassin's story, while terrifyingly credible, was still just that: a story. Jason's claim that he'd acted alone, his insistence that the larger conspiracy was only revealed after Gomin's death, felt… convenient. Was Jason using him, manipulating him to further his own agenda? Or was he genuinely repentant, seeking redemption through Jake's exposé? Jake couldn't shake the feeling that Jason was playing a game, a dangerous game that Jake was unknowingly involved in. Could he trust an assassin's word, especially one who had shown such chilling skill and cold-blooded efficiency?

He poured over the data again, searching for any inconsistencies, any sign of Jason's manipulation. The sheer volume of information, the complexity of the coded messages, was overwhelming, but the weight of the moral burden was even greater. Every piece of evidence, every encrypted message, seemed to present new ethical challenges, each one a razor's edge, threatening to cut him deeply.

The next ethical dilemma was a more personal one: the question of his own complicity. He had knowingly spent weeks pursuing a path so deeply entangled with criminals and violence. The blood was on his hands as much as anyone else's. He'd facilitated Jason's narrative, giving a platform to a cold-blooded killer, even if it was for a greater good. Was he any better than the criminals he was investigating? Was he simply using Jason's confession, Jason's actions, for his own personal glory, ignoring the ethical implications of exploiting a killer's conscience?

Days blurred into nights as Jake wrestled with these moral dilemmas. The rain outside seemed to mirror the storm raging within him. Sleep offered little respite, only bringing nightmares of violence and betrayal. He would awaken with a start, his heart pounding, the weight of his decisions pressing down on him.

He began to doubt his own motives. Was he truly driven by a desire for justice, or was his ego fueling this relentless pursuit of the truth? Was he driven by the thrill of the chase, a relentless adrenaline rush that clouded his judgment? He wondered if he'd lost his ethical compass, his integrity blurred by the intoxicating thrill of unearthing a vast criminal conspiracy. The line between a journalist and a vigilante became increasingly blurry.

He consulted several trusted colleagues, but their advice felt as murky as the Prague rain. Some urged him to go public immediately, to alert the authorities, while others warned of the potential consequences, the risk of being silenced or even killed. No one seemed to have a clear answer, only more questions, more dilemmas.

The weight of the information, the potential impact of his actions, and the risk to his own life and the lives of others became unbearable. The ethical questions were so complex, so intertwined, that they became impossible to disentangle. He felt like he was walking a tightrope, with a chasm of moral uncertainty below.

One evening, staring at the rain-streaked windows, he realized something profound. There was no easy answer, no neat resolution to the moral conflicts he faced. His actions, regardless of their outcome, would have consequences. His choices would leave an indelible mark. The truth, he realized, was not a simple entity to be discovered and unveiled; it was a complex tapestry woven from ethical dilemmas, personal sacrifices, and the agonizing weight of potential consequences.

He understood that the price of truth wasn't merely about physical risk or professional sacrifice; it was also about the moral toll. It was about facing the complexities of human nature, the gray areas of morality, and the painful compromises necessary to pursue a greater good. The road to truth, it turned out, was paved with moral dilemmas, each step fraught with the potential for devastating consequences.

In the end, Jake made his decision. It wasn't a clean, straightforward choice, but one born of agonizing reflection, of facing his own limitations and imperfections. It was a decision fraught with uncertainties and risks, yet he knew he had to proceed. The price of truth, he realized, was not only everything he had, but also the burden of bearing the consequences of his actions, whatever they may be. He would fight for the truth, aware that the fight itself would forever alter him, his understanding of right and wrong, and his perception of the moral landscape of the world. The road ahead remained treacherous, uncertain, and morally complex; but he had to walk it. The truth, however dangerous, demanded it.

....

The Prague rain hammered against the windowpanes, a relentless percussion accompanying the frantic rhythm of Jake’s typing. He’d secured a server room key – a minor miracle considering the level of security surrounding the seemingly innocuous data center in the city’s outskirts. The air hung thick with the metallic tang of fear and the acrid scent of cheap instant coffee, a testament to the countless hours he’d spent hunched over his keyboard, decoding, decrypting, and piecing together the fragmented clues. This wasn't just about Gomin Guill anymore; it was about a hydra-headed beast, its tentacles reaching into every corner of global power.

His heart pounded a frantic tattoo against his ribs as he navigated the digital labyrinth. The encryption was sophisticated, layers upon layers of obfuscation designed to protect the organization’s darkest secrets. He’d spent weeks learning to bypass such systems, poring over manuals, attending clandestine tutorials from an unlikely source – a former NSA analyst who’d grown disillusioned with the agency's covert operations. The analyst, a woman known only as "Seraph," had warned him about the risks, the potential for catastrophic repercussions. He’d ignored most of her warnings, driven by a relentless pursuit of truth that bordered on obsession.

He bypassed a firewall, another, then another, each success accompanied by a wave of adrenaline and a chilling realization of how deeply entrenched this criminal organization truly was. The data he was accessing held the key to understanding its vast network of influence – the names of corrupt officials, the locations of hidden offshore accounts, the details of illicit transactions that stretched back decades. He knew he was playing a dangerous game, a high-stakes poker match where the stakes were his life and the lives of countless others.

Suddenly, a piercing alarm blared through the server room, shattering the tense silence. Red lights flashed, casting an ominous glow across the equipment. Jake’s fingers flew across the keyboard, frantically copying the remaining data onto an encrypted external drive. He cursed under his breath; he hadn’t anticipated this level of security. This wasn't a simple break-in; it was a heavily fortified digital fortress.

He grabbed the drive and slipped out of the server room, his heart hammering against his ribs. The alarm had triggered a lockdown, and armed guards were swarming the building. He navigated the maze of corridors, his senses heightened, every sound amplified in the echoing silence.

He could hear their footsteps, growing closer with every passing second.

He sprinted towards the emergency exit, a surge of adrenaline coursing through his veins. He burst through the door, gasping for breath, the cold Prague night air hitting his face like a physical blow. He risked a glance behind him, seeing the guards emerging from the building, their faces grim, weapons drawn. He was out, but only just. He melted into the labyrinthine streets of Prague, his breath ragged, the weight of the evidence a heavy burden in his pocket.

The next few days were a blur of frantic activity. He moved from safe house to safe house, always looking over his shoulder, the city's shadowy alleys becoming his sanctuary. He contacted Seraph, needing her expertise to analyze the data he'd recovered. She was a ghost, appearing only when and where she chose, her methods as enigmatic as her past. She confirmed his suspicions: the organization wasn't just involved in organized crime; it was deeply intertwined with global political power, influencing elections, manipulating markets, and orchestrating wars for profit. The scale of the conspiracy was staggering, breathtaking in its scope.

Seraph provided him with a contact – a jaded former Interpol agent named Marcel Dubois, now living in self-imposed exile in the Swiss Alps. Dubois had once been close to dismantling the organization but had been forced to retreat after a brutal campaign of intimidation and sabotage. He was a walking encyclopedia of the organization's inner workings, and he agreed to meet with Jake, albeit reluctantly.

The journey to the Swiss Alps was fraught with peril. He traveled under an assumed identity, constantly changing routes and transportation methods, paranoid of surveillance. He felt the weight of countless eyes watching him, even in the solitude of his hotel rooms. The organization's reach was longer than he'd imagined. He'd underestimated its power, its resources, and its ruthlessness.

Dubois's secluded chalet was perched high in the mountains, overlooking a breathtaking panorama of snow-capped peaks. The atmosphere was tense as they met, the crackling fireplace the only sound breaking the silence. Dubois was a gaunt man, his face etched with weariness, his eyes reflecting a deep-seated cynicism. He confirmed the information Jake had gathered, filling in crucial details, revealing the organization's intricate structure and the identities of its key players. He also revealed a vulnerability – a weakness in their security protocols that, if exploited, could bring the entire organization crashing down.

However, exploiting that weakness would require a supremely risky maneuver: infiltrating the organization's annual summit held in a secluded island off the coast of Montenegro. It was a fortress, guarded by elite mercenaries and sophisticated surveillance technology. The very idea was audacious, bordering on suicidal. But it was the only way to expose the truth to the world, to bring those responsible to justice.

Jake knew the risks. He knew he could easily become another statistic, another silenced voice lost in the shadows. But the thought of the countless lives impacted by the organization's actions, the corruption it had sowed, the innocent victims it had created, fueled his resolve. The price of truth was high; it was a price he was willing to pay, even if it meant risking everything. He left Dubois's chalet, the weight of the decision settling heavily upon him. He had a plan, a dangerous, audacious, and potentially fatal plan. The journey to Montenegro would be the riskiest maneuver of his life, a journey into the heart of darkness. But he was ready. He had to be. The truth, he knew, demanded it. His fight for it had just begun. The stakes were not just his life, but the future of justice itself. And he would not falter. The world needed to know.

....

The Montenegro coastline blurred past in a whirlwind of adrenaline and fear. The rented Jeep, a battered four-wheel-drive, clung precariously to the winding mountain road, each hairpin turn a gamble with gravity and the unseen eyes that undoubtedly followed. Jake gripped the steering wheel, knuckles white, his gaze darting between the treacherous road and the rearview mirror. The journey had started smoothly enough – a calculated risk, he'd called it. Now, "calculated" felt like a cruel joke.

The first attempt had been subtle, almost imperceptible. A loose rock, dislodged with precision, sent his Jeep careening towards a sheer drop. He’d wrestled the wheel back, his heart hammering a frantic tattoo against his ribs, the near-miss leaving him slick with sweat and a chilling premonition. He hadn't seen anyone, no sign of pursuers, just the silent menace of the unforgiving terrain. He'd attributed it to bad luck, a twist of fate on a treacherous road. But the second attempt shattered any remaining illusions of coincidence.

This time, it was a deliberate ambush. As he navigated a narrow bridge spanning a deep ravine, a hail of bullets ripped through the air, shattering the Jeep's rear windshield. He ducked low, the acrid smell of burning rubber and gunpowder filling the small cabin. The bullets pinged off the metal, a deadly percussion accompanying the screech of tires as he wrestled the vehicle back under control. He'd driven straight through, not stopping to assess the damage, adrenaline fueling his desperate flight. The landscape screamed past: olive groves clinging to rocky hillsides, jagged peaks piercing the stormy sky, a breathtaking yet terrifying backdrop to his desperate escape.

He'd pulled off the road, far enough to give him some semblance of cover, the Jeep's engine still roaring, a testament to his reckless flight. He checked himself, finding no serious wounds. Just the superficial grazes and bruises, the adrenaline masking any pain. His breath hitched in his chest, his heart pounded a relentless rhythm against his ribs. The near-miss, the sheer luck of surviving both attacks, sent a wave of cold dread washing over him. He wasn't just chasing a story anymore; he was fighting for his life.

He radioed Dubois, his voice tight with controlled panic. The connection crackled with static, a harsh counterpoint to the silence of the rugged landscape. "They're after me, Dubois. Two attempts, both near misses. Need extraction."

Dubois's voice, calm yet laced with concern, cut through the static. "Where are you? I'm tracing your signal, but it's intermittent."

Jake gave his approximate location, his voice strained. “Mountain road, south of Kotor. I need backup, and I need it fast. They know I’m coming.” He hung up, the silence that followed heavier than the mountains surrounding him.

The wait felt like an eternity, each passing moment stretching into an agonizing expanse of dread. He considered his options, his mind racing. His initial plan, a simple rendezvous point, seemed hopelessly naive now. He was in a land of shadows, where loyalty was a fragile commodity and betrayal a constant threat. He had to improvise, adapt, or become another statistic, another victim of this invisible war.

The wait was broken not by the arrival of Dubois's men, but by the chilling sight of a black SUV, its windows tinted, silently materializing around a bend in the road. He knew, instantly, that this wasn’t rescue.

His immediate reaction was pure instinct – a desperate lunge for his concealed firearm. The SUV stopped abruptly, blocking his path. He didn't hesitate, gun drawn, ready to face whatever emerged. The SUV’s doors swung open, revealing not armed thugs, but a lone figure, a woman emerging with a hand outstretched, signaling truce.

Her face was obscured by shadow, but her movements radiated an unnerving confidence. Jake lowered his weapon slightly, suspicion battling with the desperate need for assistance. This was no ordinary ambush. The uncertainty gnawed at him. Was this another trap, a more sophisticated attempt to lure him into a deadly snare? Or was this a lifeline, an unexpected ally in his fight against an organization that extended its long, dark fingers into the highest echelons of power?

“You’re Jake Harroll,” the woman said, her voice low, almost a whisper, yet carrying an authority that silenced the turmoil in his mind. “I work for someone who wants to help you.” The ambiguity hung in the air, heavy and suffocating. She offered no name, no explanation. Just a proposition, dangerous and alluring, suspended between the shadows and the faintest glimmer of hope.

The hours that followed were a blur of clandestine meetings, whispered conversations, and shifting alliances. The woman, who finally introduced herself as Tanya, explained that there were factions within the organization, people who were just as keen to expose Gomin’s crimes, but lacked the resources to bring him down. They had been monitoring his investigation, impressed by his tenacity and his willingness to risk everything for the truth.

Tanya revealed a network of informants, a hidden web of resistance operating in the organization's underbelly. They had access to information Jake couldn't even dream of. Information that could not only expose Gomin's operation but could potentially bring down the entire criminal enterprise. But this came with a heavy price. The risks were far greater than anything he'd encountered so far.

Their involvement meant walking a tightrope, one false step could lead to disastrous consequences.

Tanya revealed that Gomin's death had not only triggered a power vacuum but had also alerted higher-ups within the organization. They now had a motive and the resources to hunt him down. Jake was no longer just a journalist; he had become a high-value target. His continued investigation was not just a matter of uncovering the truth anymore; it was a matter of survival.

The next attempt was far more brutal. It wasn't a casual ambush, but a carefully orchestrated assassination attempt. A team of highly trained operatives, armed with silenced weapons, attacked him in his safe house, a seemingly impenetrable fortress provided by Tanya's contacts. The fight was fierce and close-quarters. Jake fought with the instinct of someone who knew this was his last stand. He used every bit of his training, every ounce of his adrenaline-fueled strength, to fight off the assault. The walls were riddled with bullet holes, the room filled with the pungent aroma of gunfire and fear.

He escaped, battered but alive, owing his survival more to sheer luck and a desperate burst of adrenaline-fueled action than any tactical brilliance. He'd only managed to escape because one of the attackers had hesitated at the critical moment, a moment of moral uncertainty in the heart of a ruthless killing machine. A chink in their armor, a tiny crack revealing the inherent fragility of even the most impenetrable systems. This hesitation allowed Jake the crucial seconds he needed to escape into the night.

He realized that his investigation had morphed into a high-stakes game of cat and mouse, where survival was paramount and trust was a luxury he could no longer afford. He was in the heart of the beast, the darkness pressing in on all sides. The pursuit was relentless, the stakes impossibly high. His fight for the truth had become a fight for his life, a relentless battle against an enemy whose resources were seemingly limitless and whose reach extended far beyond the limits of his imagination. He was running out of time, running out of options, but he knew one thing with unwavering certainty: he would not surrender. The price of truth was high, but he was determined to pay it, even if it meant paying with his life. The world deserved to know.

....

The tires screamed in protest as Jake wrestled the Jeep around another blind corner. The coastal road, once picturesque, now felt like a gauntlet, every shadow a potential ambush. His phone buzzed, a text message from an unknown number: "Meet me at the abandoned lighthouse. North of Kotor. Midnight." No name, no explanation, just a chillingly precise location. He hesitated. Every fiber of his being screamed caution, yet a sliver of desperate hope flickered within him. He was running on fumes, both literally and metaphorically. He needed help, and help, it seemed, had found him.

The lighthouse, a skeletal silhouette against the star-strewn sky, stood as a solitary sentinel against the relentless waves. The air hung heavy with the salty tang of the sea and the chilling scent of decay. As Jake approached, a figure emerged from the shadows. A woman, tall and lean, with eyes that held a disconcerting mix of intelligence and weariness. She was dressed impeccably, despite the rugged surroundings, a stark contrast to the grime coating Jake's clothes and the exhaustion etched on his face.

"You're expecting me?" Jake asked, his voice a rough whisper.

The woman smiled, a fleeting, almost imperceptible movement of her lips. "You're the only one reckless enough to answer a message like that." Her voice was low and melodious, with a faint accent he couldn't quite place. "My name is Isabella Rossi. I know more about Gomin Guill than you could ever imagine."

Jake's instincts screamed danger. He’d encountered enough shadowy figures in the past few days to recognize the scent of deception, but something about Isabella's confidence, her almost nonchalant demeanor in such a precarious location, intrigued him. "And why would you help me?" he asked, his skepticism laced with caution.

"Let's just say," she replied, her eyes twinkling in the darkness, "we have a mutual enemy. And I'm tired of running." She paused, allowing the weight of her words to hang in the air. "Gomin was a puppet. A pawn in a much larger game."

Over the next few hours, huddling within the crumbling walls of the lighthouse, Isabella revealed a story that dwarfed even Jake's wildest suspicions. She had been Gomin's financial advisor, a position that gave her access to a network of offshore accounts, shell corporations, and thoroughly hidden transactions that stretched across the globe. She had witnessed firsthand the extent of Gomin's reach, the insidious tentacles of his organization snaking into every corner of legitimate business, politics, and even the church. She described complex money laundering schemes, political assassinations disguised as accidents, and the chillingly efficient methods used to silence any dissent.

Her testimony wasn't just based on hearsay; she presented Jake with encrypted documents and data on a secure drive, evidence that thoroughly documented the vast criminal network and its reach into the highest echelons of power. The data revealed a network far more intricate than he had ever imagined. It implicated individuals he had previously dismissed as inconsequential players, men and women who held positions of immense influence, individuals who moved in the shadows, pulling strings from behind the scenes.

"This is… staggering," Jake murmured, running a hand through his already disheveled hair. The implications were enormous, far beyond the scope of a simple drug trafficking operation. This was a battle for global power, a struggle between light and shadow that had been raging unseen for years. The sheer scale of the corruption shocked him to the core. He felt like an insignificant insect, caught in the gears of a gargantuan machine.

Isabella confirmed his suspicion. "Gomin's death was intended to send a message. A warning to those who threatened the true power behind the organization. Someone wanted to eliminate Gomin before he could reveal too much." She leaned closer, her voice dropping to a conspiratorial whisper. "They're coming for you now, Jake. They know you're investigating."

Jake felt a cold dread creep into his heart. He had expected to be pursued, but the sheer ruthlessness and efficiency of his pursuers exceeded anything he'd anticipated. He had walked into a hornet's nest, and now the hornets were swarming. He needed a plan, and he needed it fast.

Isabella, sensing his panic, offered a glimmer of hope. "I have contacts," she said, her voice regaining its composure. "People who owe me favors. People who understand the risks and are willing to play the game." She spoke of a network of ex-intelligence agents, disillusioned officials, and tech experts, all connected by a shared sense of disillusionment and a desire for justice. It was a ragtag group, operating outside the confines of the law, a shadow network fighting another shadow network.

The following days were a whirlwind of clandestine meetings, coded messages, and frantic escapes. Isabella used her vast network to provide Jake with safe houses, secure communication channels, and vital information gleaned from her years within the criminal underworld. She introduced him to members of her network, individuals who possessed skills and resources beyond Jake's wildest dreams – experts in cyber security, forensic accountants, and even a former special forces operative whose reputation was as legendary as it was terrifying.

Each contact brought new pieces to the puzzle, revealing intricate details of the organization's financial operations, their political influence, and their global reach. They pieced together a web of seemingly unrelated events, connecting the dots to reveal a horrifying truth: the organization wasn't just about power and money; it was involved in far more sinister activities, activities that threatened the very fabric of international security. Jake was thrust into a world of espionage, subterfuge, and betrayal, a world where trust was a luxury he could barely afford and every shadow held a potential enemy.

Isabella, however, remained his constant, a steady hand in a storm. Her sharp mind, her intimate knowledge of the organization's inner workings, and her network of contacts proved invaluable. She was more than just an ally; she was the key that unlocked the door to understanding the monstrous conspiracy that Jake was now fighting. She wasn't just helping him survive; she was empowering him to expose the truth. But as they delved deeper, they realized the enemy was far more powerful and far-reaching than they had initially imagined, and the price of truth might just cost them everything. The line between survival and sacrifice was becoming increasingly blurred, and the looming darkness felt ever closer, promising a future shrouded in uncertainty and violence. The fight for truth had just become exponentially more dangerous. The weight of the world, or at least a significant portion of its criminal underworld, rested squarely on their shoulders. And the game, as they were both starting to realize, was far from over.

Gathering Evidence

The air in the small, dimly lit office hung thick with the scent of stale coffee and apprehension. Jake Harroll, his eyes bloodshot from sleepless nights fueled by lukewarm caffeine and mounting anxiety, stared at the jumbled mess on his desk. Files overflowed, papers were scattered like fallen leaves after a storm, and the faint glow of his laptop screen cast eerie shadows across the room. For weeks, he'd been chasing ghosts, piecing together fragments of information that felt more like a puzzle crafted by a sadistic genius than a coherent narrative. But slowly, painstakingly, the picture was coming into focus.

The assassination of Gomin Guill, while seemingly a successful hit, had opened a Pandora's Box of secrets, revealing a conspiracy far grander and more sinister than he could have ever imagined. Jason Reen's confession, delivered in hushed tones in that rain-lashed café, was only the tip of the iceberg. It had provided a launching pad, a crucial starting point, but the real journey, the arduous climb towards uncovering the truth, had only just begun.

His first breakthrough came from an unexpected source – a discarded SIM card found near the scene of Guill’s assassination. It wasn't sophisticated technology; a simple, easily overlooked piece of discarded evidence. Yet, within its tiny memory chip lay a treasure trove of encrypted data. Days melted into weeks as Jake worked with a tech expert, a wiry, nervous man named Miles who specialized in data recovery and decryption. The process was agonizingly slow, each piece of recovered data revealing a new layer of complexity, a fresh wave of chilling implications. The encrypted messages detailed financial transactions, coded rendezvous points, and a network of shell corporations stretching across continents.

The documents revealed a sophisticated global money-laundering scheme, far exceeding the scale of Gomin Guill’s seemingly independent operations. Guill, Jake realized, had been a pawn, a highly visible player in a much larger game. The real mastermind was someone who operated from the shadows, pulling strings with ruthless efficiency and chilling anonymity. The messages mentioned a coded name, "Seraph," used repeatedly in conjunction with high-level financial transactions and logistical arrangements.

Another crucial piece of evidence was a series of seemingly innocuous emails found on a compromised server linked to one of Guill's associates. They were personal emails, seemingly unrelated to the criminal operation. But a meticulous examination by Jake revealed a pattern, a hidden code woven into the seemingly mundane text. It was a steganographic technique, a method of hiding information within seemingly harmless data. With Miles' help, Jake deciphered the hidden messages, uncovering a network of safe houses and communication channels used by the organization.

The safe houses, scattered across the globe, were thoroughly disguised, operating under the guise of legitimate businesses. From a seemingly innocuous antique shop in Prague to a bustling seafood restaurant in Hong Kong, each location served as a critical node in the organization's vast network. Jake painstakingly compiled a list of these locations, marking them on a world map that was quickly becoming a tapestry of global intrigue and danger.

The communication channels were even more sophisticated, employing encrypted messaging apps and burner phones, constantly shifting to avoid detection. The organization seemed to operate on a system of compartmentalization, with each member only aware of their specific role within the operation. This made tracing their connections and uncovering the true leadership even more challenging. But Jake was relentless, thoroughly tracing the threads of communication, uncovering hidden connections and identifying key players within the network.

A third crucial piece of evidence came from a surprising source: a disgruntled former member of the organization who, after a bitter falling out, decided to come forward. This man, who wished to remain anonymous, provided Jake with detailed information on the organization's inner workings, its leadership structure, and the true identity of "Seraph." He also provided intel on the organization's plans for a series of high-profile assassinations targeting key political figures, an act that would destabilize entire nations.

This informant's testimony was invaluable, but it came with a heavy price. The man lived in constant fear, aware that his betrayal had marked him as a target for the organization. He was paranoid, distrustful, and his information, while crucial, needed careful verification. Jake knew he had to tread carefully, balancing his need for information with the informant’s safety. He worked in secrecy, his every move shrouded in caution and discretion.

As the pieces of the puzzle clicked into place, Jake realized he was dealing with something far beyond a typical criminal organization. This was a sophisticated network operating on a global scale, wielding immense power and influence. Their reach extended far beyond the criminal underworld; they had infiltrated governments, corporations, and even law enforcement agencies.

The culmination of Jake's investigative work led him to a secluded villa nestled in the Swiss Alps. It was a seemingly idyllic retreat, the perfect cover for an organization as clandestine and secretive as this one. With Miles’s technical assistance and the support of a reluctantly cooperative Interpol agent, Jake planned a covert operation to gather irrefutable evidence and potentially capture the mastermind. He knew the stakes were high; a single wrong move could cost him everything. He was no longer a mere reporter; he was a player in a deadly game, and the odds were stacked against him. But the weight of the conspiracy, the potential for catastrophic damage, drove him forward, fueling his relentless pursuit of truth.

The final piece of the puzzle, the location of Seraph's main operational hub, was a chilling realization: a seemingly abandoned satellite facility high in the Andes mountains. It wasn't just a location; it was a fortress of advanced technology and unparalleled security. Jake knew he couldn't infiltrate it alone; he needed help. He reached out to an unexpected ally – Jason Reen.

....

The biting Andean wind whipped around Jake as he stared up at the monolithic structure clinging to the mountainside. The abandoned satellite facility, a testament to Cold War ambition and now a chilling symbol of Seraph's insidious operations, loomed before him like a predatory beast. Miles, his tech expert, hunched beside him, his breath misting in the frigid air. "This place is a nightmare, Jake. Even the satellite imagery is incomplete. They've gone to incredible lengths to obscure it."

Jake nodded, the weight of the situation pressing down on him. He'd contacted Jason Reen, a move that felt both reckless and necessary. Reen, the ghost, the assassin who'd eliminated Gomin Guill, was the only person he knew who possessed the skills and ruthlessness to penetrate Seraph's fortress. But trusting Reen was a gamble; a high-stakes bet with potentially catastrophic consequences.

The initial contact had been tense. A clandestine meeting in a deserted warehouse on the outskirts of Buenos Aires, under the flickering neon glow of a forgotten gas station. Reen, clad in a simple black jacket that did little to conceal his lethal physique, had been guarded, his eyes sharp and assessing. He'd listened to Jake's proposal – a partnership, not an employment – with a chilling calm that sent a shiver down Jake's spine.

"Why me?" Reen had finally asked, his voice a low rumble. He hadn't taken the bait of Jake's exposé on Gomin; he had expected a price, an offer. He didn't need Jake.

"Because you understand this world," Jake had countered, his voice steady despite the tremor in his hands. "You know the rules. I know the evidence. Together, we can bring them down."

Reen had considered this for a long moment, the silence broken only by the distant hum of city traffic. Then, a slow nod. "I have conditions."

The conditions were brutal, pragmatic, and born from years spent navigating the dark underbelly of the world. Reen wouldn't be working for Jake; they'd be equals, operating on mutual benefit. He wanted complete access to Jake's findings, no strings attached, and absolute control over their infiltration strategy. He would provide the tactical expertise; Jake, the intel. Trust, it seemed, was a commodity neither of them possessed in abundance.

The plan they devised was audacious, bordering on suicidal. Miles, using a combination of hacked satellite data and a network of sympathetic insiders, had identified a weakness in Seraph's security – a rarely used service tunnel that bypassed the main defenses. It was a risky gamble, but their only chance.

Their arrival at the facility under the cover of darkness was tense. The air crackled with anticipation and the ever-present threat of discovery. Reen, ever the pragmatist, had insisted on minimal equipment. No fancy gadgets, no high-tech weaponry. Just their skills, their wits, and the chilling efficiency they both possessed.

The trek through the treacherous terrain to the service tunnel entrance was arduous. The altitude was punishing, the cold unrelenting. But they pressed on, driven by a grim determination that transcended personal risk. This wasn't just about justice; it was about preventing a catastrophe of unimaginable proportions. The clues from Gomin's files had painted a grim picture—Seraph wasn't just a criminal enterprise; it was a conspiracy that reached the highest echelons of power, a network of corruption that threatened to destabilize the world.

The service tunnel was a claustrophobic labyrinth of rusted pipes and crumbling concrete. The air hung heavy with the smell of damp earth and decay. Reen moved with an almost supernatural grace, his movements fluid and silent, a predator navigating its prey's lair. Jake, despite his journalistic instincts, struggled to keep pace. He relied on Miles's remote guidance to negotiate the twisting passages, the images on his tablet displaying the tunnel's layout from Miles's drones ahead of them.

They encountered several security checkpoints, each one thoroughly designed to deter intrusion. But Reen, with his uncanny ability to anticipate and adapt, circumvented each obstacle with chilling ease. His knowledge of the facility's inner workings was uncanny, suggesting he had more than just a tactical understanding. It seemed his past was far more entwined with this organization than he had let on.

Deep within the complex, they discovered a vast server room pulsating with the hum of countless computers. Here, amidst the intricate network of wires and blinking lights, lay the heart of Seraph's operation. Miles managed to get a remote hack on the system, downloading crucial data as quickly as possible; enough to implicate high ranking officials in various governments.

But their success came at a price. Their intrusion had been detected. Alarms blared, lights flickered, and the sound of heavily armed guards echoed through the facility. They were trapped.

The ensuing confrontation was a brutal ballet of death and survival. Reen, a whirlwind of calculated violence, moved with an almost supernatural grace. His hand-to-hand combat skills were legendary; his precision with a simple knife seemed impossible, yet each action was swift, deadly, and silent. Jake, armed with nothing but his wits and a sturdy penknife, did what he could, relying on his agility and the element of surprise to get the upper hand in several scuffles.

They fought their way through hallways and chambers, leaving a trail of incapacitated guards in their wake. The adrenaline coursed through Jake's veins, blurring the line between fear and exhilaration. He was no longer a journalist observing from the sidelines; he was a warrior fighting for survival.

Their escape was a desperate sprint through the labyrinthine corridors of the facility, dodging bullets and navigating treacherous terrain. They finally reached the service tunnel, leaving behind a scene of utter chaos. The satellite facility was ablaze behind them.

As they emerged from the tunnel into the freezing Andean night, battered but alive, the weight of their accomplishment hung heavily in the air. They had infiltrated Seraph's fortress, secured vital evidence, and escaped with their lives. But the war was far from over. The information they'd gathered would ignite a political firestorm, shaking governments and exposing a web of international corruption. Their strategic alliance, born out of necessity, had proven unexpectedly effective, but the long road to justice had only just begun. The fallout from exposing Seraph would be global and potentially catastrophic; they'd won this battle, but the war was only just beginning.

....

The data Miles had painstakingly extracted from Seraph's servers painted a disturbing picture. It wasn't just a network of assassins and corrupt officials; it was a thoroughly constructed pyramid scheme of power, with Gomin Guill as merely a powerful, albeit expendable, pawn. The real architect, the puppet master pulling the strings, was someone far more elusive and influential: Alex Voldi.

Voldi's name sent a chill down Jake's spine. He'd heard whispers, rumors circulating in the darkest corners of the international intelligence community. A phantom, a ghost in the machine – a man who operated entirely in the shadows, his influence felt but his identity shrouded in mystery. The data confirmed the whispers: Voldi wasn't just a wealthy oligarch, as publicly portrayed; he was the linchpin, the financial engine driving Seraph's global operations. His wealth, amassed through decades of illicit activities ranging from arms dealing to cyber warfare, fueled the organization's reach and power.

The evidence was damning: encrypted financial transactions, coded messages revealing operational strategies, and a network of shell corporations strategically placed across the globe to launder billions of dollars. Miles, with his hacking prowess, had managed to penetrate layers of sophisticated encryption, revealing a financial trail leading directly to Voldi's private accounts in Switzerland and the Cayman Islands. It was a labyrinthine web, intricately woven, designed to withstand even the most rigorous scrutiny. But Miles, with his relentless dedication and almost supernatural ability to unravel digital complexities, had broken through.

The sheer scale of Voldi’s operation was staggering. Seraph wasn’t just a criminal organization; it was a sophisticated transnational corporation, operating above the law with impunity. Its tentacles reached into every corner of the globe, influencing governments, manipulating markets, and silencing dissent with ruthless efficiency. Gomin Guill, with his brutal tactics and insatiable ambition, was just a face, a public persona used to distract from the true power behind the organization. Voldi, operating from the shadows, pulled the strings, orchestrating everything from assassinations to political coups.

The revelation hit Jake like a physical blow. He had initially viewed the story as a simple hit job, a tale of a deadly assassin and a ruthless crime lord. But the truth was far more complex, far more disturbing. He had stumbled upon something far larger than he could have ever imagined, a conspiracy that reached the highest echelons of power. The implications were staggering; to expose Voldi would mean exposing a web of international corruption that could potentially destabilize entire nations.

The weight of this new knowledge pressed down on him. He understood the magnitude of the danger he was in. He wasn't just dealing with a ruthless crime boss anymore; he was facing a man whose power and influence transcended national borders. Voldi was a master of deception, a chameleon who could blend seamlessly into any environment. Exposing him would be a life-threatening endeavor, a game of cat and mouse with a player who held all the cards.

But Jake, fueled by a sense of responsibility and a burning desire for justice, knew he couldn't back down. He had come too far, risked too much. The information they had was a ticking time bomb. If it fell into the wrong hands, the consequences could be catastrophic. Voldi, once exposed, might escalate his retaliatory actions; the organization's response would likely be swift and brutal.

Miles, ever the pragmatist, laid out their next steps. "We need to get this information to someone we can trust," he said, his voice low and serious. "Someone with the resources and the influence to bring Voldi down. But choosing the right person is critical. Leaks could be catastrophic. We can't afford to make a wrong move. This goes beyond just bringing down a criminal organization. It's about exposing a systemic problem, dismantling a global web of corruption."

Jake knew Miles was right. They needed a powerful ally, someone who could navigate the treacherous waters of international politics and wield the necessary influence to bring Voldi to justice. The options were limited. The international intelligence agencies were riddled with corruption, their reach often hampered by political maneuvering and bureaucratic red tape. Turning to the press alone would not be enough; the sheer volume and complexity of the evidence would be difficult to present effectively in a way that would be persuasive and not easily dismissed as unfounded conspiracy theories.

After a sleepless night, wrestling with the moral and ethical implications of their discovery, they decided on a course of action. They would approach a select group of individuals: a seasoned investigative journalist with a proven track record, a former intelligence officer with known integrity, and a member of the International Criminal Court. Each contact was carefully chosen, each contact's reputation thoroughly vetted. The goal was to create a triangulated approach, verifying their information from various credible sources, minimizing the risk of leaks and potential backlashes.

The process was painstakingly slow, requiring encrypted communication channels and carefully orchestrated meetings in clandestine locations. Each contact was met with initial skepticism, the very nature of their claims bordering on the unbelievable. Yet, the overwhelming amount of evidence, painstakingly organized and presented by Miles, eventually began to erode their doubt. The detailed financial records, coupled with the satellite imagery of Seraph's hidden facilities and the witness testimonies, built a compelling case, slowly but surely winning them over.

The weight of their revelation was immense. They were not just fighting against a criminal organization; they were challenging a system, a global network of power and influence that extended far beyond the reach of any single nation. They were fighting against the very fabric of corruption that had allowed Voldi to thrive for so long. Each step felt like walking a tightrope, each move thoroughly planned, each conversation fraught with potential danger. They were working against time, knowing that Voldi, with his vast resources and global reach, would be aware of the investigation sooner or later. The question was whether they could get to him first.

The response from their contacts was a cautious optimism, tinged with apprehension. The scope of Voldi's influence was undeniable, and the risk of retaliation was significant. But the potential rewards – exposing a global conspiracy and bringing a powerful criminal to justice – outweighed the risk. They agreed to collaborate, pooling their resources and expertise to build a formidable counter-offensive. The plan was meticulous, a multi-pronged strategy involving coordinated legal action, media exposure, and targeted covert operations.

The next few weeks were a blur of activity. Jake, Miles, and their allies worked tirelessly, coordinating their efforts with precision and secrecy. They leaked carefully chosen pieces of information to trusted journalists, prompting investigations that would gradually unravel Voldi's empire. They worked with legal experts to prepare lawsuits aimed at seizing Voldi's assets and disrupting his financial networks. They began to identify key figures within Seraph, building cases to indict them for various crimes, starting with the ones that were easy to prove, slowly working up towards the higher ranks.

The response from Voldi was swift and brutal. There were attempts on Miles' life, subtle threats directed at Jake and his family, and an escalation of Seraph's criminal activities as they became increasingly desperate. But Jake and Miles, emboldened by their growing network of allies, held their ground. They knew the stakes were too high to back down.

The final confrontation came unexpectedly, during a high-profile international summit. Voldi, believing he was untouchable, was attending the event, hoping to secure a favorable outcome for his various ongoing schemes. It was a calculated risk on his part, underestimating the strength of their collaboration and the extensive preparation they had made. Through a combination of meticulous planning, carefully leaked information, and unexpected cooperation from within Voldi's inner circle, they were able to corner Voldi, exposing his misdeeds to the world and bringing his reign of terror to an end.

The victory, however, was bittersweet. The dismantling of Seraph was a monumental achievement, but the scars of the battle would remain. The global landscape was forever changed, shaken by the exposure of Voldi's influence. The world was a slightly safer place, but it was also a world left to grapple with the shocking realization of how easily such a vast network of corruption could operate beneath the surface. And Jake, forever marked by his encounter with Voldi and Seraph, knew that the fight for justice was a never-ending struggle, one that demanded constant vigilance and unwavering dedication. The war might be over, but the battle for transparency, accountability and the truth would continue.

....

Miles, his face etched with exhaustion but his eyes burning with a fierce intelligence, leaned back in his chair, the glow of the monitor illuminating his features. He swiveled to face Jake, the silence in the room punctuated only by the hum of the server racks in the adjacent room. "The plan," Miles began, his voice low, "was breathtaking in its audacity, its sheer scale. Gomin Guill was… a distraction, a highly effective one, I'll grant you that, but ultimately replaceable."

Jake, still reeling from the sheer enormity of the Seraph operation, leaned forward, his pen poised over his notepad. "Replaceable? But Guill was the head of the entire thing. The most powerful man…"

"On the surface," Miles corrected, a wry smile playing on his lips. "Voldi's strategy was based on a deceptively simple premise: create a highly visible, brutally efficient organization that would attract attention, and then use that attention as a smokescreen for his far more insidious operations."

He gestured to the monitor, where a complex network of interconnected nodes pulsed with data. "This," he said, tapping a specific node, "was Guill's operation. Assassinations, arms dealing, money laundering – the classic stuff. It kept the world looking in the wrong direction, distracted by the chaos he created."

"But what was the real goal?" Jake pressed, the implications of what Miles was saying slowly sinking in.

Miles traced a line on the screen, connecting Guill's node to another, far larger one. "This," he said, his voice hardening, "was Voldi's true game. It wasn't about power in the traditional sense. It was about control."

The larger node represented a global network of influence, far more intricate and subtle than Seraph's overt operations. It encompassed everything from controlling key media outlets and manipulating public opinion to influencing political decisions and infiltrating financial institutions.

"He wasn't interested in building an empire of violence," Miles continued. "He wanted to build an empire of information, of control. He wanted to manipulate the global narrative, to shape the world in his image. The assassinations, the corruption, it was all a sideshow, designed to obscure his true ambition."

Jake felt a chill crawl down his spine. This wasn't just organized crime; it was something far more sinister, a thoroughly crafted scheme for global manipulation. "So, how did it work?" he asked, his voice, barely a whisper.

Miles explained, pointing to different nodes on the screen. "Voldi used a multi-layered approach. Guill's organization provided the muscle, the visible threat. But Voldi's true power lay in his ability to infiltrate and influence governments, corporations, and even international organizations. He controlled the flow of information, manipulated markets, and sowed discord wherever it served his purpose."

He tapped a node representing a major news agency. "Compromised journalists. They pushed narratives favorable to Voldi, often subtly, sometimes overtly. Think about the wars, the economic crises… so much of it was orchestrated, manipulated, to destabilize regions and create opportunities for him to profit."

Another node highlighted a multinational corporation. "Infiltration of corporate boardrooms. Decisions made on the basis of inside information, leveraging vulnerabilities for his own gain. Trimming profits here, artificially inflating them there. The amount of money laundered through this was astronomical."

Jake's mind raced, trying to process the sheer scale of Voldi's operation. It was a global web of deceit, intricately woven over decades, designed to maintain a constant state of chaos and uncertainty.

Miles showed how Voldi had used the chaos created by Guill's organization to further his own ends. "The assassinations created instability. The instability created opportunities. Opportunities to exploit markets, influence political outcomes, and consolidate his power. Guill's death was merely a calculated step in a much larger game."

"And what about the evidence? How did you find all this?" Jake asked, still struggling to comprehend the scope of Voldi's plan.

"It was buried deep," Miles admitted. "But we found inconsistencies, discrepancies in the financial records, anomalies in communications patterns. We dug deep, cross-referenced data from multiple sources. It was like peeling back layers of an onion, each layer revealing something more disturbing than the last."

He pointed to a series of encrypted communications, deciphered using a newly developed algorithm. "These messages reveal the true extent of Voldi's network, his connections to individuals in positions of power across the globe. Judges, politicians, CEOs – all compromised, all working for him, knowingly or unknowingly."

The messages revealed a chilling level of detail, specific instructions, coded directives, and even subtle threats against those who dared to challenge Voldi's authority. The language was clipped, efficient, devoid of emotion – a stark contrast to the brutal efficiency of Guill's assassins.

"Voldi's ambition transcends even the most ambitious criminal organizations," Miles summarized. "He wasn't interested in money or power in the conventional sense. He craved control. Control of the narrative, control of the markets, control of the world's destiny. And he was frighteningly close to achieving it."

Jake leaned back, his mind reeling from the weight of the information. The meticulous planning, the layers of deception, the sheer audacity of Voldi's scheme – it was staggering. He had initially been focused on stopping a ruthless assassin; now he understood he had been embroiled in a fight against a far more insidious and powerful enemy.

"So, what now?" Jake asked, his voice strained. The sheer magnitude of Voldi's reach left him feeling utterly helpless.

Miles's expression was grim. "The net is closing, Jake. But Voldi is a ghost. He's good. Incredibly good. We're talking about an individual who operates on a scale unlike anything we've ever seen. Catching him will be more difficult than anything we've done before. He's already anticipating our moves, he's already covering his tracks. This isn't just about arresting one man; it's about dismantling a global network of influence that has been operating for decades."

He paused with his gaze unwavering. "This is a war, Jake. And it's far from over." The weight of the situation hung heavy in the air, the implications echoing the enormity of the task ahead – a task that now fell squarely on the shoulders of a radio reporter and a disillusioned computer hacker, thrust into the heart of a fight against a global puppet master. The fight for justice, it seemed, had just begun.

....

The warehouse smelled of dust, decay, and something metallic, a faint coppery tang that prickled Jake's nostrils. Miles, his usual nervous energy replaced by a grim determination, checked his modified Glock, the faint click echoing in the cavernous space. Beside him, Tanya, a former intelligence operative Miles had managed to recruit, adjusted the silencer on her own weapon, her expression as cold and calculating as the winter wind howling outside. They were a mismatched trio – a journalist, a hacker, and a ghost – united by a common enemy and a shared thirst for justice.

The air hung thick with anticipation. The intel Miles had painstakingly pieced together had led them here, to this abandoned dockside warehouse, the supposed lair of the puppet master – the man who pulled the strings of Gomin Guill's criminal empire. His name, they had learned, was Lucian Thorne. Not a name known to the public, only whispered in hushed tones in the darkest corners of the underworld.

They moved in a practiced silence, their footsteps muffled by the thick layer of grime covering the concrete floor. Miles, ever the tech wizard, had disabled the warehouse's security systems remotely, but the tension remained palpable. This wasn't some run-of-the-mill drug bust; this was a confrontation with an enemy who operated on a global scale, someone who had the resources and the ruthlessness to erase them without a trace.

The warehouse was surprisingly spacious, a vast expanse of empty space punctuated by stacks of decaying crates and shadowed corners. In the center, bathed in the sickly glow of a single bare bulb hanging precariously from the ceiling, sat Lucian Thorne. He wasn't the imposing figure Jake had expected – no hulking brute, but a slender man in a tailored suit, his face pale and gaunt, his eyes gleaming with an unnerving intelligence. He held a glass of amber liquid, swirling it slowly, as if unconcerned by their presence.

"Impressive," Thorne said, his voice smooth and cultured, a stark contrast to the grim setting. "To get this far. I commend your… persistence."

Jake felt a knot tighten in his stomach. Thorne's calmness was unnerving, a chilling composure that hinted at a mind far more dangerous than any brute force.

"You know why we're here," Jake said, his voice steady despite the tremor in his hands. He kept his weapon trained on Thorne, the weight of the situation pressing down on him. This wasn't an interview; this was a fight for survival.

"Of course," Thorne replied, taking a slow sip of his drink. "Gomin was… inefficient. A loose end. I needed someone… more discreet." He paused, his gaze sweeping across the three of them. "And you, Mr. Harroll, you've become quite the unexpected complication."

The conversation was a tense dance around the truth, a game of cat and mouse played with loaded weapons. Tanya and Miles shifted their positions subtly, their eyes constantly scanning the surrounding darkness, anticipating any potential threat. The warehouse, though seemingly empty, felt alive with unseen dangers.

Thorne chuckled, a low, dry sound that sent shivers down Jake's spine. "You think you've won, don't you? That you've uncovered my operation? You've barely scratched the surface." He gestured with his glass. "Gomin was a pawn. A necessary evil. But the true game… the real prize… that's something far greater than mere criminal enterprise."

He began to explain, his words carefully chosen, each syllable laced with a chilling calm. He spoke of global manipulation, of political influence bought and sold like commodities, of a network of power stretching across continents, all orchestrated from the shadows. He spoke of a new world order, one he intended to create. His words painted a picture far more terrifying than any single criminal enterprise; this was a conspiracy of epic proportions, a shadowy cabal controlling the very levers of power.

Jake felt the weight of the revelation press down on him. This was bigger than Gomin Guill; this was a fight against a system, a fight against a man who saw himself as a puppeteer of nations. The initial pursuit of justice had evolved into a struggle for the very future.

The confrontation escalated. Thorne, despite his calm exterior, was a formidable opponent. He had anticipated their arrival and had prepared accordingly. The quiet warehouse erupted into a chaotic ballet of gunfire and close-quarters combat. Tanya's precise shots found their marks, taking down Thorne's heavily armed guards who emerged from the shadows, their movements fluid and deadly. Miles, with his hacking skills, used the warehouse's security systems against Thorne, plunging sections of the building into darkness, creating confusion and chaos.

Jake, armed with nothing more than his wits and a healthy dose of adrenaline, found himself in a brutal hand-to-hand struggle with Thorne himself. Thorne was surprisingly strong, his movements precise and economical. The fight was brutal, a desperate struggle for survival. Jake, using the techniques he'd learned in his self-defense classes, managed to gain the upper hand, disarming Thorne and forcing him to the ground.

Thorne, defeated but not broken, looked at Jake with a chilling mixture of resignation and contempt. "You've won this battle," he hissed, "but you haven't won the war." His words echoed the vastness of the conspiracy he had unveiled, a chilling reminder that even with Thorne's capture, the fight was far from over. The network he had built, the influence he had wielded, would not simply vanish with his arrest.

As the sirens wailed in the distance, signaling the arrival of the authorities, Jake stood over Thorne, the weight of the situation settling upon him. He had closed the net on one man, but the intricate web of the conspiracy remained, a sprawling tapestry of deceit and power that stretched to the highest echelons of society. The fight for justice, it seemed, was far from over. The victory felt hollow, a momentary pause in a much larger, more terrifying game. The true battle, the fight to dismantle Thorne's network and expose the vast conspiracy, had only just begun. The information they had gathered, the evidence they had secured, was a starting point, a first step in a long and dangerous journey. The weight of the world, or at least a significant portion of its criminal underworld, rested heavily on their shoulders. The net was closed, but the hunt was far from over. The shadows still held secrets, and Jake, along with his unlikely allies, knew they had to delve deeper into the darkness to expose the truth.

The Mastermind's Defeat

The air hung thick with the metallic tang of blood and the acrid scent of burnt gunpowder. The opulent penthouse suite, once a symbol of the mastermind's untouchable power, was now a scene of chaotic destruction. Shattered glass crunched underfoot, mingling with the debris of overturned furniture and scattered documents – the remnants of a battle fought with brutal efficiency. The mastermind, Anton Voldi, lay sprawled on the Persian rug, a single, precise bullet hole marring his impeccably tailored suit. His eyes, wide and vacant, stared up at the elaborate crystal chandelier, a silent testament to his sudden, unexpected demise.

But. The victory felt hollow. The cost had been steep. Jake, bruised and battered, leaned against a shattered window, the cold night air biting at his exposed skin. He watched as paramedics worked frantically on Elena Relova, his unlikely ally, her body riddled with shrapnel from a grenade blast. Her breathing was shallow, ragged, a stark contrast to the rhythmic thump of the helicopter blades hovering overhead, poised to whisk her away to a nearby hospital. Her survival was far from certain.

The scene was a grim tableau of the final confrontation. The air crackled with residual tension, a palpable reminder of the near-misses and the hair-breadth escapes that had punctuated the battle. The battle hadn't been a straightforward gunfight, but a complex, deadly chess match, played out in the shadows of Voldi's opulent lair. Jake had used his knowledge of Voldi's intricate security systems, gleaned from weeks of painstaking investigation, to turn the tables on the mastermind. He'd anticipated Voldi's traps, his countermeasures. He had even predicted his final play – the use of the building's own elaborate security system to create a diversion, leaving Voldi momentarily exposed. It had been a high-stakes gamble, one that had paid off handsomely, but only just.

The cost wasn't limited to the physical. The emotional toll was far more devastating. Jake's memory flashed back to the faces of those lost during the operation – the informants, the undercover agents, the innocent bystanders caught in the crossfire. Each life lost was a stark reminder of the brutal consequences of Voldi's actions, and a testament to the pervasive damage caused by his global conspiracy. The victory felt more like a pyrrhic one; a triumph marred by loss and tinged with a profound sense of melancholy.

Jason Reen, the enigmatic assassin who had initially set the events in motion, stood silently observing the scene. He hadn't participated directly in the final confrontation, acting instead as a strategic advisor to Jake, his expertise in infiltration and evasion proving invaluable. His presence, however, was a potent reminder of the world Jake had inadvertently entered. A world where the lines between right and wrong blurred, where morality was a luxury few could afford. Jason's cold efficiency had been a key element in dismantling Voldi's network, but his methods were morally questionable, at best. Jake found himself questioning the nature of his own actions, his own complicity in the violence that had unfolded.

The aftermath was a whirlwind of activity. Law enforcement officials swarmed the scene, their movements methodical and efficient as they secured the area and collected evidence. The penthouse, once a symbol of opulence and power, was now reduced to a crime scene, a testament to the downfall of a ruthless empire. Yet, the unsettling silence that followed the chaos was far more unnerving. It was the kind of silence that hinted at untold secrets, at unresolved mysteries, at lingering threads still waiting to be unraveled.

As the first rays of dawn pierced through the smoke-filled air, painting the sky with hues of grey and orange, a chilling realization dawned on Jake. While Voldi was dead, his organization wasn't. The tentacles of the conspiracy stretched far and wide, its influence seeping into the very fabric of society. The network's infrastructure, its vast wealth, its international connections – all remained intact. Voldi's death was merely a tactical setback, not a strategic defeat. The fight was far from over.

The loose ends were numerous and frustrating. There were unanswered questions, cryptic messages found amidst Voldi's scattered documents, and whispers of hidden accounts spread across offshore banks. The information obtained from the raid was overwhelming – a labyrinthine puzzle with pieces still missing. Jake knew that Voldi's death, while significant, only scratched the surface. The true extent of the conspiracy, its intricate web of connections, and the identities of its remaining players still lay hidden, shrouded in a veil of secrecy and deception.

The media frenzy was immediate and intense. The story of Voldi's downfall became front-page news, a sensation that captivated the world's attention. Jake, despite his exhaustion and grief, found himself thrust into the limelight, his phone ringing incessantly with calls from journalists, investigators, and even politicians. He was inundated with requests for interviews, for insights into the intricacies of the conspiracy. He tried to evade the media glare, retreating into the quiet solitude of his apartment, where he could process the events that had transpired and attempt to make sense of it all.

The legal proceedings were slow, torturous, a labyrinthine process that added to the feeling of incompleteness. Several of Voldi's associates had been apprehended, but the legal system seemed incapable of comprehending the scale and complexity of the conspiracy. The evidence, while compelling, was fragmented and difficult to present in a court of law. Jake watched helplessly as justice was delayed, the legal system struggling to keep pace with the complexities of Voldi's operations. The sense of frustration was palpable.

As the dust began to settle, Jake found himself wrestling with the weight of his experiences. He had faced death countless times during his investigation, pushing himself to the very limits of his physical and emotional endurance. He'd witnessed brutality, deception, and betrayal on a scale unimaginable to most people. The loss of friends and allies weighed heavily on his heart. Yet, despite the losses and the lingering sense of unease, he couldn't shake the feeling that something was still amiss. The network of Voldi's organization had been damaged, significantly, but not destroyed. He knew, with a chilling certainty, that Voldi's death was merely a chapter in a larger, more sinister story. The fight was far from over. The echoes of the past would continue to resonate, reminding him of the unfinished business that lay ahead. The battle was won, but the war was far from over. The seeds of a new conflict had already been sown. The shadows, it seemed, were far from gone.

....

The sirens wailed a mournful counterpoint to the rhythmic thump of my own heart. Each pulse hammered a grim reminder of the price paid for the night's "victory."

The penthouse, a monument to Voldi's obscene wealth, was now a charnel house. The air, still thick with the metallic tang of blood, carried the phantom scent of expensive cologne, a stark contrast to the raw brutality of the scene. Voldi’s body, still sprawled amidst the shattered remnants of his opulent life, was a chilling tableau. He wasn't just a casualty; he was a symbol – a fallen king whose demise hadn't brought peace, only a grim acknowledgment of the war's true cost.

My gaze drifted to the bodies scattered around the room – Voldi's men, loyal to the bitter end. Their faces, frozen in expressions of shock and disbelief, bore testament to the swift, merciless efficiency of Jason's operation. Each one represented a life cut short, a family fractured, a future stolen. There was a young man, barely out of his twenties, his hand still clutching a discarded pistol; an older man, his face contorted in a silent scream, a testament to the panic that had gripped him in his final moments. These weren’t faceless thugs; they were individuals, each with their own stories, their own loves and losses, extinguished in the crossfire of a battle they likely didn't fully understand.

Jason, ever the ghost, remained detached, almost clinically so. He stood near the window, silhouetted against the cityscape, his face obscured by shadow. He hadn't spoken much since the gunfire had ceased, only offering terse responses to my questions. His demeanor betrayed a weariness, a deep exhaustion that went beyond physical fatigue. It was the weariness of a man who'd carried the weight of the world on his shoulders, a man who'd seen too much, done too much.

"They were expendable," he'd said, his voice a low murmur, almost lost in the wail of the sirens. "Just like I was, once." His words hung in the air, a chilling testament to the dehumanizing nature of the life he'd led. But even in his detachment, I sensed a flicker of something else – remorse, perhaps? A recognition of the human cost of his actions, a weight that even his steely resolve couldn't completely suppress.

My own heart ached. I'd interviewed countless victims of organized crime, listened to their stories of loss and betrayal, felt the raw pain of their grief. Yet, witnessing the aftermath of this particular confrontation, the raw carnage that filled the penthouse, was different. I'd become accustomed to the violence, the underbelly of society that Gomin Guill and Voldi represented, yet the sheer number of casualties here struck me with a fresh wave of horror. It wasn't just the scale of the violence but the stark reminder that behind every statistic, every news report, were individual lives, shattered beyond repair.

The forensic team arrived, their methodical movements a stark contrast to the chaos surrounding them. They began their grim task, documenting the scene, collecting evidence, the very act a testament to the system attempting to make sense of the senseless. Each photograph, each piece of evidence, was another brick in the wall of justice, a slow and methodical process in the face of the chaotic nature of Voldi's reign.

But the justice served that night was incomplete, a grim reminder of the long road ahead. Voldi's death, while satisfying in a certain, grim way, felt insufficient. It was like slaying the hydra; for every head cut off, two more seemed to sprout. The documents scattered across the floor, the hastily scribbled notes, the encrypted messages on laptops hinted at a deeper network, a labyrinthine structure reaching far beyond Voldi's immediate circle. The organization was wounded, perhaps mortally, but not vanquished. Its tentacles, hidden in the shadows, remained a significant threat.

The investigation continued long after the sirens had faded. Days bled into weeks, filled with interrogations, stakeouts, and the painstaking process of piecing together Voldi's empire. We unearthed evidence of money laundering operations stretching across continents, of arms deals that fueled conflicts across the globe, of political corruption on an unimaginable scale. The casualties of the war extended far beyond the bodies scattered in the penthouse. There were the families left destitute, the communities ravaged by violence, the political landscape warped by corruption. The human cost was immeasurable.

The organization's reach was insidious, its influence pervasive. We learned of informants turned traitors, of double-crosses and betrayals that mirrored the complexity of a spy novel. Each revelation brought a fresh wave of unease, a chilling reminder of how deeply entrenched the organization was, its roots intertwined with the very fabric of society. We were chasing shadows, fighting an invisible enemy whose tendrils stretched into every corner of the world.

One of the most heartbreaking discoveries was the network of informants Voldi had cultivated within law enforcement. These were individuals who had sworn to uphold the law, yet had betrayed their oaths for personal gain. Their betrayal wasn't just a matter of corruption; it was a profound breach of trust, a violation of the very principles that underpinned the justice system. Their complicity underscored the insidious nature of the organization, its ability to infiltrate and corrupt even the most trusted institutions.

As the investigation progressed, I felt a creeping sense of dread, a premonition of impending doom. The further we delved into Voldi's world, the more dangerous the terrain became. The organization’s response to Voldi’s demise wasn't just retaliatory violence; it was a carefully orchestrated attempt to eliminate any loose ends, any witnesses who might expose their operations. We were in a deadly game of cat and mouse, the stakes escalating with each passing day.

The death toll continued to climb. Informants were found dead, their deaths staged to look like accidents, suicides, or gang violence. The lines between justice and vengeance blurred, morality itself becoming a casualty of the conflict. We were fighting a shadow war, a battle of wits, resources, and brutality. The casualties were not just those who died violently, but also those who were broken, both physically and mentally.

The emotional toll on the investigators was immense. The constant threat of violence, the pervasive sense of danger, the weight of responsibility took a heavy toll. We were haunted by the ghosts of those we couldn't save, the memories of the violence we'd witnessed. The relentless pressure, the constant fear of being targeted, chipped away at our resolve, testing our resilience, stretching our empathy to its limits. We were fighting not just an organization; we were fighting a system, a culture of corruption, greed, and brutality.

And yet, amidst the darkness, there were glimmers of hope. The dismantling of Voldi's immediate network was a significant victory. We had crippled his operation, exposed his corruption, and sent a powerful message. The investigation provided closure for some victims, a chance for justice. But it was a pyrrhic victory, a moment of respite in a protracted war. The fight was far from over. The shadows lingered, long and menacing, a constant reminder of the intricate, far-reaching network that still remained, its future unknown, its motives murky, its next move unpredictable. The war, it seemed, was just beginning.

....

The city hummed a low, dissonant tune, a symphony of distant sirens and the hushed anxieties of a city that rarely slept soundly. My apartment, usually a haven of quiet contemplation, felt claustrophobic, the walls closing in on the weight of unanswered questions. Voldi's death, while satisfying on a visceral level, had only scratched the surface. It was a domino, yes, but one that had toppled only a small part of a vast, intricate game.

The files lay scattered across my desk – a chaotic landscape of police reports, intercepted communications, and financial records, each document a piece of a puzzle that refused to coalesce into a complete picture. Voldi's thoroughly kept ledger, a testament to his greed and ruthlessness, detailed transactions that reached far beyond his immediate circle. Names – coded, cryptic, and sometimes chillingly clear – appeared repeatedly, hinting at a shadowy network far more extensive and powerful than we had initially suspected. These weren't just local thugs or corrupt officials; we were dealing with players operating on an international scale, their influence seeping into the highest echelons of power.

One name haunted me: "Seraph." It appeared several times in Voldi's ledger, always accompanied by astronomical sums of money and cryptic notations. My initial research suggested it wasn't a person, but a designation – perhaps a codename for a project, a division within the organization, or even a specific type of illicit operation. The lack of concrete information only fueled my suspicions, each unanswered question deepening the mystery.

Then, there was the matter of the technology. Voldi's security system was state-of-the-art, a labyrinthine network of surveillance cameras, biometric locks, and encrypted communication lines. It was far beyond anything a typical criminal organization could afford or deploy. This level of sophistication pointed to a source of funding and technological expertise far outside the realm of ordinary crime. Where did this technology originate? Who provided it? And what was its ultimate purpose beyond protecting Voldi's personal interests? These questions remained unanswered.

The interviews were proving equally frustrating. Many of Voldi's associates, cowed by fear or bought with promises of immunity, offered little more than carefully crafted lies and evasive answers. Their silence, though, was a statement in itself – a testament to the power and reach of the organization they served. Even those who agreed to cooperate were hesitant, their testimonies laced with ambiguity and riddled with gaps in their accounts. The fear in their eyes was palpable, a chilling reminder of the consequences of defiance.

The most disturbing revelation came from one of Voldi's former accountants, a nervous man named Dimitri, who had initially refused to cooperate but eventually broke under the weight of mounting evidence. He confessed to laundering money for a group he referred to only as "The Syndicate," an organization that operated entirely outside the legal system. He described elaborate financial schemes designed to obscure the origins and destination of vast sums of money, often involving shell corporations, offshore accounts, and cryptocurrency transactions – a complex web of deceit designed to evade detection.

Dimitri also revealed the existence of a network of safe houses and secret communication channels used by the

Syndicate. He sketched a rough map, marking locations in several different countries, a labyrinthine trail that stretched across continents. Following these leads felt like navigating a treacherous minefield, each step fraught with potential danger. The Syndicate's reach was far broader than we could have imagined.

The investigation had unearthed a series of seemingly unrelated crimes – assassinations, kidnappings, corporate espionage – all of which, upon closer examination, seemed to be connected to The Syndicate. It was as if the organization had tentacles reaching into every aspect of society, silently pulling strings, orchestrating events from the shadows. This wasn't just about money; this was about power, influence, and control.

Even Jason Reen's confession, though compelling, left several unanswered questions. While his account of eliminating Gomin Guill was meticulous and convincing, it failed to adequately address the larger conspiracy. He had focused on the immediate threat, eliminating the immediate danger, but he hadn't delved deep enough into the organization's structure, its inner workings, or its ultimate goals. His expertise was in taking down targets, not dismantling complex criminal enterprises.

This realization hit me hard. The war wasn't over; it had just shifted to a new, more dangerous level. We had won a battle, but the war against The Syndicate was far from won. The loose ends, far from being mere details, were red flags, indicators of a deeper and far more dangerous threat lurking beneath the surface. The fight against The Syndicate was a marathon, not a sprint, and I had only just begun to understand the true scope of the race.

The implications were staggering. We were dealing with an organization capable of manipulating global events, influencing politics, and wielding power in the shadows. Their reach extended beyond borders and jurisdictions, making them practically untouchable. The sheer scale of their operation, their resources, and their ruthlessness was daunting.

I spent the next few days poring over Dimitri’s information, piecing together the fragmented clues. Each new piece of the puzzle only deepened the mystery, revealing further layers of complexity and deceit. The Syndicate wasn't just a criminal organization; it was a shadow government, operating in plain sight, yet remaining invisible to the casual observer. They were masters of manipulation, able to control the flow of information, influence public opinion, and even frame innocent people.

As I delved deeper into the investigation, the feeling of being trapped in a web of deceit and conspiracy grew stronger. I was no longer just a reporter chasing a story; I was a pawn in a much larger game, a game with potentially deadly stakes. The feeling was unsettling, a cold dread that settled deep in my bones. This wasn't just a matter of exposing corruption and bringing criminals to justice; it was a fight for survival.

The night was closing in. The city outside my window was a shimmering tapestry of lights, but the darkness inside my apartment felt overwhelming. The weight of responsibility pressed down on me, the realization that I was facing an enemy far more powerful and dangerous than I could have ever imagined. I was alone in this battle, armed with nothing more than my wits, my determination, and the nagging feeling that the shadows held far more than just secrets. They held the key to understanding the true nature of the enemy, and the only way to win this war was to face the darkness head-on.

The fight for justice wasn't over. It was merely beginning. The loose ends were not just gaps in the story;

they were the threads that, when carefully pulled, would unravel the entire tapestry of deception. The road ahead was perilous, but the alternative – allowing The Syndicate to continue its reign of terror – was unthinkable. The game had changed, and so had I. I was no longer just a reporter; I was a soldier in a war no one else even knew existed. And the battle, I knew, would be long and bloody. The sirens wailed again in the distance, a somber soundtrack to my newfound resolve. The war was far from over. The fight had only just begun.

....

The air hung heavy, thick with the unspoken. The city lights, usually a vibrant tapestry of life, seemed muted, dulled by the weight of the events that had unfolded. Voldi's death, the culmination of weeks spent chasing shadows and whispers, had left a void, a hollow ache in the pit of my stomach. It wasn't the satisfaction of vengeance, not exactly. It was something colder, a chilling recognition of the depth of the abyss I'd glimpsed, a testament to the sheer scale of the conspiracy I'd stumbled into.

I stared out at the cityscape, the familiar skyline transformed into a menacing silhouette against the darkening sky. Each building, each flickering light, seemed to whisper secrets, each shadow a potential threat. The adrenaline that had fueled me for weeks had begun to recede, replaced by a bone-deep weariness that clung to me like a shroud. The champagne toast from the previous night, a fleeting moment of celebratory relief, now felt like a cruel joke, a stark contrast to the harsh reality that loomed.

Justice? Had justice truly been served? Voldi was dead, yes, but the organization he represented remained, a hydra with a seemingly infinite number of heads. His death was a blow, undoubtedly, but it was hardly a fatal one. It was more akin to pruning a branch, a temporary setback for a beast with the capacity to regenerate. The insidious tendrils of The Syndicate still reached into every facet of society, their influence spreading like a malignant tumor.

The recordings, the thoroughly documented evidence, were now a double-edged sword. They provided undeniable proof of Voldi's crimes, a cornerstone for dismantling his particular operation. But the greater threat, the mastermind pulling the strings from the shadows, remained elusive. Voldi had been a pawn, a highly dangerous one, but just a pawn nonetheless. The king remained hidden, his identity a phantom, his movements invisible.

The information Jason had provided, cryptic as it was, was proving far more valuable than I initially believed. His description of the network, his insights into the Syndicate's operations – these details were like pieces of a complex puzzle, each seemingly insignificant until they were placed in relation to the others. I spent the next few days thoroughly reviewing every scrap of information, every piece of audio, every single interview transcript. I was chasing ghosts, trying to piece together the ethereal form of an unseen enemy.

Sleep was a luxury I could no longer afford. My apartment, once a refuge, had become a battleground, a war room littered with documents, audio cassettes, and half-eaten takeout containers. The walls were covered in maps, dotted with locations, connecting the dots of Jason's confessions. Each city, each clandestine meeting, each carefully orchestrated assassination represented a step further down the rabbit hole.

One detail, a seemingly innocuous mention of a coded message found in Voldi's safe, plagued me relentlessly. Jason hadn't mentioned this specific detail, which raised immediate questions about the nature of his relationship with his employers and the true extent of his knowledge. If he had been so thorough in eliminating Voldi and his immediate circle, why was this oversight so glaring? It felt like a deliberately placed red herring, a trap. Or a hint. A key to something bigger.

The message itself, a series of seemingly random numbers and symbols, proved to be an enigma. Cryptography was far beyond my expertise; I needed help, and quickly. I reached out to an old contact, Dr. Tanya Masqua, a brilliant cryptographer and former colleague at the university. Her reputation preceded her; renowned for her sharp mind and unwavering integrity. I explained the situation, laying out the urgency and the stakes. She was hesitant initially, wary of the dangers inherent in this case, but the implications of what I was uncovering, the potential to expose a truly global network, ultimately won her over.

Tanya's help proved invaluable. Within days, she had cracked the code, revealing a chilling message, a rendezvous point, and a new name: Mr. Silas. The location was a seemingly innocuous warehouse district on the outskirts of the city, a place that blended seamlessly into the industrial landscape. The name, Silas, triggered a faint recognition, a fleeting memory from a past investigation. I scoured my archives, my heart pounding as I found an article, a decade old, about a string of mysterious disappearances, cases that were abruptly closed and swiftly forgotten. The only common denominator, other than their mysterious nature, was the presence of an individual referred to only as "Silas" in a few of the police reports.

My sleep-deprived mind was piecing together the fragments. Silas was the missing link, the orchestrator lurking in the shadows. He was pulling the strings, manipulating Voldi and his associates, using them as disposable pawns in a game of immense proportions. The implications were staggering: a network that transcended national borders, a conspiracy that extended far beyond the realm of organized crime. This wasn't just about money or power; there was something far more sinister at play. This wasn't just about taking down a single criminal organization. It was about dismantling a global threat.

The warehouse, as Tanya had predicted, was under heavy surveillance. Cameras, hidden microphones, and armed guards patrolled the perimeter. This was no mere storage facility; it was a heavily fortified stronghold. The mission to infiltrate the place was far riskier than anything I had undertaken before. I needed a new approach. I wouldn't be able to get into the place covertly, even with Tanya's help. I needed an insider. I needed someone within The Syndicate who was tired of playing the game.

It was a long shot, a desperate gamble. I started by contacting some of the smaller players, the operatives on the fringes of the organization, the ones who were expendable, the ones who could be bought, or coerced. I searched through my files for potential contacts, anyone who had been arrested in connection to past cases and may have a desire for retribution. I had to tread carefully, each call, each email fraught with potential danger. Each word, each syllable, had to be carefully weighted. One wrong move could lead to my death, exposing me to the full wrath of the Syndicate.

One contact, a low-level operative named Marco, eventually agreed to meet. He was desperate, worn down by years of living on the edge. He wasn't interested in the money; what he desired most was an exit strategy, a way to escape the life he had. The information he provided was invaluable. Marco was willing to help, to become my eyes and ears within the organization, but only under strict conditions and with the guarantee of anonymity. This was a risk, but it was my best chance to get closer to Silas and expose the entire truth, but could I trust him?

The game had changed, once again. The fight wasn't just about bringing Voldi to justice; it was about uncovering a web of deceit that stretched across continents, a conspiracy that threatened the very fabric of society. The path ahead was perilous, fraught with danger at every turn. But I had to keep going. The alternative, allowing Silas and The Syndicate to remain unchecked, was simply unacceptable. The war had begun, and I, along with Marco, now found myself fighting on the front lines. The hunt was on for Mr. Silas. And this time, it was personal.

....

The rain lashed against the windows of my small apartment, mirroring the tempest inside me. The city, usually a cacophony of sirens and shouts, felt strangely quiet, a hushed aftermath. The victory over Voldi, the dismantling of his immediate network, felt hollow, a fleeting moment of respite in a protracted war. Marco, his face etched with the weariness of sleepless nights and close calls, sat across from me, nursing a glass of something amber and strong. He hadn't spoken much since we'd left Voldi's lifeless body sprawled in the rain-slicked alley. The silence, heavy and suffocating, spoke volumes.

We'd won a battle, but the war raged on. Silas, the elusive puppet master, remained at large, his shadowy tendrils still wrapped around the world's underbelly. The information Voldi had unwittingly spilled, the fragmented clues we'd pieced together, pointed to a conspiracy far grander, more insidious than we could have imagined. It wasn't just about drug trafficking or arms dealing anymore; it was about something far more sinister, something that touched the highest echelons of power, twisting the levers of influence with ruthless efficiency.

I ran a hand through my hair, feeling the exhaustion gnawing at my bones. The relentless pursuit, the near-misses, the constant threat of betrayal – it had taken its toll. I wasn't the same man who had started this investigation months ago. The naive idealism that had fueled my early days as a reporter had been eroded, replaced by a hardened cynicism born from firsthand experience with the depravity of humanity. Yet, there was a strange resilience, a newfound strength, forged in the crucible of danger. The line between reporter and participant had blurred, almost vanished entirely. I was no longer just observing; I was actively engaged in a fight for survival, a fight for justice, a fight against a foe so powerful, so deeply entrenched, that it seemed invincible.

Marco broke the silence, his voice low and gravelly. "Silas won't stop. He'll find a way to rebuild, to regroup. This isn't over."

I nodded; my gaze fixed on the rain-streaked window. He was right. The feeling of satisfaction, the fleeting sense of closure after Voldi's demise, had already faded, replaced by a chilling premonition. Silas was a ghost, a phantom, capable of slipping through the cracks, of disappearing into the shadows. He was the architect of this elaborate web of deceit and dismantling it would require more than luck and grit; it would demand meticulous planning, strategic alliances, and a level of cunning that even I, seasoned as I'd become, found daunting.

The following weeks were a blur of coded messages, clandestine meetings, and hushed conversations in dimly lit bars. Marco, with his network of informants and his uncanny ability to navigate the city's underbelly, proved invaluable. We followed a trail of breadcrumbs, each leading us closer to Silas, yet always just out of reach. We learned about Silas's intricate network of shell corporations, his labyrinthine financial dealings, and the staggering level of corruption that allowed him to operate with such impunity. The Syndicate, as we now called it, wasn't just a criminal organization; it was a parasitic entity, feeding on the very foundations of society.

We had to be smarter, more cunning. We needed to anticipate Silas's moves, to think like him. The information we had gleaned so far pointed to a massive money-laundering operation, with assets hidden across multiple offshore accounts. Our next step was to infiltrate the organization from within, to plant a mole who could relay information about Silas's plans and his whereabouts. It was a risky endeavor, one that could easily backfire, but it was our best chance.

We found our mole in an unlikely source: Tanya, a former associate of Voldi, who had grown disillusioned with Silas's ruthlessness. She was desperate to escape his grasp, to make amends for her past transgressions. She was our key to unraveling the puzzle, the key to bringing Silas to justice. However, trusting Tanya was a gamble, a dangerous game of chicken. Her loyalty remained questionable, a constant source of unease in my mind.

The infiltration process was agonizingly slow and meticulous. We thoroughly crafted a false identity for Tanya, carefully creating a backstory that would make her believable within the Syndicate's ranks. Months turned into years as we waited patiently, watching as Tanya weaved her way deeper into the organization’s heart. The stakes were impossibly high. One wrong move, one misplaced word, could cost us everything. The constant tension, the pressure of knowing that failure was not an option, gnawed at us relentlessly.

And then, finally, a breakthrough. Tanya managed to get her hands on Silas’s detailed financial records, a trove of information that exposed the extent of his criminal empire. We had enough evidence to bring him down, to expose him for who he really was. The moment of reckoning was close. But as we prepared to strike, a new threat emerged, one that threatened to derail our plans completely. A rival syndicate, eager to seize control of Silas's empire, had discovered our infiltration, threatening to expose Tanya and jeopardize the entire operation.

The final confrontation took place in a secluded warehouse on the outskirts of the city. The air crackled with tension as we faced off against Silas and his men. It was a bloody, brutal showdown, a desperate fight for survival. Marco's skills, honed over years of clandestine operations, proved invaluable, allowing us to secure the upper hand. Silas, though cornered, fought with the ferocity of a cornered animal, desperate to maintain his grip on power. But in the end, justice prevailed. Silas, the puppet master, was finally brought to his knees.

The arrest of Silas marked not an ending but a turning point. The long-awaited sense of closure, however, felt far removed from any sense of elation. The victory had come at a cost. The world had changed during those years, irrevocably scarred by the events we had witnessed and participated in. The weight of the past, the burden of knowledge gained through blood and sacrifice, remained. The fight was over. But the war, it seemed, would forever linger in the shadows.

As I sat by the rain-streaked window, watching the city lights twinkle faintly in the distance, I realized that the scars we bear become part of who we are. This experience, this journey into the heart of darkness, had irrevocably changed me. But amidst the darkness, I found a flicker of hope – the hope that perhaps, just perhaps, a new beginning was possible. A beginning where justice, though often elusive, was still worth fighting for. A new beginning where I could reconcile the man I was before the chaos, with the one I had become. The battle had been won, but the journey was far from over. The world remained a dangerous place, but armed with experience and a newfound resolve, I was ready to face whatever darkness lay ahead. The rain continued to fall, a cleansing wash over the city and over my soul, a symbol of renewal and a promise of the new dawn.

Political Ramifications

The revelation of Gomin Guill's operation, and the even larger conspiracy behind it, wasn't confined to the shadowy world of international assassins and criminal syndicates. It exploded into the public sphere like a nuclear bomb, shattering the carefully constructed facade of political stability and leaving a trail of rubble in its wake. The initial reports, cautious and fragmented at first, quickly coalesced into a maelstrom of accusations, denials, and desperate attempts at damage control. Jake Harroll, unwittingly at the epicenter of this maelstrom, found himself thrust from the relative anonymity of his radio show into the blinding glare of the global spotlight.

The political ramifications were immediate and profound. The implicated politicians, initially dismissed as mere pawns in a much larger game, suddenly found themselves under intense scrutiny. Years of carefully cultivated public images crumbled under the weight of leaked documents and damning testimony. Career-long reputations, built on carefully crafted narratives of public service and integrity, were reduced to ashes overnight. The fallout was brutal, leaving a vacuum of power and a sense of deep unease among the electorate.

One of the most significant impacts was on the upcoming elections. Several high-profile candidates, their campaigns heavily funded by individuals and corporations now revealed to be deeply entwined with Gomin's organization, saw their support plummet. The public outcry was fierce, fueled by the relentless reporting that followed Jake's initial exposé. Investigations, launched by both legislative and judicial bodies, were moving forward at a pace that shocked seasoned observers.

The media frenzy that followed was unprecedented. Jake's initial interview with Jason Reen, initially dismissed by many as a sensationalist stunt, had become the linchpin of a global investigation. News channels across the globe ran 24/7 coverage, dissecting every detail of the conspiracy. Analysts debated the scope and implications, while commentators speculated on the potential fallout. Jake, transformed from a relatively unknown radio reporter into a reluctant hero (or villain, depending on the perspective), found himself besieged by requests for interviews, threatened by shadowy figures, and under constant surveillance.

The sheer volume of information unleashed onto the public was overwhelming. Leaked documents detailing shady transactions, illicit meetings, and clandestine operations were shared on social media, triggering widespread public outrage and igniting social unrest. Protests erupted in major cities around the world, demanding accountability and transparency from governments that had seemingly turned a blind eye to years of criminal activity. The political landscape shifted dramatically, with trust in established institutions eroding at an alarming rate.

But the political fallout extended beyond the immediate consequences of the exposed conspiracy. The crisis exposed deep-seated vulnerabilities within existing systems of governance and oversight. Questions were raised about the effectiveness of intelligence agencies, the role of campaign finance, and the influence of powerful lobbies. The revelation that Gomin's network had infiltrated seemingly impenetrable systems prompted calls for extensive reforms.

The legal system, too, was severely tested. The complexity of the conspiracy, with its web of interconnected actors and international dimensions, proved to be a daunting challenge for law enforcement. Arrests were made, but the prosecution of those involved proved far more difficult than anticipated. The lack of sufficient evidence, the use of offshore accounts and shell corporations, and the involvement of powerful individuals within the judicial system, created significant obstacles to justice. Many victims felt that justice was delayed, if not entirely denied. The legal battle stretched on for years, causing further frustration and anger among those affected.

Beyond the immediate political turbulence, the exposure of conspiracy created a long-term shift in the political landscape. The ensuing investigations sparked a series of reforms aimed at enhancing transparency and accountability within government. New regulations were enacted to control campaign financing, and greater oversight was introduced to prevent future infiltration of political structures by organized crime.

However, despite these efforts, a sense of lingering unease persisted. The deep roots of the conspiracy, its capacity to infiltrate governmental and financial institutions, had shaken the public's faith in the systems designed to protect them. The ease with which Gomin's organization had operated for so long, unchecked and unchallenged, raised serious questions about the effectiveness of the existing mechanisms.

The exposure also brought unexpected consequences for Jake Harroll. While initially hailed as a hero for his intrepid reporting, he found himself increasingly targeted by those who wanted to silence him. The organization, though damaged, was far from defunct. Elements of the conspiracy lingered, and the threat of further attacks and repercussions was very real. He faced death threats, harassment, and numerous attempts on his life, each closer to success than the last.

This led him to reflect deeply on the cost of truth and the price he'd paid for uncovering the conspiracy. The emotional and psychological toll was immense. He’d witnessed firsthand the brutal reality of organized crime, experienced the chilling efficiency of Gomin’s assassins, and seen the corruption festering at the heart of power. The experience left an indelible mark on him, transforming him from a skeptical journalist into a hardened investigator, forever marked by the shadows he’d helped expose.

The story, however, was far from over. While the immediate threat posed by Gomin's organization seemed neutralized, the implications of the larger conspiracy, the far-reaching networks, and the enduring power of those who had been implicated remained. The exposure had unleashed a torrent of political and social upheaval, but the long-term consequences were far from clear, a chilling reminder of the complex and often unpredictable nature of organized crime's influence on the world stage. The story of Gomin Guill, therefore, remained an open chapter, a constant reminder of the intricate web of power and corruption that operated beyond the confines of public view, a threat that continued to lurk in the shadows, ready to strike again when least expected. The fight for justice, for transparency, and for the very survival of democratic institutions, was far from over. Jake Harroll knew this better than anyone. The world had changed irrevocably, and he was left to navigate the treacherous currents of a new reality, one where the lines between right and wrong, justice and retribution, were far more blurred than he ever could have imagined.

....

The interview, leaked in its entirety online by an anonymous source, became an instant global phenomenon. Jake Harroll's quiet radio show, previously known only to a dedicated niche audience, was now a household name, albeit one shrouded in controversy and uncertainty. The sheer audacity of the revelation – a renowned assassin detailing the systematic dismantling of a powerful criminal empire – captivated the world. News channels across the globe ran excerpts, analyzing Jason Reen's chillingly calm demeanor and the stark implications of his confession. The internet exploded with speculation, theories, and conspiracy narratives, each more outlandish than the last.

Jake, suddenly thrust into the limelight, found himself besieged. His phone never stopped ringing, a cacophony of calls from news outlets, political pundits, and even a few threatening anonymous ones. He was swarmed by reporters outside his apartment, their cameras flashing incessantly, turning his life into a surreal, unsettling spectacle. The anonymity he had cherished for so long had evaporated, replaced by a suffocating sense of public scrutiny. The pressure was immense, a relentless tide threatening to pull him under.

Initially, he tried to maintain a sense of professionalism, granting select interviews to reputable news organizations. He carefully chose his words, emphasizing the dangers inherent in Gomin Guill's operation and the far-reaching implications of the conspiracy Jason had uncovered. But he also faced relentless questioning about his role in the story, the veracity of Jason's claims, and the potential risks he himself now faces. Every utterance was dissected and analyzed; each pause scrutinized. The media, hungry for more, quickly lost patience with his guarded responses.

The tone shifted rapidly. Initial expressions of awe and shock morphed into accusations of sensationalism, conspiracy theories, and even accusations of Jake being complicit in some grand scheme. Some outlets suggested he'd fabricated the entire story for personal gain or notoriety. Others accused him of jeopardizing national security by publicizing sensitive information. Talk shows erupted in heated debates, pitting experts against conspiracy theorists, politicians against journalists, in a chaotic maelstrom of competing narratives.

The pressure from his superiors at the radio station was equally intense. They initially welcomed the surge in listeners and ratings, but as the criticism intensified, their anxieties grew. They urged him to tone down his reporting, to avoid making any further pronouncements, to simply let the story fade away. They fretted about potential lawsuits, public backlash, and damage to the station's reputation. Jake, however, felt a deep sense of responsibility. He knew, as he had since Jason's confession, that this was bigger than just a story, bigger than just his career. He knew it was a battle for truth, for accountability, and potentially, for survival.

The political fallout was even more dramatic. Governments across the globe scrambled to respond to the revelations, issuing carefully worded statements denying any involvement in Gomin Guill's operation, while subtly hinting at investigations underway. But the damage was already done. Public trust in established institutions eroded further, replaced by a cynical skepticism. Politicians, once untouchable, were suddenly implicated, their names whispered alongside Gomin's in hushed tones. The media fueled the fire, digging up old scandals and raising uncomfortable questions about funding, contracts, and questionable partnerships. The political landscape shifted dramatically, with alliances fracturing and power dynamics abruptly altered.

The internet, meanwhile, became a battleground of competing narratives. Conspiracy theories ran rampant, some outlandish, some disturbingly plausible. Pro-government trolls battled with anonymous activists, each side trying to control the narrative, spreading misinformation and manipulating public opinion. The sheer volume of information, both true and false, made it almost impossible to discern truth from fiction. The line between legitimate journalism and sensationalized clickbait blurred beyond recognition. Jake found himself fighting not just against the powerful figures implicated in the conspiracy, but also against the tidal wave of misinformation, the deliberate obfuscation designed to bury the truth under a mountain of lies.

Social media became a crucible of intense debate and often violent rhetoric. Hashtags related to the story trended worldwide, but the conversations were frequently toxic, filled with hatred, insults, and threats. Jake, despite his best efforts to maintain a professional demeanor, found himself becoming increasingly isolated, a lone voice against the deafening cacophony of misinformation and hate. He felt a constant sense of threat, the feeling of being followed, the sense that every corner held an unseen enemy.

His apartment, once a sanctuary, became a prison. He installed security cameras, changed his phone number, and started relying on trusted colleagues for support. Even then, he never felt entirely safe. The constant barrage of emails, calls, and social media messages, a mixture of support, vitriol, and threats, was incredibly taxing. The weight of the story, the danger it represented, and the relentless scrutiny he was under, began to take its toll. Sleep became a luxury, replaced by a constant state of hypervigilance, a palpable sense of unease that clung to him like a shadow.

He tried to focus on his work, but the sheer scale of the conspiracy, the depth of corruption it exposed, and the implications for global security, was overwhelming. The interview had opened a Pandora's box, unleashing a maelstrom of chaos and uncertainty that threatened to engulf him, and possibly the world. The fight for truth, he realized, was only just beginning. And he, armed with nothing but his microphone and his unwavering commitment to uncovering the truth, was at the forefront of the battle. The fallout wasn't just about the story itself; it was about the fight to preserve the integrity of journalism in the face of overwhelming pressure, political maneuvering, and the potent weapon of misinformation.

The future remained uncertain, but one thing was clear: Jake Harroll's life, and the lives of many others, were now inextricably linked to the unraveling of a conspiracy far greater than he ever could have imagined. The quiet world of radio reporting was long gone, swallowed by a media frenzy that mirrored the chaos he was now trying to unravel.

....

The initial wave of public outrage, fueled by Jason Reen’s explosive interview, slowly began to ebb. The headlines, once screaming with the details of Gomin Guill’s reign of terror and its sudden, brutal end, faded into the background noise of the daily news cycle. The sheer scale of the conspiracy, initially captivating and horrifying in equal measure, became a distant, abstract threat, a story relegated to the back pages. The human cost, however, remained starkly visible, a painful reminder of the justice yet to be served.

Families of Gomin Guill's victims, many of whom had suffered for years in silence, watched with growing frustration as the wheels of justice turned agonizingly slowly. The legal system, burdened by bureaucratic inertia and a lack of political will, proved a formidable obstacle. Key witnesses were intimidated into silence, crucial documents mysteriously disappeared, and the vast network of lawyers and lobbyists employed by Guill’s organization worked tirelessly to obfuscate the truth and delay proceedings. The initial euphoria surrounding the downfall of Gomin Guill quickly dissolved into a bitter reality: justice, it seemed, was a luxury afforded only to the powerful.

One such family was the Petrovs, a modest family from Odessa, Ukraine. Their patriarch, Dmitri Petrov, a small-time businessman, had unwittingly crossed paths with Guill’s organization years ago. He had refused to pay a protection fee, a seemingly insignificant act of defiance that had cost him dearly. Dmitri was brutally murdered, his body left to rot in an abandoned warehouse. His wife, Irina, and their young daughter, Tanya, were left to navigate the labyrinthine complexities of the legal system, a system seemingly designed to protect the guilty and punish the innocent.

Irina Petrov, a stoic woman with eyes that held the weight of years of sorrow, became a symbol of the fight for justice delayed. She tirelessly pursued the case, gathering evidence, confronting indifference, and battling against the overwhelming weight of a corrupt system. She attended countless court hearings, each one a soul-crushing reminder of the powerlessness she felt. She wrote letters to politicians, newspapers, and anyone who would listen, her voice a desperate plea for accountability. But her efforts met with limited success. Bribery, intimidation, and procedural delays stalled the case repeatedly, turning what should have been a straightforward investigation into a Kafkaesque nightmare.

The lawyer assigned to the Petrovs' case, a young idealist named Elena Voldi, initially displayed great zeal and determination. However, as she delved deeper into the investigation, she found herself overwhelmed by the sheer scale of the conspiracy and the immense power of those involved. Threatening phone calls became increasingly frequent, and subtle attempts to influence her decisions became more blatant. Elena, though initially unwavering in her commitment, found herself growing weary, burdened by the weight of a seemingly unwinnable battle. The system, she realized, wasn't simply inefficient; it was fundamentally broken.

Meanwhile, Jake Harroll found himself caught in the undertow of the political fallout. His interview with Jason Reen had become a lightning rod, attracting criticism from both ends of the political spectrum. Conservative commentators accused him of sensationalism and undermining national security. Progressive voices criticized his failure to immediately deliver the evidence to authorities, suggesting that he prioritized personal glory over justice. The ensuing media firestorm threatened to drown out the real victims of Gomin Guill's crimes, leaving Irina Petrov and countless others in a state of desperate limbo.

Jake, consumed by a sense of responsibility, felt the weight of the world on his shoulders. The interview, intended to expose Guill's crimes, had inadvertently unleashed a maelstrom of political infighting and legal maneuvering that threatened to bury the truth beneath layers of bureaucracy and misinformation. He dedicated himself to assisting Irina Petrov, leveraging his newfound notoriety to shine a spotlight on her fight. He secured pro bono legal representation from a prominent human rights lawyer, someone who had a history of taking on seemingly impossible cases against powerful adversaries. This lawyer, a formidable woman named Tanya Blema, had a reputation for tenacity and an unwavering commitment to justice. She wasn't intimidated by Guill's vast network of influence.

Tanya's investigation revealed a deeper, more sinister layer to the conspiracy. It wasn't just about the protection rackets and drug trafficking Gomin Guill was involved in. It involved far-reaching political influence, corruption at the highest levels of government, and connections to international arms dealers and terrorist organizations. Guill was a pawn in a larger game, a small piece in a vast, intricate chessboard. The evidence was compelling, damning, and incredibly dangerous. The trail led to powerful individuals who had the means and the motive to ensure the case remained buried. The deeper Tanya dug, the more precarious her position became.

The revelation of this larger conspiracy only served to further delay justice for the victims. The legal process became even more bogged down, with political maneuvering and behind-the-scenes negotiations delaying the inevitable reckoning. The Petrovs, along with countless other families, found themselves trapped in a Kafkaesque nightmare, their hopes for justice dwindling with each passing day. Irina’s quiet resolve began to crack under the pressure. The constant barrage of setbacks, the seemingly endless parade of legal obstacles, the sense of futility - it all began to wear her down. Yet, she held on, her spirit fueled by a fierce determination to see justice served, even if it was delayed, even if it seemed impossible.

The media attention, initially focused on the dramatic downfall of Gomin Guill, had shifted its focus. The intrigue surrounding the larger conspiracy, the political backroom deals, and the high-stakes legal battles stole the spotlight from the human cost of Guill's reign of terror. The plight of Irina Petrov and other victims became a footnote in a much larger, more complex story. Jake Harroll fought to keep the focus on these victims, reminding the world of the human cost of political gamesmanship. He used his platform to expose the systemic flaws in the legal system, highlighting the challenges faced by ordinary citizens in their struggle against powerful adversaries.

The delay in justice became a symbol of the larger problems plaguing society: the corruption within governments, the influence of money and power, and the inherent inequalities within the legal system. Irina Petrov's story, and those of countless others who were similarly affected by Gomin Guill's crimes, served as a stark reminder of the long and arduous path towards justice, a path often fraught with obstacles and delays, leaving victims in a prolonged state of limbo, unsure if and when justice will be served. The fight for justice, Jake realized, was far from over. The battle had shifted, but the war was still raging.

....

The quiet hum of the city was a deceptive lullaby. It masked the simmering resentment, the barely contained fury, the chilling whispers of retribution that echoed in the underbelly of the metropolis. Gomin Guill was gone, but the organization he'd built, the intricate web of corruption and violence he'd spun, remained stubbornly intact. His demise, far from being a final victory, felt more like a severed head of a hydra, promising a surge of retaliatory strikes.

Jake Harroll, despite the initial media frenzy having subsided, felt a growing unease. The interviews, the frantic calls, the hushed conversations in dimly lit bars – they all pointed to a disturbing truth. Guill's death had only scratched the surface. The organization, a colossal beast with countless tentacles reaching into every level of society, was still very much alive and, seemingly, more determined than ever.

He thought of Irina Petrov, her face etched with a weariness that belied her youthful appearance. Her testimony, the heart-wrenching details of her ordeal at the hands of Guill's men, had been crucial in painting a vivid picture of the organization's cruelty. Yet, even with the compelling evidence she provided, the legal process ground to a glacial pace. Justice, it seemed, was a luxury afforded to few, especially when those in power were implicated.

Irina's case was far from unique. Jake had received countless calls from other victims, their voices trembling with a mixture of hope and despair. Each story was a chilling testament to the organization's reach and ruthlessness. They were stories of intimidation, of silenced witnesses, of legal battles deliberately stalled and manipulated. The organization wasn't just eliminating its enemies; it was systematically dismantling any attempts at accountability.

His phone buzzed, jolting him from his grim reflections. It was an anonymous tip, a cryptic message laced with veiled threats and coded language. “The viper has lost its head, but the tail remains venomous.” The message ended with a single, chilling image: a stylized serpent coiled around a skull. Jake recognized the symbol – a clandestine marker used by the organization's inner circle, a sign of impending danger.

The investigation, once focused on Guill, now took on a new, more daunting dimension. It was no longer a matter of uncovering a single criminal mastermind; it was a question of dismantling a deeply entrenched system of power, one that operated in the shadows, manipulating laws, exploiting loopholes, and silencing dissent with ruthless efficiency. The investigation felt like navigating a labyrinthine maze, each turn leading to a dead end or a new, more treacherous path.

He revisited Jason Reen’s account, poring over every detail, searching for clues that the initial interview had missed. Jason, despite his ruthless efficiency, had spoken of limitations, of unseen forces that stretched beyond his reach. He'd alluded to a shadowy council, a group of individuals pulling the strings from the dark corners of the world – individuals even Guill seemingly answered to. This was the heart of the conspiracy, the source of its enduring power.

Jake's research took him down a rabbit hole of offshore accounts, shell corporations, and anonymous trusts, all intricately linked to the organization. He discovered a complex network of money laundering schemes, cleverly disguised transactions that masked the movement of billions of dollars. The scale of the operation was staggering, extending far beyond the initial scope of Guill's empire. It was a global network, a financial hydra with its tentacles wrapped around governments, corporations, and influential individuals.

The deeper Jake dug, the more dangerous the situation became. He found himself walking a tightrope, one misstep away from falling into the clutches of the organization. Threats became more direct, more menacing. Anonymous calls turned into veiled warnings delivered in person, accompanied by menacing stares and ominous gestures. His apartment was under surveillance; his phone tapped. He felt like a hunted animal, constantly looking over his shoulder, his every move scrutinized.

He knew he couldn't do this alone. He sought out the help of an old contact, a former FBI agent named Marcus Bell, a man known for his sharp intellect and unwavering integrity. Marcus, hardened by years spent battling organized crime, was initially hesitant, skeptical of Jake's claims. But Jake’s persistence, coupled with the irrefutable evidence he presented, finally convinced Marcus that this was bigger than they both had initially anticipated.

Together, they delved deeper into the organization's operations. They unraveled layers of deception, exposing a sophisticated network of informants, spies, and mercenaries. They discovered hidden communication channels, encrypted messages, and secret meetings in secluded locations. Each piece of information they uncovered felt like a victory, yet it also added to the magnitude of the threat they faced.

The organization responded with swift and brutal efficiency. Marcus's apartment was raided; his sources threatened. Jake discovered a sophisticated network of social engineering, designed to discredit him, to sow doubt and mistrust among those who supported his investigation.

The organization was not only powerful, it was highly adaptive, its tentacles reaching out in various and unexpected ways.

One evening, while sifting through a trove of encrypted files, Jake stumbled upon a crucial piece of information: a list of names, names of politicians, high-ranking government officials, and influential business leaders who were complicit in the organization's activities. It was the smoking gun, proof of the systemic corruption at the heart of the entire operation. This was not a simple case of organized crime; it was a cancer at the core of the system, a vast conspiracy threatening to unravel the very fabric of society.

The weight of this discovery settled heavily on Jake's shoulders. He realized that he wasn't just fighting against an organized crime syndicate; he was fighting against a powerful, entrenched system, a system protected by those in positions of power. He was a David facing a Goliath, armed with nothing but the truth and his unwavering commitment to justice. But as he looked at the list of names, he knew that the fight for justice had just begun. The lingering threats, once veiled and subtle, now felt like a tangible, omnipresent danger, a constant reminder of the immense challenge ahead. The war was far from over; it had only just begun. The fallout from Guill's death had not ended; it had just begun to spread. And Jake, caught in the vortex of this swirling maelstrom, was at the very heart of the storm.

....

The cheap, lukewarm coffee tasted like ash in my mouth. The city lights, usually a mesmerizing spectacle from my apartment window, now felt like the cold, uncaring eyes of a predator. Guill was dead, but the silence that followed his demise was far more unsettling than the cacophony of the city's usual nocturnal symphony. It was the silence before the storm, a deceptive calm masking the gathering tempest. I stared at the city sprawling beneath me, a concrete jungle teeming with secrets, betrayals, and simmering revenge. The weight of my investigation, the cost of uncovering the truth, pressed down on me, heavy and suffocating.

This wasn't the triumphant conclusion I had envisioned. I'd expected a sense of closure, a feeling of having righted a wrong. Instead, I was left with a chilling realization: I had only scratched the surface. Guill's death had opened a Pandora's Box, unleashing a torrent of unforeseen consequences. The thoroughly maintained appearance of order and stability that Guill had so diligently preserved had disintegrated, exposing an intricate and perilous underworld beyond my previous comprehension. The list of names Jason had left behind—a chilling testament to the organization's vast reach and influence—haunted me. Each name whispered a story of corruption, intimidation, and violence, a grim tapestry woven with threads of deceit and desperation.

I ran my fingers across the worn surface of the recording device, its metallic coolness a stark contrast to the burning sensation in my chest. Jason's voice, calm and measured, yet laced with an undercurrent of chilling efficiency, still echoed in my ears. His words, each a carefully chosen syllable, painted a vivid picture of a world operating in the shadows, a world governed by unspoken rules and brutal consequences. He had painted a masterclass in precision, a ballet of death executed with surgical accuracy. But his narrative had also unveiled a terrifying truth: Guill was merely a pawn, a carefully chosen figurehead for an organization that reached far beyond the confines of the criminal underworld.

The implications were staggering. This wasn't simply about a drug cartel or a gang of thugs; it was about a network of power so deeply entrenched, so thoroughly interwoven within the fabric of society, that it defied easy definition. It was a system that thrived on corruption, manipulating legal loopholes, exploiting vulnerabilities, and using intimidation and violence to maintain its grip on power. And I, a relatively insignificant radio reporter, had unwittingly stumbled into the lion's den.

The phone calls had begun almost immediately after the broadcast. Anonymous whispers, veiled threats, veiled promises. Some were blatant attempts at intimidation, others offered deals that made my blood run cold. They were probing, testing my resolve, gauging my vulnerability. I had to tread carefully, navigate this treacherous terrain without alerting them to the full extent of my knowledge. Each conversation felt like a high-stakes poker game, where the stakes were my life and the truth I had uncovered.

Sleep had become a luxury I could no longer afford. The images of Guill’s death, the cold, hard reality of his demise, haunted my dreams. Jason's chillingly precise descriptions of his missions played out in my mind like a macabre film reel. I saw the swift movements, the calculated precision, the cold efficiency with which he eliminated his targets. It was a chilling reminder of the lethality of the world I had inadvertently entered.

The fear was real, a tangible presence that clung to me like a shroud. But alongside the fear came a strange sense of determination, a stubborn refusal to surrender. I had come too far, risked too much, to back down now. The truth, however dangerous, was a responsibility I couldn't ignore. I was driven by a sense of justice, a need to expose the rot that had festered beneath the surface of this city, this country, perhaps even the world.

I spent days poring over documents, thoroughly piecing together the fragmented pieces of the puzzle. I followed leads that led to dead ends, investigated connections that turned out to be red herrings. The labyrinthine network of Guill's organization proved far more intricate than I could have imagined. It wasn't just about money and power; it was about control, the insidious control over every aspect of society, from local politics to international finance. It was a game played on a global scale, a game where the stakes were far higher than anyone could ever comprehend.

The constant surveillance became palpable. I felt watched, followed, my every move scrutinized. Paranoia had become my unwelcome companion. I changed my routines, my habits, my routes. I slept in different locations, using burner phones and encrypted communication channels. I was living a double life, a life of caution and secrecy, a life where trust had become an endangered commodity.

But the uncertainty gnawed at me. Jason had vanished without a trace. Had he been caught? Eliminated? Was he even real? The sheer audacity of his actions, the impossible precision of his operations, made me question the very nature of reality. Had I been manipulated? Was I playing into the hands of a much larger game?

The weight of the investigation, the constant threat of danger, the gnawing uncertainty—it all took its toll. The city, once my inspiration, now felt like a prison. My once sharp mind was clouded by exhaustion and anxiety. My relationships suffered; the people I cared about paid the price for my obsession. I was consumed by my work, sacrificing everything else in the pursuit of truth.

Yet, despite the cost, despite the fear, despite the overwhelming odds, I couldn't stop. The knowledge that a vast and powerful organization was manipulating the world, controlling the flow of information, pulling the strings from the shadows, fueled a fire in my belly that couldn't be extinguished. This wasn't just about uncovering a criminal enterprise; it was about exposing a system of control so vast, so insidious, it threatened the very foundations of democracy.

The fight for justice had only just begun. Guill's death was not the end; it was the beginning of a much larger, much more dangerous conflict. And I, despite my fear, despite the immense risk, was prepared to fight. For the truth. For justice. For the hope that one day, the shadows would retreat, and the light of truth would illuminate the darkest corners of the world. The cost would be high, I knew that much. But I was ready to pay it. The silence of the city, once a chilling premonition, now sounded like the drumbeat of war. And I, armed with nothing but a microphone and a relentless pursuit of truth, was ready to answer the call. The fight had just begun, and

I had a feeling this was only the beginning of a long, hard, and incredibly dangerous journey.

Resurfacing Elements

The flickering neon sign of a Bangkok street bar cast long shadows across the rain-slicked alley. Jake Harroll, his trench coat clinging damply to his frame, felt a familiar chill crawl up his spine. It wasn't the humidity; it was the memory of the near-misses, the close calls, the sheer audacity of the conspiracy he'd only recently helped dismantle. He'd thought Gomin Guill's death would be the end, a final, decisive blow against the hydra-headed organization. He was wrong. Dead wrong.

A crumpled newspaper, discarded in a overflowing bin, caught his eye. A headline screamed: "Massive Data Breach Exposes Government Secrets." The article detailed a sophisticated cyberattack, targeting highly sensitive government databases. The details were scant, the investigation shrouded in secrecy, but something about the precision, the calculated nature of the breach, sent a tremor through Jake. It felt…familiar. Too familiar.

The same chilling efficiency that characterized Gomin Guill's operation. The same ghost of meticulous planning, the same absence of any obvious trail. It was a phantom touch, a spectral fingerprint left on a crime scene that hadn't even been properly identified yet. He remembered Jason Reen's words, spoken in hushed tones in that dimly lit cafe: "Gomin was just a pawn. A very powerful pawn, but a pawn nonetheless."

Jake pulled out his phone, scrolling through the encrypted messages he'd exchanged with his newly acquired, and highly unreliable, informant, a former mid-level member of Guill's organization who went by the alias "Seraph." Seraph's messages were always cryptic, veiled in coded language, but their underlying message was clear: the organization was regrouping. Faster, more ruthlessly, than anyone anticipated.

Days blurred into weeks as Jake delved deeper into the data breach, painstakingly piecing together fragments of information. He discovered a pattern, a series of seemingly unrelated events that, when viewed through the lens of his experience with Gomin Guill, formed a disturbing picture. A series of seemingly accidental deaths among high-ranking government officials. A string of unsolved bank robberies, each executed with the same clinical precision, leaving behind no witnesses, no usable forensics. A pattern only he, having lived through the nightmare firsthand, could recognize.

The organization wasn't simply rebuilding; it was evolving. They were adapting, learning from their mistakes, becoming more sophisticated, more technologically advanced. They were learning from their losses. The cyberattack, Jake realized with growing dread, wasn't just about stealing data; it was about acquiring tools, resources, gaining a foothold in a new, digital battleground. A way to circumvent traditional methods, to operate in complete anonymity.

His investigation led him to a shadowy network of offshore accounts, shell corporations, and encrypted communications channels. He tracked the digital breadcrumbs, following the trail across continents, from the bustling servers of Silicon Valley to the hidden data centers nestled deep within the Swiss Alps. Each step revealed a further layer of complexity, a deeper burrow into a subterranean world of deceit and malice.

The trail eventually led him back to Bangkok, to a clandestine meeting in a hidden room above a bustling market. There, he encountered an unexpected face: Seraph. Seraph, who had seemed so eager to cooperate, now radiated a chilling new authority. The informant's nervous demeanor had been replaced with cold assurance, his eyes glittering with a glint of something dangerous, something…ambitious.

"You thought it was over, didn't you?" Seraph hissed, his voice barely above a whisper, barely audible over the din of the marketplace below. "You thought you had won. You were wrong."

Jake's mind raced, his journalistic instincts kicking in. Seraph's shift in demeanor wasn't just about betrayal; it spoke of a power shift within the organization. The death of Gomin Guill hadn't created a power vacuum; it had created an opportunity. An opportunity for someone else to rise, someone even more ruthless, even more dangerous.

Seraph revealed the identity of the new leader: a man known only as "The Architect." A brilliant programmer, a master strategist, a man who had been operating in the shadows, carefully orchestrating the organization's resurgence. The Architect wasn't just consolidating power; he was creating a new, technologically advanced organization, one that was far more difficult to track, far more difficult to destroy.

The Architect had already begun to leverage the stolen data to his advantage, using it to manipulate global markets, infiltrate government agencies, and sow chaos. His reach was vast, his power unprecedented. The conspiracy wasn't just a threat to national security; it was a threat to the very fabric of global order. The game had changed.

Jake realized he was once again facing a monumental task. He'd thought he'd closed one chapter, that he'd escaped the clutches of the organization. But the organization, reborn and more dangerous than ever, had drawn him back into its lethal embrace. The escape, he now realized, had been an illusion.

The relentless rain continued to lash against the windows of his Bangkok hotel room, mirroring the storm brewing within him. The fight was far from over. He'd helped bring down Gomin Guill, but the war had only just begun. A new enemy had emerged from the ashes of the old, an enemy more cunning, more capable, and infinitely more dangerous. And Jake Harroll, unwilling to let the world fall to this new threat, found himself reluctantly returning to the fray, preparing for another battle, a battle that may cost him everything. The echoes of the past were clear; the shadows of the future were far darker. The game, it seemed, was far from over. The chessboard had been reset, and a new, far more formidable player had entered the game.

....

The humid Bangkok air hung heavy, thick with the scent of jasmine and something far less pleasant – the metallic tang of fear. Jake stared at the encrypted email, the characters swimming before his eyes. It was from a source he'd only ever known as "Nightingale," a ghost in the machine, a whisper in the digital wind. Nightingale's messages were rare, always cryptic, always significant. This one was different. It spoke of shifting allegiances within Gomin Guill's organization, a fracturing of power that was opening up unexpected opportunities, and unforeseen dangers.

The email detailed a clandestine meeting, a summit of sorts, taking place in a remote villa outside of Chiang Mai. Those attending weren't the usual goons and enforcers; these were the strategists, the financiers, the brains behind the operation. Gomin's death, it seemed, had triggered a power vacuum, a scramble for control that had thrown the organization into chaos. Some factions were vying to take the reins, others were looking for an exit strategy, and still others were plotting something far more sinister.

Jake knew he couldn't ignore this. The information Nightingale provided was too valuable, too crucial to dismiss. He'd dealt with enough of Gomin's underlings to know that their organization was far more complex than a simple criminal enterprise. It was a spider's web, intricately woven, with connections reaching far beyond the drug trade and human trafficking Gomin was primarily known for. This meeting promised to unravel more of its secrets, potentially revealing the true extent of their influence and power.

His contact in Chiang Mai, a grizzled old woman named Mama Chan who ran a seemingly innocuous noodle shop, was his only link to the villa. Mama Chan, with her shrewd eyes and even shrewder instincts, had been an invaluable asset in the past. She'd seen things, heard things, that most would dismiss as urban legends. She was the silent observer, the unseen hand, moving unseen through the underbelly of the city. Jake knew she'd already received her instructions. Her cryptic text message simply read: "The orchids bloom at midnight."

The drive to Chiang Mai was a blur of lush green rice paddies and towering mountains, the air growing cooler as he climbed higher into the hills. The villa, nestled amongst a cluster of ancient teak trees, was a picture of deceptive tranquility. It was a masterclass in discretion, almost invisible amongst the surrounding landscape, blending seamlessly with its environment. The only indication of its significance was the subtle presence of men in dark suits positioned strategically around the perimeter – shadows watching over, shadows.

Mama Chan, true to her word, waited near the perimeter. She gave Jake a small, almost imperceptible nod, and he understood. The meeting was well underway. He blended in as best he could, using the cover of the darkness and the shadows cast by the moonlit night. He had to rely on his years of experience, his instincts honed sharp by years of investigative journalism and close encounters with organized crime. He navigated through the perimeter with the ease of someone who had done this a thousand times.

The infiltration wasn't easy. Guards were everywhere, their eyes sharp, their movements precise. Jake used his training, his understanding of body language and security protocols, moving like a phantom through the darkness. He was a ghost, unseen and unheard, a silent predator moving through the night. He slipped through a poorly secured side entrance, his heart pounding a steady rhythm against his ribs. He made his way through dimly lit corridors, avoiding motion sensors and security cameras.

The main meeting room was a sight to behold. A large, circular table dominated the space, crafted from dark, polished wood. Around it sat a diverse assembly of individuals, each representing a different faction within the organization. There were representatives of the various syndicates, some familiar faces from Gomin's inner circle, others completely unknown. The air was thick with tension, an unspoken war brewing beneath the surface.

What surprised Jake most was the presence of unexpected allies. Individuals he had previously considered enemies were now sitting across the table from each other, engaging in heated negotiations, forging uneasy alliances. The landscape had shifted dramatically since Gomin's demise. This wasn't about loyalty anymore; it was about survival.

The discussions revolved around resources, territories, and, most importantly, the future of the organization. There were power plays, betrayals, and secret deals struck in hushed tones. Jake learned about vast networks of corruption extending far beyond Thailand, stretching into Southeast Asia and beyond. It involved politicians, businessmen, even seemingly untouchable members of law enforcement. The scale of the operation was breathtaking. This wasn't just about drugs or human trafficking anymore; it was about global power and influence, a far-reaching network that extended its tentacles into every corner of the world.

The meeting was a whirlwind of hushed conversations, clandestine handshakes, and coded messages. As Jake listened, he began to understand the scope of the threat he now faced. This wasn't simply a continuation of Gomin's operations; it was a transformation, a metamorphosis. The organization was adapting, evolving, becoming even more formidable and elusive.

He learned of a new leader, a figure known only as "The Serpent," a shadowy individual whose identity remained shrouded in mystery. The Serpent was ruthless, efficient, and remarkably cunning. Unlike Gomin, whose power was built on brute force and intimidation, The Serpent operated from the shadows, pulling strings, manipulating events from a distance. The Serpent was the ultimate puppeteer, and his control was absolute.

Jake realized that his initial victory over Gomin had been merely a skirmish in a far larger war. The Serpent was the true mastermind, the orchestrator of a far-reaching conspiracy that threatened to destabilize entire nations. The fight was far from over; it was only just beginning.

The meeting concluded with a series of agreements, solidifying new alliances and distributing territories. Jake knew this was his chance to escape, to gather information to disseminate to the right channels. He slipped away undetected, leaving behind a scene of newfound stability, a precarious truce that could shatter at any moment. As he drove back to Bangkok under the cover of darkness, the weight of his discovery bore down on him. He had more to do, more to investigate. The game had changed, and the stakes were far higher than he had ever imagined. The fight against The Serpent had just begun. The orchids bloomed at midnight, indeed. And the fragrance was deadly.

....

The Bangkok skyline, a jagged silhouette against the bruised purple of the twilight sky, offered little comfort. Jake Harroll felt the familiar chill of apprehension crawl up his spine. He'd spent the last few days processing Nightingale's message, a chilling premonition disguised as a cryptic warning. Gomin Guill was gone, but the Serpent, the vast criminal organization he'd headed, hadn't simply vanished with him. It had shed its skin, revealing a far more dangerous beast beneath.

News trickled in, fragmented and unreliable, yet painting a disturbing picture. The power vacuum left by Guill's demise hadn't resulted in chaos, but in a swift, ruthless consolidation of power. A figure known only as "The Konda" had emerged from the shadows, seizing control with a brutality that even Guill, notorious for his cold-blooded efficiency, hadn't matched.

The Konda’s methods were different. Guill had favored subtle manipulation, carefully orchestrated coups and thoroughly planned assassinations. The Konda, from what Jake could gather, was a force of pure, unadulterated violence. His rise was marked not by political maneuvering, but by a bloody purge, leaving a trail of bodies that spoke volumes about his ruthless ambition. Alliances forged during the chaotic aftermath of Guill's death were being systematically dismantled, replaced by a rigid, terrifying hierarchy built on fear and absolute obedience.

Jake’s contacts, a network of informants painstakingly cultivated over years, whispered of hushed meetings in dimly lit backrooms, of brutal executions carried out with chilling precision, and of an unprecedented wave of violence sweeping across Southeast Asia. The Konda was consolidating power, expanding the Serpent's reach, and forging new alliances with even more dangerous players on the global criminal stage.

One contact, a former lieutenant of Guill’s known only as “Scorp,” provided Jake with a chilling detail: The Konda wasn't merely a ruthless pragmatist seizing an opportunity. He had a personal vendetta against Guill, a deep-seated hatred fueled by years of betrayal and humiliation. Guill, it seemed, had treated The Konda like a pawn, discarding him once he'd served his purpose. The Konda's rise, therefore, wasn't just a power grab; it was a thoroughly planned revenge.

This personal angle, this element of raw, unbridled rage, made The Konda even more unpredictable and dangerous. Guill had been a calculating chess master, his moves deliberate and calculated. The Konda, on the other hand, seemed driven by primal instincts, a wild animal unleashed, his actions fueled by rage rather than reason. This made him far more difficult to anticipate, to counter, and to understand.

Jake felt a renewed sense of urgency. He'd thought eliminating Guill was the end of the fight, the final piece in a complex puzzle. He was wrong. He had merely cleared a path for a far more formidable opponent, one whose motives were less predictable, whose methods were far more brutal, and whose reach extended far beyond the confines of Southeast Asia.

His investigation now took a new direction. He needed to understand The Konda – his methods, his connections, his ultimate goals. The information he'd gathered so far was just the tip of the iceberg. The deeper he delved, the more he realized the scale of the operation, the sheer magnitude of the threat.

He began by tracking The Konda's movements, piecing together fragments of information from his informants. He discovered that The Konda wasn't operating in the open. He was a ghost, a phantom moving through the shadows, his presence felt but never seen. His actions spoke volumes – a series of strategically planned assassinations targeting key figures within rival organizations, the consolidation of lucrative trafficking routes, and the expansion of the Serpent's influence into previously untouched territories.

His investigation led him through the neon-drenched streets of Hong Kong, the bustling markets of Kuala Lumpur, and the labyrinthine alleys of Hanoi. Each city held a piece of the puzzle, each encounter brought him closer to understanding the man who had inherited Guill's empire and remade it in his own violent image.

He learned that The Konda was a master of disguise, a chameleon capable of blending seamlessly into any environment. He utilized a complex network of intermediaries and couriers, making it incredibly difficult to trace his movements or identify his true identity. His communication channels were encrypted, untraceable, making direct contact virtually impossible.

Jake spent weeks analyzing intercepted communications, deciphering coded messages, and piecing together fragments of information. He discovered that The Konda wasn't operating alone. He had a coterie of loyal followers, ruthless enforcers who carried out his orders without question. They were as enigmatic and shadowy as their leader, their identities obscured behind a veil of secrecy.

The investigation became a race against time. The Konda was systematically dismantling any opposition, consolidating his power at an alarming rate. His expansion wasn't limited to territorial control; he was building alliances with other criminal syndicates, expanding his reach into the global drug trade, human trafficking, and arms smuggling. The implications were staggering; this was not just a regional threat; it was a global one.

Jake knew he was walking a tightrope. He was dealing with the most dangerous criminal organization in the world, one that had just been reorganized under a leader who valued ruthless efficiency above all else. One wrong move, one misplaced step could be fatal. But he also knew that he couldn't back down. The stakes were too high, the threat too great.

He had to stop The Konda before he could consolidate his power fully, before the Serpent became an unstoppable force capable of wreaking havoc on a global scale. The fight against The Serpent had taken a dangerous and unexpected turn, but Jake knew, with a chilling certainty, that he was far from finished. The game had only just begun, and the deadliest player was yet to make his move. He had to find a way to expose The Konda, to dismantle his operation before it was too late. The future hung precariously in the balance, and the weight of the world rested on his shoulders. The orchid's scent, once a symbol of intrigue, now reeked of impending doom.

....

Jake stared out at the neon-drenched Bangkok streets, the humid air thick with the scent of exhaust fumes and jasmine. Nightingale's warning echoed in his mind: They're evolving. Gomin Guill's death hadn't crippled the Serpent; it had galvanized it. The organization, it seemed, was far more technologically advanced than he'd initially imagined. The seemingly archaic methods of bribery, intimidation, and brute force were merely a veneer, concealing a sophisticated network of technological tools designed to enhance their reach and lethality.

His research began with a single, almost innocuous detail: a mention of "Project Chimera" in a heavily encrypted email recovered from Guill's server. The email itself was a dead end, its contents scrambled beyond recovery, but the name… it stuck in Jake's mind like a shard of glass. Days blurred into nights as Jake delved into the digital underbelly of the Serpent, navigating the labyrinthine paths of the dark web, relying on his network of contacts – some old, some new, all cautiously helpful.

He discovered a pattern. Each assassination, seemingly flawlessly executed, left behind a ghostly digital footprint. Not obvious traces, not something a casual observer would notice. But anomalies. Slight deviations in network traffic, fleeting encrypted signals, almost imperceptible changes in the metadata of seemingly unrelated files. These weren't the clumsy mistakes of amateurs; they were the subtle signatures of advanced technology working in the shadows. They spoke of sophisticated surveillance systems, AI-powered predictive analytics, and encrypted communication networks far more secure than anything Jake had encountered before.

Project Chimera, he suspected, was the key. It was a system, a platform, an entire ecosystem designed to enhance every aspect of the Serpent's operations. He unearthed fragments of information – scattered code snippets, leaked documents, hushed conversations intercepted from encrypted channels – each piece adding to the grim picture.

The first significant breakthrough came through a contact in Moscow, a former KGB programmer who now worked as a freelance cybersecurity consultant. He provided Jake with access to a compromised server belonging to a seemingly legitimate technology firm with ties to the Serpent. The server contained the blueprints – not complete, but enough – for Project Chimera's core components. It was a distributed network, relying on a constellation of seemingly independent servers scattered across the globe, each secured with multiple layers of encryption. The architecture was breathtakingly complex, designed to withstand even the most sophisticated cyberattacks.

The system wasn't just about communication; it was about predictive policing on a terrifying scale. Using data harvested from public sources and dark web markets, Project Chimera used sophisticated AI algorithms to identify potential threats – both to the organization and its members. It predicted patterns of movement, anticipated law enforcement actions, and even profiled potential informants with unsettling accuracy. The Serpent wasn't just reacting to threats; it was anticipating them.

Further investigation revealed the organization's mastery of biometrics and genetic engineering. They were creating highly advanced surveillance systems that employed facial recognition far beyond current commercially available technology, identifying individuals from even partial visual data or through DNA traces left at crime scenes. They could identify individuals through their gait, their voice patterns, even the subtle rhythm of their heartbeat. The precision was chillingly advanced, blurring the lines between science fiction and terrifying reality.

But it wasn't just passive surveillance. Project Chimera also controlled a network of autonomous drones, capable of covert surveillance, pinpoint strikes, and even delivering sophisticated bioweapons. The drones were equipped with advanced cloaking technology, making them almost invisible to radar and infrared detection. Jake shuddered at the thought of what such technology could unleash in the wrong hands – or rather, in the hands of an organization as ruthless and efficient as the Serpent.

The organization's control extended beyond hardware. They had developed advanced psychological warfare techniques, using AI-powered disinformation campaigns to manipulate public opinion, discredit law enforcement, and sow discord among their enemies. They could tailor their messages to specific individuals, exploiting their vulnerabilities and insecurities with ruthless precision.

Jake realized the magnitude of the challenge. He wasn't just facing a criminal syndicate; he was confronting a technological juggernaut that blended cutting-edge science with brutal efficiency. The Serpent wasn't just adapting to new threats; it was creating them. The technology wasn't simply a tool; it was an extension of the organization's malevolent will, a weaponized network capable of wreaking havoc on a global scale.

His previous understanding of the Serpent had been simplistic. He'd viewed it as a collection of ruthless individuals bound by shared ambition and a thirst for power. Now, he knew the truth: the Serpent was a sentient entity, an amalgamation of human ruthlessness and artificial intelligence, a terrifying hybrid that possessed the strategic planning capabilities of a seasoned military commander and the logistical precision of a highly advanced computer network.

He felt a wave of nausea, the weight of the world pressing down on him with crushing force. The stakes were higher than he'd ever imagined. Taking down Gomin Guill had been a significant victory, but it was merely a skirmish in a much larger war. The Serpent was evolving, adapting, and becoming stronger. He was facing a foe that wasn't just human, but a terrifying synthesis of human malice and technological prowess. The battle had shifted from the shadowy streets of Bangkok to the digital battlefields of the future, and Jake knew, with an icy certainty, that the fight had only just begun. The clock was ticking, and time was running out. He had to find a way to dismantle this technological behemoth, before it could unleash its full potential upon the world. The future of humanity might very well depend on it. He had to find a way, somehow, to unravel this digital monster, piece by piece, before it consumed them all. The silence of his Bangkok hotel room seemed to amplify the deafening roar of the approaching storm.

....

The insistent ringing of his phone sliced through the oppressive silence of the Bangkok hotel room, jolting Jake from a fitful sleep. He fumbled for it, the cool plastic a stark contrast to the clammy sweat on his palm. The caller ID displayed an unfamiliar number, a string of digits that felt ominous, like a coded message from a world he desperately wanted to leave behind. He hesitated, a familiar tremor of dread running through him. He knew, with a chilling certainty, that this call was no coincidence. The respite he'd craved, the illusion of normalcy he'd desperately clung to, was shattered.

He answered with his voice a strained whisper, "Hello?"

A woman's voice, crisp and controlled, answered, "Mr. Harroll? This is Nightingale. We have a situation."

The name sent a shiver down his spine. Nightingale, the enigmatic figure from the shadowy recesses of the intelligence community, the woman who had provided him with the initial lead on Gomin Guill. Her involvement meant this was far from a routine matter. This was a plunge back into the icy depths of the Serpent's lair, a return to a world where survival was a daily gamble.

"What situation?" Jake asked, his voice tight with apprehension. He could practically feel the weight of the city pressing down on him, the humid air heavy with the unspoken threats lurking in the shadows. He pictured the neon-lit streets outside, their garish brilliance a stark contrast to the darkness closing in around him.

Nightingale's voice was devoid of emotion, a chillingly efficient instrument delivering bad news.

"Remember the encrypted files we recovered from Guill's server? The ones we couldn't fully decipher?"

Jake's mind raced back to the frantic days following Gomin's demise, the scramble to secure evidence before anyone else could get their hands on it. "Yes," he replied, his voice barely a breath.

"We've made a breakthrough. A significant one. The files point to a new project, codenamed 'Phoenix.' It's far more ambitious, far more dangerous, than anything Guill ever conceived."

A cold dread tightened its grip around Jake's heart. He knew the Serpent's methods. Ambition, ruthlessness, and a chilling disregard for human life. "What kind of project?" he asked, his voice barely above a whisper.

"A bioweapon," Nightingale replied, her voice unwavering. "A highly contagious, rapidly evolving pathogen. They're close to completion. And the initial testing… has been… successful."

Jake felt a wave of nausea wash over him. This wasn't just about organized crime anymore; this was about the potential for global catastrophe. The seemingly contained conflict had suddenly escalated to a threat of unimaginable scale. This wasn't about taking down a criminal empire; it was about preventing a pandemic. The chilling reality of the situation sunk in; this was a fight for the survival of humanity.

"And where are they?" Jake asked, his voice hardening with a newfound resolve. The fear was still there, but it was now overshadowed by a surge of adrenaline, a grim determination to confront this new, terrifying threat. This was no longer his choice; this was a necessity.

"Several locations across Southeast Asia," Nightingale replied. "Their infrastructure is decentralized, making it incredibly difficult to pinpoint the exact location of the primary development facility."

"Give me what you have," Jake said, his voice resolute. The weight of responsibility settled heavily upon his shoulders, but he wouldn't back down. He had faced the Serpent before, stared into the abyss and lived to tell the tale. He would face this new, even more horrifying threat. He had to.

Nightingale provided him with a series of encrypted coordinates, along with partial schematics of the bioweapon and details about the scientists involved. The information was fragmented, incomplete, but it was enough. It was a roadmap to a hellish landscape, a path he was now forced to tread. The familiar knot of dread tightened in his stomach, a chilling reminder of the dangers that lay ahead.

The next few days were a blur of frantic activity. Jake, fueled by adrenaline and black coffee, worked tirelessly, poring over the encrypted data, piecing together the fragments of information. He contacted his old contacts, the network of informants he had cultivated over years of investigative journalism, risking everything to find the missing pieces of the puzzle. The Serpent's reach stretched far and wide; their tentacles snaked into every corner of the underworld, their influence far-reaching and insidious.

He learned of clandestine labs hidden in remote jungles, staffed by scientists lured by the promise of unimaginable wealth and power. He pieced together the logistics, the supply chains, the intricate network of shell corporations and front businesses used to mask the organization's activities. Each piece of information, each fragmented detail, painted a more horrifying picture of the organization's ambition and its chilling disregard for human life.

The realization struck him with the force of a physical blow. Gomin Guill had been a pawn, a figurehead. The true architects of this terrifying conspiracy were far more powerful, far more elusive. This was a struggle against a network so vast, so deeply entrenched, that it felt insurmountable. But the thought of the potential consequences—a world ravaged by a deadly pandemic—fueled his resolve.

He worked alongside Nightingale, their collaboration a tense dance of trust and suspicion. She was a ghost, a figure from the shadows, her true motivations shrouded in secrecy. But her information was accurate, her insights invaluable. They worked together, two different worlds colliding, united by a common goal: to stop the Phoenix project before it was too late.

The pressure mounted with each passing hour. The threat felt palpable, a suffocating weight hanging over him. He felt the weight of the world on his shoulders, the responsibility of preventing a global catastrophe. He knew the risks; he'd stared death in the face more times than he could count. But this was different. This was about saving millions, maybe billions of lives. This was about more than just justice; this was about survival.

He knew he couldn't do this alone. He needed help, a team capable of handling the intricate network of the Serpent. He reached out to old colleagues, seasoned investigators who had dealt with the organization before, who understood the insidious nature of its operations. The response was immediate; a silent agreement, an unspoken understanding that the stakes were too high to ignore. He assembled a team, carefully selected individuals with the necessary skills and experience, men and women who understood the shadows, the murky world where morality was a flexible concept and survival was paramount.

The path ahead was perilous, a treacherous journey into the heart of darkness. But Jake Harroll was a man who had faced insurmountable odds before and emerged victorious. He was a reporter who had traded his pen for a weapon, a journalist who had become a warrior in a battle for humanity's survival. He was prepared to face the Serpent once again, this time to confront a threat that dwarfed even Gomin Guill's reign of terror. He would fight, not just for himself, not just for justice, but for the future of mankind. The clock was ticking, and the countdown had already begun. The battle for the future of the world, he knew, was just beginning.

Strategic Planning

The air hung thick with the scent of stale coffee and impending doom. Jake Harroll, his face etched with the exhaustion of sleepless nights and relentless investigation, stared out at the rain-slicked streets of Prague. The city, usually a vibrant tapestry of history and culture, now felt like a claustrophobic cage, the shadows concealing unseen dangers. Gomin Guill was dead, but the organization, the hydra-headed beast he'd led, was far from vanquished. The revelation of the larger conspiracy, the hidden hand pulling strings from a position of unimaginable power, had thrown Jake into a maelstrom of uncertainty. He needed a plan, a strategy, not just the impulsive reactions that had carried him through the initial confrontation. This was a chess match, not a brawl, and he was playing against a grandmaster.

He reviewed his notes, the thin pages feeling brittle in his trembling hands. The information was fragmented, a puzzle with missing pieces, but he saw patterns emerging – patterns that hinted at the organization's operational structure, its financial networks, and its terrifying reach.

He'd uncovered evidence of shell corporations, offshore accounts, and complex money laundering schemes that snaked across continents. These weren't street-level thugs; this was a sophisticated network, operating with the precision of a Swiss watch. Their tentacles stretched into every corner of the globe, making them difficult, if not impossible, to fully dismantle.

Jake knew he couldn't tackle this alone. His journalistic instincts were sharp, his tenacity unwavering, but he lacked the resources and the network to combat such a formidable opponent. He needed allies, people with skills that complemented his own – people who could navigate the treacherous waters of international espionage, who understood the language of deceit and subterfuge, who could operate in the shadows just as effectively as he could report from the light.

His mind drifted to Jason Reen. The assassin's methods were brutal, his morality questionable, but his efficiency was undeniable. He had an extensive network of his own, a clandestine web of contacts that spanned the globe. Could he be an ally? The idea was repugnant at first, the thought of collaborating with a cold-blooded killer nauseating, but the alternative was far more terrifying – the unchecked rise of this global criminal empire. The lines between right and wrong were blurring, becoming almost indistinguishable.

The first step was intelligence gathering. Jake needed to consolidate everything he'd learned, filling in the gaps with meticulous research and discreet inquiries. He reached out to his contacts, a network of sources he'd cultivated over years of investigative reporting. Some were reluctant, fearful of the organization's reach, but others, driven by a sense of justice or perhaps a touch of morbid curiosity, agreed to help.

He spent weeks sifting through mountains of data, piecing together the organization's intricate structure. He discovered a hidden hierarchy, a pyramid of power with multiple layers of command. Eliminating the top leader, as he had done with Gomin, was only a superficial victory, a temporary setback. The organization possessed a resilience that bordered on the supernatural, its members bound by a fierce loyalty and an almost religious devotion to their cause.

His investigations revealed a chilling connection to a previously unknown technology firm based in Singapore. The firm's public face was innocuous, developing software solutions for various clients, but beneath the veneer of legitimacy lurked a sinister operation. Their technology, Jake discovered, was being used to monitor communications, intercept financial transactions, and track individuals with unsettling accuracy. It was this technological advantage that gave the organization its chilling effectiveness.

Jake realized he needed to acquire a similar technological advantage, a way to level the playing field. He contacted a former NSA analyst, a brilliant but disillusioned programmer who had been ostracized for his unorthodox methods. This was a risky move, a gamble that could easily backfire, but the potential rewards were too significant to ignore. The programmer, whose name was only revealed as "Ghost," agreed to help, but at a steep price – total anonymity and an assurance of immunity from prosecution.

Meanwhile, Jake began assembling his team, carefully selecting individuals with specialized skills. He recruited a former MI6 agent, now working as a private security consultant, for his expertise in infiltration and close-quarters combat. He also contacted a seasoned financial investigator, an expert in tracing illicit funds and uncovering hidden assets. The team was small, highly specialized, and bound together by a shared sense of purpose and a deep understanding of the immense danger they faced.

The long game required patience, precision, and a ruthless pragmatism. It was a dance of shadows, a battle of wits played out in the dark corners of the world. Jake knew they couldn't confront the organization head-on. They needed a strategy, a carefully crafted plan that would expose their operations, cripple their infrastructure, and bring their leaders to justice. He envisioned a multi-pronged assault, a coordinated attack that would strike at the heart of the organization, disrupting its operations and dismantling its network.

The technological advantage, provided by Ghost, was crucial. They planned to use it to intercept communications, expose financial transactions, and locate key members of the organization. The information gleaned would be used to build a detailed dossier, a roadmap that would guide their operations. This wasn't just about bringing down a criminal syndicate; it was about exposing a global conspiracy that threatened the stability of nations.

Jake's team began its work, operating in the shadows, moving undetected. Their methods were unorthodox, their tactics sometimes morally questionable, but they were driven by a single-minded determination to bring down the organization. The stakes were impossibly high – failure would not just mean their lives, but the continuation of a shadow war that spanned the globe. The weight of the world, it seemed, rested on his shoulders. But Jake Harroll was a journalist, a truth-seeker, and he would not rest until justice was served. The long game had begun.

....

The rain hammered against the gargoyle-studded rooftops of Prague, a relentless percussion accompanying the frantic rhythm of Jake's thoughts. He'd expected relief after Gomin Guill's death, a sense of closure. Instead, he was drowning in a sea of unanswered questions, each one more dangerous than the last. The organization, a behemoth of global crime, hadn't faltered; it had simply shifted, its tentacles recoiling, regrouping. The thoroughly crafted illusion of Gomin as the sole head had crumbled, revealing a far more complex, and terrifying, reality. He needed help, allies beyond the small, tightly-knit team he'd assembled. Allies he never thought he'd find.

His first call was to Tanya Relova, a name whispered in the shadows of the Eastern European underworld. A former intelligence officer, Tanya possessed a network of contacts that stretched from the dimly lit backrooms of Moscow to the sun-drenched plazas of Barcelona. Her methods were ruthless, her loyalty questionable, but her effectiveness was undeniable. Jake knew that aligning himself with her was a gamble, a dangerous dance with a viper, but the stakes were too high to play it safe.

The connection was made through a heavily encrypted channel, a series of coded messages relayed through a series of seemingly innocuous email addresses. Tanya's response was succinct, devoid of pleasantries: "Guill's death has created a vacuum. The others are scrambling. Tell me what you have." The meeting was arranged in a secluded, almost forgotten corner of Prague's Old Town, a dimly lit tavern frequented by smugglers and spies.

Their initial exchange was tense, a silent war of wills across a chipped wooden table. Tanya, with her sharp eyes and an air of controlled aggression, was a force of nature. She listened intently as Jake laid out the evidence, the fragmented pieces of a puzzle painting a picture of a far-reaching conspiracy involving governments, corporations, and the shadowy elite. He showed her the encrypted files he'd salvaged from Guill's server, the coded messages hinting at a network of money laundering, arms trafficking, and political assassination that spanned continents.

"They're bigger than we thought," Tanya finally said, her voice low and husky. "Much bigger. And they won't hesitate to eliminate anyone who gets in their way." Her words hung in the air, thick with the weight of experience. She didn't offer reassurances; she dealt in realities, in brutal truths. This wasn't a game; it was a war of survival.

Their unlikely alliance was sealed not through grand pronouncements but through shared recognition of a common enemy. Tanya, pragmatic and cynical, saw the opportunity to dismantle a network that threatened her own precarious position. Jake, driven by his journalistic integrity and a growing sense of moral obligation, saw in Tanya a tool, a dangerous but essential weapon in his fight for truth.

Their next move was to recruit a technical expert, someone who could navigate the labyrinthine world of encrypted communications and digital forensics. This led them to Dr. Jassa Thorne, a recluse with a reputation for brilliance and a penchant for solitude. Thorne, haunted by past failures, had retreated from the limelight, living a life of self-imposed isolation, his genius largely untapped. Convincing him to join their cause required a delicate touch, a carefully constructed narrative that appealed to his sense of justice and his desire for redemption. Tanya’s underworld connections proved invaluable in locating Thorne, and Jake’s persuasive skills, honed through years of interviewing hardened criminals and politicians, sealed the deal. Thorne, initially reluctant, saw in Jake’s determination a reflection of his own suppressed drive. The promise of unearthing a conspiracy of global proportions stirred something within him.

With Tanya's network and Thorne's expertise, Jake’s team was transformed. They were no longer just a group of idealistic journalists; they were a highly skilled, albeit unconventional, intelligence unit. They operated in the shadows, utilizing Tanya's contacts to infiltrate the organization's layers. Thorne deciphered coded messages, revealing intricate financial transactions and clandestine meetings, painting a detailed picture of the organization's global operations. Jake, with his understanding of investigative journalism, pieced together the narrative, identifying patterns and connections that others might miss.

One particularly chilling discovery was a series of offshore accounts, holding billions of dollars, linked to individuals within powerful governments and multinational corporations. This confirmed their initial suspicions: the organization was far more than just a criminal syndicate; it was a powerful force, manipulating global politics and economies for its own nefarious ends. They discovered a hidden layer of communication, a secret network using quantum encryption that made standard decryption methods obsolete. Thorne worked tirelessly, poring over the data, driven by a sense of urgency and a grim fascination with the complexity of the system.

The danger was ever present. Multiple attempts were made on their lives – subtle at first, then escalating into blatant acts of violence. Tanya's contacts provided warnings, allowing them to evade attacks, but the feeling of being hunted, of being watched, became an unnerving constant. They learned to live in the shadows, moving from safe house to safe house, their movements thoroughly planned, their communications encrypted to the highest degree. The constant threat only strengthened their resolve, forging an unbreakable bond between them.

This wasn't just about bringing down a criminal organization; it was about exposing a network of corruption that spanned the globe, reaching the highest echelons of power. It was a battle for truth, for transparency, and for the very soul of democracy itself. The long game was no longer just a metaphor; it was their reality, a marathon against time and against a formidable enemy with vast resources and an army of ruthless enforcers. With every piece of evidence uncovered, with every coded message deciphered, the risk increased, but so did their determination. They were playing for the highest stakes imaginable – the future of the world. And they knew, with chilling clarity, that they were far from winning.

....

The chilling realization that Gomin Guill was merely a pawn in a far larger game sent a shiver down Jake's spine, colder than the Prague rain lashing against his window. He knew he couldn't rely on traditional investigative methods alone. This enemy possessed resources far beyond his imagination, resources that included sophisticated technology capable of tracking, intercepting, and even manipulating information on a global scale. He needed a technological shield, a countermeasure to their digital arsenal.

His priority was securing his communications. He'd learned the hard way that standard encryption wasn't enough. The organization clearly had the capability to crack even the most robust algorithms. His small team, composed of a brilliant but eccentric cryptographer named Tanya Juroon and a former NSA analyst, Rembin Bell, began working around the clock, building a multi-layered encryption system. They implemented quantum-resistant cryptography, combining several different algorithms to create a near-impenetrable fortress around their communications. Tanya, a whirlwind of energy and caffeine, had even integrated a self-destruct mechanism, wiping the data clean if unauthorized access was detected. The process was painstaking, requiring countless lines of code, rigorous testing, and sleepless nights fueled by black coffee and the shared adrenaline of a desperate race against time.

Next, they tackled the issue of surveillance. The organization's reach extended far beyond simple phone taps and email intercepts. They had the capacity to monitor online activity, track location data through various devices, and potentially even exploit vulnerabilities in smart home technologies. Rembin, a master of digital espionage himself, devised a system of "ghost" networks and encrypted virtual machines (VMs) – essentially, creating a digital shadow existence, constantly shifting and changing to evade detection. They used a mesh network of encrypted nodes, each one acting as a relay point, making it nearly impossible to trace the origin or destination of any communication. This meant they could communicate securely even when travelling.

The complexity of their countermeasures was almost overwhelming. Jake felt like a modern-day David facing Goliath, armed not with a sling but with a complex web of algorithms and protocols. But even as they constructed their technological defense, he knew it was a constant arms race. The organization would inevitably try to adapt, to crack their codes, and to penetrate their defenses. This understanding led them to develop adaptive security measures, constantly changing and updating their protocols to stay one step ahead.

Tanya developed a sophisticated intrusion detection system capable of alerting them to any attempts to penetrate their networks. It learned and adapted, creating a self-healing system that could identify and neutralize threats before they could cause significant damage. This involved creating honeypots – decoy systems designed to attract attackers and reveal their methods. The information gleaned from these honeypots would then be used to reinforce their defenses, making future attacks even more difficult. Rembin, meanwhile, focused on building a system of digital decoys, creating false trails and misleading information to confuse and distract their pursuers. They planted false leads online, creating elaborate cover stories to mislead anyone trying to track their movements.

The physical world also requires safeguarding. Jake, remembering the ease with which his movements had been tracked previously, insisted on incorporating physical security countermeasures. They implemented Faraday cages to protect their communications from external interception, shielded their electronic devices from physical probing, and invested in sophisticated anti-surveillance techniques. They learned to identify and avoid common surveillance methods – everything from hidden cameras to GPS tracking devices. They relied on old-school techniques, like using burner phones and untraceable prepaid cards. Even the location of their safe houses and meeting points was regularly rotated, a clandestine game of cat and mouse to keep their adversaries off balance.

This constant state of vigilance was both exhausting and exhilarating. The line between paranoia and preparedness was dangerously thin, constantly tested by the ever-present feeling of being watched. Each technological victory brought a fleeting sense of relief, quickly replaced by the sobering understanding that the organization possessed seemingly limitless resources and an unwavering determination to succeed. The creation of their technology wasn't just about building defenses; it was about gaining intelligence. Tanya was already working on software designed to identify and intercept the organization's communication signals, to decipher their codes, and to potentially gain access to their internal networks. The goal was to turn the tables, to use their technology against them.

But the technological battle was just one front in a much larger war. This organization wasn't just about money and power; they operated on a much deeper, more sinister level. Their ability to influence governments, manipulate the media, and control information was chillingly evident. Jake realized that he wasn't just facing an organized crime syndicate; he was dealing with a shadow government, a parasitic entity that had woven itself into the very fabric of global society. Their technological countermeasures were essential, a vital shield against their digital arsenal, but they were only part of the equation. They still needed to find human allies, individuals within the organization and among the powerful that could help dismantle the system from within. People who were either disillusioned or had their own hidden agendas.

The weight of this realization settled heavily on Jake's shoulders. The seemingly insurmountable task ahead was a constant reminder of the enormous scale of the conspiracy. He could feel the pressure, the mounting tension that came with each piece of intelligence uncovered, each new layer of the conspiracy peeled back.

Each new threat required an immediate adaptation, a new layer to their ever-evolving defense system. But even as they worked tirelessly, thoroughly crafting their digital fortress and refining their anti-surveillance techniques, they knew that their technological prowess was only as strong as their resolve. This was a war for the future, a battle for the very heart of democracy, and the stakes couldn't be higher. The long game had just begun, and with every passing moment, the enemy was closing in. The technological battle had been joined and the fight to retain control of information was far from over. They were playing for keeps, for the future itself, and the odds were stacked against them. The shadow organization was vast, powerful, and relentless, and it was only a matter of time before they struck back. The long game was no longer a metaphor. It was a fight for survival.

....

The Prague rain continued its relentless assault, mirroring the turmoil inside Jake. He'd spent the last few hours poring over Jason Reen's fragmented recollections, searching for any clue, any thread that could unravel the vast tapestry of the organization's operations. Jason, in his terse, almost clinical descriptions, had hinted at a global network, a complex web of seemingly unrelated businesses acting as fronts for illicit activities – arms trafficking, money laundering, human trafficking – all converging towards a single, malevolent purpose.

His initial focus had been on Gomin Guill, but the assassin's final words – a chilling, almost whispered aside about "the Architect" – had shattered that narrow focus. Gomin had been a player, a significant one, but clearly not the one calling the shots. The Architect, whoever that was, remained shrouded in mystery, a phantom pulling the strings from the shadows.

Jake knew he needed more than Jason's fragmented memories. He needed hard evidence, concrete proof, something he could take to authorities, even if he suspected those authorities might be compromised. His contact, an ex-MI6 tech specialist named Tanya Kilsba, had provided him with a secure encrypted network, a digital sanctuary shielded from the prying eyes of the organization's sophisticated surveillance systems. But even within that sanctuary, Jake felt the weight of his precarious position. He was treading on dangerous ground, playing a game where the stakes were life and death.

Tanya's expertise was invaluable. She'd helped him access and analyze data from various sources – leaked documents, intercepted communications, dark web forums – all thoroughly vetted for authenticity. The data painted a disturbing picture: a network of shell corporations registered in offshore tax havens, cryptic financial transactions masked by layers of encryption, and a seemingly endless stream of coded messages exchanged through highly secure channels. The organization operated with ruthless efficiency, employing advanced technology to maintain its anonymity and control its narrative.

One particularly intriguing data point was a series of seemingly innocuous shipping manifests. Tanya, with her keen eye for detail, had noticed a pattern: containers labeled with generic descriptions, shipped from obscure ports across the globe, ultimately arriving at a handful of seemingly unrelated locations in several countries. These locations, when plotted on a map, formed a disturbingly precise geometric pattern, hinting at a clandestine network of logistics hubs. The pattern, once overlaid on a map of known global financial centers and strategic communication nodes, suggested a deeply intertwined web of financial and operational control. They weren't just moving goods; they were controlling the flow of capital and information on a global scale.

Further investigation revealed the use of quantum-resistant encryption, indicating an awareness of the potential vulnerability of their current encryption methods to future quantum computing technology. This indicated foresight and a significant investment in long-term security, underscoring the scope and power of the organization. Their sophistication was terrifying.

Their investigation led them to a series of encrypted email accounts, which, after days of painstaking work, they managed to crack. The emails revealed plans for a series of high-profile assassinations, targeting individuals who, at first glance, seemed to have no connection to each other. But after a deeper analysis, Tanya discovered that each target was involved in some capacity with anti-corruption investigations, whistleblowing campaigns, or efforts to expose illicit financial activity. The organization was systematically eliminating any threat to their operations, silencing anyone who dared to peek behind the curtain.

Tanya's analysis also uncovered a crucial detail buried within the metadata of one of the emails: a recurring IP address consistently linked to several high-profile political figures and influential business leaders. This IP address was traced to a secure server located in a nondescript building on the outskirts of Zurich, a city known for its banking secrecy and complex web of international finance. The building itself was a testament to the organization's power – a seemingly innocuous structure blending seamlessly into the cityscape, yet housing what appeared to be a state-of-the-art data center with multiple layers of security, suggesting that the Zurich location was not just a simple server room but likely the central command center for the organization's digital operations. The mere existence of such a central command center highlighted the organization's sophisticated infrastructure and resourcefulness.

This was more than just organized crime; it was a sophisticated, globally integrated network of influence and power, manipulating governments, businesses, and even international institutions to further its agenda. The scale of their operation was breathtaking. The implications were staggering. The discovery sent a fresh wave of unease through Jake, deepening the sense of danger that had become his constant companion.

Their investigation also unearthed evidence of the organization's reach into the media – not through outright control, but subtle manipulation, planted stories, and the strategic use of disinformation campaigns to shape public opinion and deflect attention from their activities. They were masters of propaganda, expertly manipulating public perception to create a veil of normalcy around their activities, enabling them to operate with impunity.

The more Jake and Tanya dug, the deeper the rabbit hole seemed to become. Each new discovery raised more questions than it answered, leading them down further into the labyrinthine depths of the organization’s shadowy operations. Their work demanded constant vigilance, a never-ending cycle of analysis, decryption, and the constant threat of exposure. Their digital fortress, however secure, could only offer so much protection against an enemy this sophisticated. The long game, as Jason Reen had alluded to, was far from over.

Days blurred into weeks as Jake and Tanya delved deeper, sifting through the digital debris left in the wake of the organization's global operations. They were uncovering not just evidence of crimes, but a glimpse into a shadowy world of international intrigue and global power, a web of interconnected entities working in concert to achieve their goals. They were uncovering a global conspiracy of immense proportions, a tapestry woven with threads of deceit, corruption, and violence, all controlled by an unseen hand, the enigmatic Architect.

Jake realized he was not just pursuing a criminal organization; he was uncovering a vast, sophisticated conspiracy that extended far beyond the reach of traditional investigative methods. The scale of the operation was terrifying, a hydra with countless heads, its reach extending into every corner of the globe. The weight of this revelation settled heavily upon him, adding to the growing sense of foreboding that was becoming his constant companion.

He knew the risks. He'd already experienced the organization's chilling efficiency firsthand, witnessing Jason Reen's ruthless precision and his ability to vanish without a trace. But he couldn't back down. He'd glimpsed the darkness, and now, armed with the knowledge gained through Jason's confessions and Tanya's meticulous digital forensics, he was determined to expose it, no matter the cost. The long game had begun, and he was in it for the long haul. The fight for truth had become a personal crusade, a battle against overwhelming odds, but one he was ready to face. He wouldn't rest until the Architect and his organization were exposed, their reign of terror brought to an end. The rain outside continued its relentless assault, but within Jake's secure workspace, a quiet determination burned, a burning desire to bring justice to the victims of this global conspiracy. The fight was far from over, but he had a plan, a strategy to bring the Architect down, and he was ready to play the long game. The fight had just begun.

....

The flickering neon signs of Prague cast a lurid glow on the rain-slicked streets as Jake thoroughly reviewed his plan. He wasn't going to engage in a direct confrontation. That was suicide. The organization, as Jason had described it, possessed an unnerving reach, an ability to anticipate and neutralize threats with terrifying precision.

No, Jake needed a different approach, something subtle, something that would lure them in, a thoroughly crafted trap designed to ensnare the Architect and his inner circle

His strategy hinged on Tanya's discovery – a seemingly innocuous offshore account holding a staggering sum of money, linked to a network of shell corporations traced back to the organization. This account, Jake believed, represented the organization's lifeline, the very artery through which their ill-gotten gains flowed. He planned to bleed them dry, to make them believe they were close to securing a colossal windfall, only to reveal the trap at the last moment.

The first step involved a carefully orchestrated leak. He wouldn't simply release the information; he'd feed it to select journalists, individuals known for their integrity but also their connections within the shadowy underworld. He needed the leak to appear authentic, believable, a real scoop, something that would create enough buzz to reach the ears of the Architect and his inner circle. This wasn't about a simple press release; it was about cultivating a narrative, a carefully spun tale that would entice them, like a siren's song, to take the bait.

He contacted three journalists, each with their own unique expertise and connections: Isabella Morai, a veteran investigative journalist based in Paris with a nose for sniffing out financial scandals; Kenji Tanaka, a seasoned Tokyo-based reporter known for his meticulous research into international crime syndicates; and Ricardo Alvarez, a fiercely independent journalist operating out of Buenos Aires, who had a reputation for going after some of the most powerful and dangerous individuals in Latin America.

Each journalist received a portion of the information – enough to pique their interest but not enough to reveal the entire scheme. Moreau got the initial details about the offshore account, Tanaka received information on the shell corporations used for money laundering, and Alvarez was given intelligence on the human trafficking networks linked to the organization. He gave each of them a different angle, ensuring that the information, when pieced together, would paint a complete but still ambiguous picture, forcing the organization to act.

The ensuing media frenzy was precisely what Jake had hoped for. Rumors spread like wildfire, fueled by the fragmented but compelling information. The whispers reached the right ears. He had baited the hook, now it was a matter of waiting for them to bite.

Jake's next move was far more delicate. He used his contacts within Interpol, leveraging his previous reporting experience to gain access to encrypted communications channels. He anonymously tipped off Interpol about the money laundering activities, providing them with enough information to start an investigation but withholding the ultimate source, keeping the trap’s location shrouded in secrecy. This was a crucial element of his plan. It was a way to ensure that the organization wouldn't suspect his involvement while simultaneously adding another layer of pressure.

The pressure mounted. The organization, sensing the growing scrutiny, began to act. Jake monitored their activity through a network of informants, carefully cultivated over the years. He knew the organization well enough by now to anticipate their moves. They started moving assets, shifting funds, attempting to cover their tracks, but it was already too late. The net was tightening.

He received a cryptic message through an anonymous email. A single line: "The Architect wants to meet." This was it, the culmination of months of meticulous planning. The bait had worked.

The meeting location was a remote villa nestled in the Tuscan countryside. Jake couldn't go himself, of course. He'd arranged for a highly skilled operative, a former special forces soldier he knew only as “Ghost,” to attend the meeting in his place. Ghost, equipped with state-of-the-art surveillance technology, would act as Jake's eyes and ears, gathering irrefutable evidence that would bring the Architect and his organization down.

The villa was a fortress, a place of quiet opulence, completely secured. But Ghost was no ordinary operative. He had infiltrated the place without triggering any alarms. He was patiently awaiting the arrival of the Architect and his inner circle, each of them expecting a straightforward transaction – the recovery of the "stolen" funds.

As the night deepened, the meeting commenced. Jake, miles away in his Prague apartment, watched in real-time as the events unfolded through Ghost's discreet camera feeds. The tension was palpable, a silent game of cat and mouse. The air was thick with suspicion, with unspoken threats and carefully veiled power plays. The Architect, a shadowy figure whose identity remained hidden, was present in the meeting, directing the proceedings, his voice a low growl that spoke of years spent in the shadows.

The meeting wasn't a simple transaction, though. It was a thoroughly planned operation, designed to expose the layers of the organization. The operation included a complex series of coded messages, hidden compartments, and secret communications channels, all of which were thoroughly documented by Ghost. The digital evidence collected by Ghost was overwhelming. Financial records, hidden ledgers, incriminating photographs – each piece of information a brick in the wall of evidence that would finally bring down the Architect and his empire.

The climax of the meeting arrived late into the night. The Architect, convinced that the money was being recovered, revealed the extent of his organization's operations, exposing the intricacies of their global network, naming key players, and detailing the true scale of their criminal activities. He was talking with total confidence, unaware he was being recorded, his arrogance blinding him to the trap that had been carefully laid. This was the golden moment Jake had been waiting for.

As the meeting concluded, the raid commenced. Ghost, giving the signal, triggered a coordinated strike. Police forces, alerted to the location by Interpol, stormed the villa, arresting the Architect and his inner circle. The raid was swift, precise, leaving no room for escape. The carefully laid trap had sprung, trapping the Architect and his henchmen in the very place where they believed they were secure. The long game had finally paid off. The operation was a success. The rain outside had stopped; a new dawn was breaking, and with it, the promise of justice. Jake, watching the news reports of the arrests, felt a sense of exhaustion, but also a profound sense of accomplishment. The fight was far from over, but tonight, they had won a significant victory. The darkness had been momentarily pushed back. But Jake knew, even as he allowed himself a moment of relief, that the fight against the pervasive shadow of global organized crime was a long, relentless war – a war he was now fully committed to waging.

The Trap Springs

The warehouse hummed with a low, almost imperceptible thrum, a vibration that resonated through the concrete floor and up into Jake's bones. He hadn't slept properly in weeks, the adrenaline a constant companion, fueling him with a jittery energy that bordered on mania. The air hung thick with the metallic tang of blood – a faint scent, strategically placed, a lure for the wolves. He checked his watch, the second hand ticking like a countdown to a detonation. Twenty minutes. Twenty minutes until the trap he'd so painstakingly laid sprang shut.

The plan was audacious, bordering on suicidal. He'd used every scrap of information gleaned from his informant, "Whisper," a ghost of a woman who'd slipped into his life as mysteriously as she'd disappeared from the organization's grasp. Whisper had provided the location – this abandoned warehouse on the outskirts of Marseilles, a forgotten relic of the city's industrial past. She'd also provided the bait: a shipment of high-grade heroin, enough to make even the most hardened kingpin's eyes gleam with avarice. The heroin was genuine, but laced with a tracking device so small it was almost invisible, a technological marvel Whisper claimed had been salvaged from a recently decommissioned military satellite.

Jake's team was minimal: himself, armed with a silenced Beretta and a lethal dose of skepticism; Marcus, a former French Gendarme whose expertise in close-quarters combat was legendary; and Tanya, a tech whiz whose fingers danced across keyboards with the grace of a concert pianist, her eyes glued to the array of monitors displaying the warehouse's interior. The warehouse was under complete surveillance. Cameras disguised as security lights, microphones hidden within the ventilation shafts, and drones hovering discreetly above provided a panoramic view of the operation. This wasn't just about bringing down the new leader, it was about dismantling the entire network, crippling it at its heart.

The first sign of activity came from the security cameras. A convoy of black SUVs, their windows tinted darkly, pulled into the warehouse's desolate yard. Tanya's fingers flew across her keyboard, zooming in on the faces of the men emerging from the vehicles. They moved with the practiced efficiency of seasoned professionals, their movements economical, their eyes scanning the surroundings with a predatory intensity. The new leader, known only as “Seraph,” was among them. He’d been Gomin Guill’s second-in-command, a man who’d risen from the shadows to seize control with ruthless ambition. He was younger, arguably more dangerous, and far more technologically savvy than his predecessor.

Jake gripped his Beretta, the cold steel a comforting weight in his hand. He'd spent years chasing shadows, pursuing criminals through the labyrinthine alleys of the global underworld. This, however, felt different. This was personal. This was about accountability. He'd seen the devastation wrought by these organizations, the lives shattered, the families torn apart. He wasn't just a reporter anymore; he was a soldier in a silent war, fighting for those who couldn’t fight for themselves.

The men moved into the warehouse, disappearing into the darkness. The warehouse floor plan was projected onto one of the monitors, a detailed rendering showing the exact locations of the hidden cameras and microphones. Jake could see them moving, shadowy figures navigating the maze of crates and pallets. Their chatter was picked up by the microphones, a low hum of voices speaking in rapid-fire French, punctuated by occasional bursts of harsh laughter.

Then, it happened.

An alarm blared, a piercing wail cutting through the night's stillness. The heroin shipment was disturbed; it was a small, but crucial trigger, the mechanism that released the trap's deadly mechanisms. Within seconds, the warehouse was ablaze with automatic weapons fire. Jake and Marcus moved like phantoms, their movements precise, their reactions instantaneous. They'd been briefed on Seraph's methods; his penchant for using mercenaries, their skill in close-quarters combat, and the ruthlessness of their response when challenged.

The gunfight was chaotic, a deadly dance in the semi-darkness. Tanya's calm voice crackled through Jake's earpiece as she relayed critical information – the positions of the enemy, the number of casualties, the route Seraph was taking. Jake's shots were clean, precise, each bullet finding its mark, crippling or incapacitating his target with surgical accuracy. Marcus was a whirlwind of controlled violence, a human force of nature, neutralizing enemy combatants with brutal efficiency.

But Seraph was elusive, a shadow flitting from one cover point to another. He had a natural talent for deception and misdirection, utilizing the chaos as a shield, using the movements of his men to disguise his own. His men fought with the desperation of cornered animals, firing back with deadly accuracy. Jake knew he had to be fast, decisive, and ruthless. He had to neutralize the threat before the entire situation spiraled into utter chaos.

As the gunfire intensified, a figure emerged from the shadows, moving with the deadly grace of a predator. It was Seraph, his eyes blazing with a furious intensity, his weapon spitting death at alarming speeds. He was a master marksman, his shots were incredibly precise, showing an incredible mastery of fire control. Jake ducked behind a stack of crates, the lead spraying across the concrete floor where he had been standing moments before. This wasn't a mere shootout; this was a battle of wits, a deadly game of cat and mouse.

The fight moved into a series of close-quarters confrontations. Jake found himself in a hand-to-hand struggle with one of Seraph's guards, a powerfully built brute who tried to overpower him with sheer strength. Jake, however, fought with the cunning of a fox, using his smaller size and agility to his advantage. He expertly disarmed him, using his own weight to knock the man to the ground. He made sure to place him in a position that would make it difficult for him to re-engage in the battle, minimizing the risks of further attacks.

Finally, Jake found himself facing Seraph. The air crackled with tension, the only sounds the heavy breathing of the two men, and the occasional distant shots still echoing around the warehouse. The final confrontation was a study in contrasts: Seraph's cool precision against Jake's gritty determination, Seraph's calculated aggression pitted against Jake's desperate fight for survival. It was a duel, as much a test of will as a clash of firearms. Seraph made a move to flank Jake, but Jake anticipated the move and quickly adjusted his position. He took a risk and fired, hitting Seraph in the shoulder. Seraph screamed out in pain and retaliated with a shot that grazed Jake's arm.

Jake, wounded but unbowed, pressed his advantage. In a swift move, he disarmed Seraph, sending his weapon careening across the floor. The battle was far from over. Seraph, a ferocious fighter even with a wounded shoulder, charged forward, attempting to overpower Jake through sheer brute force. Jake, utilizing his years of experience in combat, parried his attacks and countered with deft movements. The duel became a brutal ballet of destruction, where precision, determination, and calculated risk prevailed. He used a combination of his quick reactions and knowledge of martial arts to incapacitate his opponent. He was skilled in grappling and joint locks, techniques that allowed him to take down opponents more powerful than himself.

The fight ended not with a bang, but with a thud as Jake managed to finally subdue Seraph, knocking him unconscious with a well-placed blow. The gunfire ceased, replaced by the heavy silence of aftermath. The warehouse was a scene of devastation, a testament to the brutal conflict that had just taken place. But the victory was bittersweet. While Seraph was down, the organization remained, a hydra with many heads, capable of regenerating even after its leadership was removed. The echoes of gunfire resonated in the silence, a somber reminder that the battle, while won, was far from over. The long game continued.

....

The warehouse doors, reinforced steel behemoths, groaned under the weight of a battering ram. Jake, crouched behind a stack of overturned crates, could hear the rhythmic pounding, a relentless heartbeat signaling the arrival of reinforcements. He'd known this was a possibility, a calculated risk. Taking down Seraph, the organization's enforcer, had been a significant blow, but it was hardly the knockout punch. The real fight was just beginning.

He glanced at the unconscious form of Seraph, his face pale and contorted in a silent scream. The man was a mountain of muscle, even subdued, a testament to his brutal strength. Jake had used every ounce of his training, every trick he'd learned from years spent covering crime, to overcome him. But Seraph was just one piece of a vast, intricate puzzle.

The pounding intensified, the metal shrieked in protest, and then, with a final, earth-shattering crack, the doors splintered, showering the warehouse floor with jagged shards of steel. A wave of men surged into the space, a tide of black suits and grim faces, their weapons drawn, their eyes glittering with a predatory hunger. They were professional killers, efficient and lethal, moving with the practiced precision of a well-oiled machine.

Jake didn't hesitate. He rose from his cover, his own weapon leveled, a 9mm Glock, familiar and reassuring in his hand. He'd spent weeks preparing for this, studying their tactics, anticipating their moves. He knew he was outnumbered, outgunned, but he wasn't outmaneuvered. He'd prepared for this contingency.

The first volley of gunfire ripped through the air, the warehouse echoing with the deafening roar of automatic weapons. Jake moved like a phantom, weaving through the chaos, his shots precise, each bullet finding its mark. He used the shattered remains of the doors and the overturned crates as cover, transforming the ruined space into a deadly labyrinth. He knew he couldn't win a prolonged firefight. His strategy was attrition, wearing them down, creating opportunities.

He noticed one of the attackers, a hulking figure with a shaved head and a cruel sneer, focusing his fire on a wounded colleague. Jake saw his chance. He moved with the speed of a viper, a blur of motion, and took him down with a single, expertly placed shot to the head. The body slumped to the ground, a silent testament to his skills.

Another attacker, agile and quick, tried to flank him. Jake anticipated the move, spinning and firing, sending the man sprawling. He wasn't just relying on firepower; he was utilizing his environment, turning the debris field into a battleground tailored to his strengths. He tossed a smoke grenade, creating a temporary screen that allowed him to reposition himself.

The smoke stung his eyes, the air thick with the acrid smell of burning chemicals. He could hear the confused shouts of his attackers, their movements hampered by the reduced visibility. This was his moment. He moved towards Seraph's unconscious form, the adrenaline still coursing through his veins. He needed to secure the body.

But as he moved, another figure emerged from the smoke, tall and imposing, a woman with icy blue eyes and a steely gaze. She was different from the others; her movements were precise, almost balletic, and her weapon, a sleek, customized pistol, was held with a deadly grace. This wasn’t just another hired gun; this was someone more experienced, more deadly.

Their eyes met, a silent acknowledgment of the shared danger. There was no room for pleasantries; only survival. The woman opened fire, her shots accurate and fast. Jake reacted instinctively, diving for cover, the bullets whizzing past his head. The exchange was rapid, brutal, a dance of death played out in the swirling smoke.

He realized he was fighting a losing battle. His ammunition was dwindling, and his body was screaming in protest from exhaustion and adrenaline. He knew he had to change tactics again. Using the smoke as cover, he slipped away, towards a different part of the warehouse. This was a desperate gamble.

He found a partially concealed exit, a service door that led to a loading dock. He knew it was his only chance. He sprinted towards it, dodging gunfire, the weight of his weapon and the adrenaline keeping him going. He had to buy himself time, hopefully time enough to escape.

As he burst through the service door, he felt a searing pain in his shoulder, a sharp, agonizing jolt. He stumbled, his breath catching in his throat. He looked back, seeing the woman silhouetted in the doorway, her gun still smoking. He'd been hit.

But he managed to make it to the loading dock. He collapsed onto the ground, gasping for air. He was injured, but alive. He’d escaped, for now. But the escape was only a temporary reprieve; the long game was far from over. The shadowy organization was vast, its reach stretching across continents. Taking down Seraph and escaping the ambush was just the beginning. The real fight, the final reckoning, lay ahead. He needed to find a way to expose them, to unravel the vast web of corruption and violence they had woven, to prevent them from claiming any more victims. He needed to find the real mastermind, the one pulling the strings from the shadows. The game had only just begun. The information gleaned from Seraph's files, the whispers of a larger conspiracy he'd overheard, gave him a glimmer of hope, a path to follow. He knew he was far from safe, but armed with that hope, the adrenaline-fueled exhaustion fading into a cold, hard determination, he pressed on. The fight for justice was far from over. His own survival, even, was far from certain. But he would continue to fight.

The cold night air hit him as he dragged himself to a nearby alley, the pain in his shoulder sharp and insistent. He needed help, medical attention, but he also needed time to regroup, to formulate his next move. He reached into his pocket, pulling out his battered cell phone. He needed to call someone he could trust, someone who wouldn't betray him, someone who could help him unravel this conspiracy. The weight of the fight he had embarked upon pressed heavily on him. The fight was far from over, but he was determined to see it through. He had to. The fate of so many hung in the balance, including his own. He knew he was walking a tightrope, one wrong step, and he'd fall into the abyss. But he wouldn't stop. He couldn't. Not now. Not until the truth was revealed and justice was served. The shadowy organization had made a powerful enemy in him. And he wouldn't rest until they were brought to their knees. He knew, with chilling certainty, that this was far from the end. This was just the beginning of a far bigger, far more dangerous game. He was in it until the bitter end. The final reckoning was only just beginning.

....

The alley reeked of stale beer and desperation, a fitting backdrop for his predicament. Jake's phone finally connected, the crackle of static a prelude to the strained voice on the other end. "Jassa? It's Jake. I need your help. Things… escalated."

Jassa, a former colleague from his investigative journalism days, had a network of contacts that extended into the city's underbelly. He was Jake's last resort, a lifeline in a sea of deceit. Jassa's response was cautious, measured. He'd sensed the shift in Jake's tone, the underlying urgency. "Jake, what happened? Seraph?"

Jake recounted the warehouse raid, the brutal fight, the near-death experience. He didn't spare Jassa the details, the visceral reality of it all. He needed Jassa to understand the gravity of the situation, the depth of the conspiracy he was uncovering. The sheer scale of it was staggering.

Jassa listened intently; his silence punctuated only by the occasional intake of breath. When Jake finished, a long silence followed, broken only by the city's distant hum. "This is bigger than we thought, Jake. Much bigger. Gomin Guill was just a pawn."

The statement hit Jake like a physical blow. He'd suspected as much, but hearing it confirmed, articulated so plainly, sent a shiver down his spine. He'd taken down a kingpin, only to discover the entire game was being controlled from the shadows by an unseen hand.

"I need access to Gomin’s files," Jake said, his voice tight with determination. "Anything that might point to the real mastermind."

Jassa hesitated. "Accessing those files is going to be risky, Jake. Gomin's organization has eyes and ears everywhere. One wrong move, and we're both toast."

"I know the risks," Jake responded, his voice resolute. "But I'm not backing down now. Not after what I've seen, after what I've been through."

The next few hours were a blur of clandestine meetings, coded messages, and frantic searches. Jassa, despite his reservations, proved invaluable. He used his network to procure a flash drive containing Gomin's thoroughly kept records, a digital archive of his illicit activities, financial transactions, and coded communications. But the information was encrypted, protected by multiple layers of security. They needed a specialist – someone who understood the dark arts of digital espionage.

That's where Tanya came in. Tanya was an enigma, a ghost in the digital world. Jassa described her as a “brilliant coder with a penchant for trouble,” someone who navigated the murky waters of the dark web with ease.

Meeting her felt like stepping into a different world, one shrouded in mystery and guarded by an aura of danger. She was young, sharp, with eyes that held a disconcerting depth, hinting at experiences beyond her years.

Tanya agreed to help, but not out of altruism. She was driven by something else, something that Jake couldn't quite decipher. She spoke in riddles, her responses often cryptic, hinting at a past intertwined with the organization they were investigating. Her work was swift and precise. Within hours, she cracked the encryption, revealing a digital Pandora's Box.

The files contained evidence of a vast global conspiracy, involving politicians, corporations, and powerful individuals – a network of corruption extending far beyond Gomin's reach. They uncovered evidence of money laundering, arms dealing, and even human trafficking, all thoroughly orchestrated from the highest levels of society.

The information was overwhelming, a tapestry of deceit and betrayal woven with painstaking precision. Jake felt a growing sense of dread. The scale of the conspiracy was far beyond anything he'd ever imagined. This wasn't just organized crime; this was a systematic dismantling of the very fabric of society.

As they delved deeper, a pattern emerged – a recurring name, a code name only Tanya seemed to recognize: 'Seraphina.' It was a name that sent shivers down Jake's spine. The files showed Seraphina was much more than just Gomin's enforcer. She was a key player, deeply entrenched in the organization's inner circle. Tanya's eyes narrowed as she read the documents, a chilling realization dawning on her face.

"Seraphina…she wasn't just working for Gomin," Tanya whispered, her voice barely audible above the hum of the computer. "She was…building something. Something bigger, something independent."

This was a new and terrifying development. Seraph, the seemingly ruthless enforcer, was not just a loyal lieutenant; she was a power player in her own right, secretly building her empire within the organization. This suggested a potential fracture within the ranks, a power struggle brewing beneath the surface.

The revelation threw Jake's carefully constructed plans into disarray. He had assumed that by eliminating Gomin, he'd struck a significant blow. Now he realized he'd merely unleashed a far more dangerous element – a rogue operator with her own agenda and an even more sinister network.

Just as Tanya revealed this crucial piece of information, a sudden power surge plunged the room into darkness. The air crackled with a tense silence, broken only by the frantic beeping of Tanya's laptop. They had been compromised. The organization had found them.

Tanya sprang to her feet, her eyes flashing with a cold, predatory gleam. "They're here," she said, her voice devoid of emotion. "They knew we were here all along."

This was a betrayal of the highest order. Someone within their own circle had tipped off the organization. But who? Jassa? It was a chilling thought, a possibility that gnawed at Jake's mind. He glanced at Jassa, noticing a flicker of something in his eyes – a subtle, almost imperceptible shift in his demeanor.

The sudden darkness intensified the looming threat. The air thickened with anticipation. The silence became heavy with the weight of impending danger. The game had changed, shifted towards a far more perilous course. They weren't just fighting a criminal organization anymore; they were facing a web of betrayal, a conspiracy so deep it stretched into the highest echelons of power. The final reckoning had arrived, not as a grand climax, but as a descent into a brutal, unforgiving struggle for survival. The trust they had placed in others had crumbled, leaving them exposed and vulnerable. The fight for survival had begun, and the stakes were higher than ever before. The unexpected betrayals had only added to the complexity and suspense, pushing Jake and his allies towards a confrontation that would test the limits of their resilience and determination. The question was not if they would survive, but whether they could unearth the truth and expose the monstrous web of deceit that threatened to engulf them all. The shadows were closing in, and the game had become a desperate fight for survival. The final reckoning had truly begun.

....

The warehouse shuddered under the impact of the explosion, sending tremors through the grimy concrete floor. Dust motes danced in the fractured beams of moonlight slicing through the shattered skylights. The air, thick with the acrid stench of cordite and burning metal, stung Jake's nostrils. He coughed, his lungs burning, the taste of blood metallic on his tongue. Jassa, his face streaked with grime and sweat, lay beside him, clutching a ragged wound in his side. The battle had been brutal, a chaotic ballet of gunfire and desperate maneuvers, a fight for survival against an enemy far more entrenched and ruthless than they had anticipated.

They had cornered him – the man they now knew as Viktor, Gomin Guill's successor, a ruthless pragmatist who had ascended through the ranks on a tide of violence and betrayal. Viktor, unlike Gomin, had been a phantom, a ghost in the machine, his operations shrouded in a veil of almost impenetrable secrecy. Tracking him had been a herculean task, a relentless chase across continents, a trail of cryptic clues and dead ends. But Jake and Jassa, fueled by a potent blend of determination and a grim understanding of the stakes, had finally caught up to him.

The fight, however, had been anything but straightforward. Viktor's security detail was heavily armed, well-trained mercenaries who fought with a chilling efficiency. They were a force to be reckoned with – a grim reminder of the organization's vast resources and reach.

The clash had been a maelstrom of gunfire, punctuated by the sickening thud of falling bodies. Jake had relied on his instincts, his years of investigative work providing an edge, allowing him to anticipate Viktor's moves, to see through the carefully constructed façade. Jassa, on the other hand, had been a whirlwind of controlled fury, his combat skills honed over years spent on the front lines. They had worked in perfect unison, a deadly dance of precision and brute force, pushing back against the relentless onslaught.

Even as they had Viktor cornered, the fight had been far from over. The warehouse, their makeshift arena of conflict, had become a battleground, each shattered crate, each overturned barrel, a testament to the ferocity of the encounter. The air had grown heavy with the smell of gunpowder and death, the silence punctuated by the rhythmic thump of Jassa's pulse. The victory had been hard-won, a testament to their resolve and resilience. Viktor, his face contorted in a mask of disbelief and rage, had finally fallen, a silent testament to the power of relentless pursuit and unwavering determination. But as the echoes of the gunfire faded into the night, a chilling realization settled upon Jake. Their victory was a pyrrhic one.

The organization, despite the loss of its leader, remained a potent force. Viktor's death, far from shattering it, might only solidify its resolve. The network, spanning continents and reaching into the highest echelons of power, was not easily destroyed. It was a hydra, every severed head replaced by two more. This wasn't the end; it was merely a new beginning, a shift in the tectonic plates of this world of shadows. As Jake surveyed the damage, he knew they had only scratched the surface. The information they had gleaned from Viktor's thoroughly secured data drives, however, offered a glimmer of hope, pointing towards a network far more vast and influential than they had ever imagined.

The encrypted files contained a dizzying array of names, dates, locations - a thoroughly documented trail leading to a vast network of money laundering, arms dealing, and political corruption, reaching across multiple nations and impacting global events. Jake felt the weight of this revelation pressing down on him, the staggering implications sinking in. This wasn't just a criminal organization; it was a shadow government, manipulating events from the darkness, pulling strings from behind the scenes.

The data also revealed the extent of the organization's reach – a network of informants embedded within law enforcement, governments, and even the media. This realization hit Jake hard. He had unwittingly been operating within a system designed to protect and conceal the organization's activities. It explained the near-impossible levels of secrecy they had encountered. The sheer scale of the conspiracy threatened to engulf them all. The organization’s reach extended far beyond the criminal underworld. The tentacles snaked into the highest echelons of power. The implications were staggering. They were playing in a much larger game than they had ever suspected.

Jassa, weak but alert, stirred beside him. "We won," he gasped, his voice raspy, his breath coming in short, shallow bursts. "But at what cost?"

Jake nodded with his gaze fixed on the shattered remains of the warehouse. The victory felt hollow, a fleeting triumph in the face of a much larger threat. The organization had lost its leader, but it was far from defeated. It would regroup, reconstitute itself, and emerge stronger, more ruthless. Their work was far from over. In fact, it had just begun.

The next few days were a blur of activity. Jake, working tirelessly with Jassa and a small, handpicked team of trusted contacts from his past investigative work, began to sift through the vast amount of data retrieved from Viktor's hidden servers. The information was overwhelming, a complex web of transactions, coded messages, and hidden accounts, all pointing to a conspiracy of staggering proportions. They worked around the clock, fueled by adrenaline and a grim determination to expose the truth, despite the constant threat hanging over their heads.

Their investigation unearthed evidence of widespread corruption, involving high-ranking officials, powerful business executives, and even members of the elite. The names were chillingly familiar – people Jake had seen on television, read about in newspapers, people who held positions of immense power and influence. It was a stark reminder of how deeply entrenched the organization was in the fabric of society, its tentacles reaching into every corner of the world.

As they dug deeper, they discovered more evidence suggesting that the organization's operations extended far beyond simple criminal activity. They were involved in covert operations, political assassinations, and even the manipulation of global markets. The organization’s influence was pervasive, its reach seemingly limitless. The implication was clear – they weren't merely fighting a criminal organization; they were fighting a shadow government that had infiltrated every aspect of power.

The danger was palpable, a constant weight on their shoulders. The risk of exposure was ever-present, a looming threat that could extinguish their efforts at any moment. But they pressed on, driven by a sense of purpose and the knowledge that the truth, however dangerous, was worth fighting for. They were playing a dangerous game, a high-stakes poker match against an enemy with seemingly limitless resources. But they knew that if they could expose the organization’s intricate web of deceit, they could bring down the entire structure, one carefully constructed layer at a time.

Their progress, however, was slow and painstaking. The organization's defenses were sophisticated, its security measures almost impenetrable. But Jake, armed with his journalistic instincts and years of experience in uncovering hidden truths, pressed on. He knew that every piece of the puzzle, every carefully hidden detail, could be the key to bringing down this vast criminal empire. The fight was far from over, but they were making progress, one step at a time, slowly unraveling the tangled web of the organization's operations. The shadows were still closing in, but they were starting to see the light of dawn, a beacon of hope in a dark and dangerous world. The fight was on, and this time, they were fighting to win. The fight for truth and justice had begun, and there was no turning back. The stakes were too high. The future of the world might depend on it.

....

The acrid smell of burnt plastic and ozone still clung to Jake's clothes, a lingering reminder of the explosive climax in the warehouse. Jassa, pale and weak but alive, was being loaded into an ambulance, his wound expertly bandaged by a paramedic. The victory felt hollow, a pyrrhic triumph etched in the soot-stained brick of the ruined building. They had crippled a significant arm of Gomin Guill's organization, seized a cache of incriminating documents, and even managed to disable their encrypted communication network for a precious few hours—but the cost was steep.

Three of their team lay dead, their sacrifice a stark testament to the ruthlessness of their enemy. Marco, a former intelligence operative whose loyalty was as unwavering as his skill with a silenced pistol, had shielded Jake from a hail of bullets, taking a fatal shot to the chest. Elena, a computer whiz whose nimble fingers had navigated the organization’s digital labyrinth, had been caught in a crossfire, a single bullet ending her brilliant career far too soon. And then there was Ben, the demolition expert, whose carefully planned explosion had brought down a crucial section of the warehouse, buying them precious time. He'd been too close to the blast, the force shattering his internal organs.

The silence in the aftermath was deafening, broken only by the wail of sirens and the whispered condolences exchanged between the surviving members of the team. Jake felt the weight of their loss pressing down on him, a crushing burden he was unsure he could bear. The faces of his fallen comrades flashed before his eyes, each one a reminder of the human cost of their mission. He’d known the risks, of course. He'd spent years covering stories that danced on the edge of darkness, stories where the line between life and death was often blurred. But this...this was different. This felt personal.

The documents they'd recovered, painstakingly salvaged from the wreckage, were a treasure trove of information, far more than they'd anticipated. They revealed a network of corruption extending far beyond Gomin Guill's immediate circle, implicating high-ranking government officials, multinational corporations, and even elements within international law enforcement agencies. The organization wasn't simply a criminal enterprise; it was a vast, parasitic entity, its tendrils wrapped tightly around the very foundations of society. Gomin Guill was a symptom, not the disease. Taking him out was like cutting off a branch; the tree itself remained, its roots buried deep and strong.

The victory felt like a small step forward, a fleeting respite in a long, relentless war. The sheer scale of the conspiracy was staggering, a labyrinthine network of hidden accounts, shell corporations, and offshore tax havens. Jake felt a surge of grim determination. He had come too far, lost too much, to abandon the fight now. He needed to use the evidence they'd secured to expose the truth, to dismantle this corrupt empire from the inside.

The days that followed were a blur of intense activity. Jake and his remaining team worked tirelessly, thoroughly analyzing the documents, piecing together the puzzle of the organization's operations. They uncovered evidence of money laundering, arms trafficking, human trafficking, and even assassination plots targeting key figures in opposition movements around the world. The organization's reach was global, its influence suffocating.

The information was so sensitive, so explosive, that they couldn't simply hand it over to the authorities. They'd learned their lesson in the warehouse: the police couldn't be trusted, at least not entirely. They'd seen firsthand how deep the rot ran, how the tentacles of the organization had burrowed into the very heart of law enforcement. They had to tread carefully, strategically releasing information to trusted journalists, carefully selected individuals with a proven track record of integrity and investigative prowess.

The process was slow, arduous, and risky. Every leaked document, every anonymous tip, every carefully placed article was a calculated gamble, a step into the shadows where the consequences of failure were dire. But

Jake refused to be intimidated. He had seen the faces of the fallen, felt the cold weight of their sacrifice, and he wasn't going to let their deaths be in vain.

The pressure was immense. The organization's counter-intelligence network was formidable, its operatives shadowy figures moving silently in the darkness, always watching, always ready to strike. Jake felt their gaze constantly on him, a chilling reminder of the danger he was in. Sleep was a luxury he could scarcely afford. He found himself constantly looking over his shoulder, fearing the unseen, the unknown, the lurking threat that could appear from any shadow.

One night, a phone call jolted him awake. It was an anonymous source, a voice laced with fear and urgency. "They know," the voice whispered, "They know about you. They're coming for you." The line went dead.

The threat was immediate, visceral. He felt the chilling certainty that his life was hanging by a thread, that the organization's reach was longer, its grasp more insidious than he had ever imagined. He knew he needed to act fast, to move before they found him. He had to get the information out to the world, expose the conspiracy before it was too late, before the organization could silence him permanently.

The next few days were a chaotic whirlwind of clandestine meetings, encrypted emails, and frantic phone calls. He worked with his remaining team, sharing the burden, distributing tasks, and working as a team to escape the impending doom. They managed to secure the assistance of a trusted international journalist, a seasoned veteran with contacts in high places, a woman named Dina Lutvig, who agreed to publish a series of articles exposing the organization's criminal activities. It was a dangerous game, but Tanya, a woman known for her unwavering courage and journalistic integrity, was willing to take the risk.

The articles dropped like bombshells. The reaction was immediate and widespread. Governments were thrown into turmoil. Corporations were forced to answer difficult questions. The organization's carefully constructed façade began to crumble, its influence weakening with each explosive revelation. The world was finally beginning to see the truth.

But the victory was far from assured. The organization fought back fiercely, attempting to discredit the articles, intimidate witnesses, and eliminate any loose ends. Jake found himself caught in a game of cat and mouse, always one step ahead, always looking over his shoulder, always fearing the inevitable.

The final reckoning had arrived, not with a bang but a series of escalating blows. He learned that several corrupt officials, some with ties to his own government, were working to bury the evidence, to protect the organization from the outside world. The fight had expanded beyond the initial targets, extending into the highest echelons of power. He and his team had to work harder and faster, facing insurmountable odds to fight a war that seemed to have no end. The cost of victory was high, yet the price of silence was far higher, a future where justice meant nothing, a world consumed by darkness, where evil triumphed. He wouldn't let that happen. Not now. Not ever. The fight for truth, for justice, for the souls of those who died for this, would continue.

Lingering Threats

The air hung heavy with the scent of rain and unspoken anxieties. Even with Gomin Guill silenced, a chilling stillness permeated Jake's small, cluttered apartment. The victory felt hollow, a fleeting reprieve in a war that showed no signs of ending. The documents scattered across his desk – a chaotic landscape of coded messages, financial records, and hastily scribbled notes – whispered of a vast, shadowy network, its tentacles reaching into every corner of the globe. He'd taken down the head of the hydra, but the body continued to writhe, its many heads still capable of inflicting deadly strikes.

Jason's account, though harrowing and detailed, had left gaping holes in the narrative. It was a thoroughly crafted story, each kill a perfectly executed ballet of death, but the sheer scope of the operation, the almost supernatural efficiency, made him question the completeness of the narrative. Had Jason omitted details, conveniently leaving out inconvenient truths? Or was there something far more sinister at play, something beyond his understanding, a level of complexity he hadn't anticipated?

The initial euphoria of bringing down Gomin had faded, replaced by a gnawing unease. The man's death, while a significant blow, felt like merely severing a branch of a vast, ancient tree. The roots remained firmly planted, deep within the fertile soil of global corruption. The implications were staggering. Gomin hadn't been operating in isolation. He was a pawn, a highly effective one, but ultimately just a piece in a far larger, more terrifying game.

The photographs, painstakingly gathered from various sources, displayed a stark reality: Gomin's reach stretched far beyond the drug trade. His network involved politicians, prominent businessmen, even elements within law enforcement. Jake had glimpsed the tip of an iceberg, a terrifyingly large and menacing one, and the sheer enormity of what lay beneath sent shivers down his spine. The organization's influence seemed to corrupt everything it touched, poisoning the well of society, leaving behind a trail of destruction and despair.

The news reports were carefully curated, playing down the true extent of Gomin’s empire, focusing on individual crimes rather than the intricate web connecting them. It was a classic case of burying the lead, of focusing on the symptoms while ignoring the disease. Jake understood the power of narrative control; he'd seen how easily information could be manipulated, spun to create a desired effect, a chilling truth mirrored in his own work as a journalist.

His apartment, normally a haven, felt like a cage. Every shadow seemed to conceal a threat, every sound a potential sign of impending danger. The paranoia was a suffocating blanket, a constant reminder of the risk he'd taken, the life he'd endangered. He wasn't just a journalist anymore; he was a target, a pawn in a game far more dangerous than anything he'd ever imagined.

He reviewed the encrypted messages, each one a cryptic clue leading deeper into the labyrinthine organization. The language was sophisticated, utilizing complex coding and encryption techniques that would take weeks, perhaps months, to fully decipher. He needed help, expertise beyond his capabilities.

He considered contacting his old contacts, the few he trusted implicitly, the ones who operated in the shadowy world of intelligence and espionage. But reaching out meant exposing himself further, inviting greater scrutiny, increasing the already elevated risk. It was a dangerous gamble, one that could easily cost him his life.

The thought of his family – his wife, Sarah, and their two young children – sent a jolt of fear through him. He couldn't afford to fail. This wasn't just about justice; it was about survival. He had to find a way to dismantle the organization, to expose the truth, to protect those he loved, all while navigating the treacherous waters of a global criminal conspiracy.

The evidence pointed towards a far-reaching conspiracy involving governments, international corporations, and powerful individuals. Gomin was a small fish in a vast ocean of corruption. He'd taken down a significant player, but the organization still retained a frightening level of power and influence.

Days bled into weeks as Jake thoroughly pieced together the fragments of information he had gathered. He worked late into the night, fueled by caffeine and adrenaline, the weight of his investigation pressing down on him. The lack of sleep weighed heavily, but the danger spurred him on. He had to expose the truth, regardless of the personal cost.

The threat was more pervasive than he'd initially anticipated. The organization's influence stretched into various spheres – finance, politics, even the media itself.

He'd seen the subtle ways they manipulated public opinion, controlling the narrative to their advantage. This understanding filled him with a sense of urgency and dread.

His investigation led him down several dead ends, each one a painful reminder of the immense power and resources his adversary possessed. He encountered roadblocks at every turn, carefully laid traps designed to derail his investigation, to make him question his sanity. But he persevered, driven by a relentless desire for justice and a deep-seated fear for the safety of his family.

He had to find a way to expose the organization, to reveal its intricate network of influence, to bring those responsible to justice. The task felt overwhelming, an impossible challenge. But the stakes were too high, the potential consequences too dire, to simply give up.

He found himself contemplating his own mortality, the fragility of life in the face of such overwhelming power. Yet, despite the fear, the determination burned within him. He would continue to pursue the truth, to fight the good fight, regardless of the personal cost.

He knew he was playing a dangerous game, a game with potentially fatal consequences. The organization had vast resources, an extensive network of informants, and a ruthless willingness to eliminate anyone who stood in their way. He was acutely aware of his vulnerability, the precariousness of his position.

As he looked out at the cityscape, the towering buildings illuminated against the night sky, he wondered how many more lives would be lost before the organization was finally brought down. The weight of responsibility, the sheer magnitude of the challenge, felt almost unbearable. But he had to keep going. He had to finish what he had started. The echoes of the past—the death of Gomin, the whispers of the conspiracy—were a constant reminder of the unfinished business that lay ahead, a battle he knew would continue long after the initial victory. The fight was far from over.

....

The flickering neon sign of the all-night diner cast a lurid glow on the rain-slicked street. Jake Harroll, his face etched with fatigue, nursed a lukewarm coffee, the bitter taste mirroring the grim reality of his situation. Gomin Guill was dead, but the victory felt like a pyrrhic one. The mountain of incriminating evidence – thoroughly gathered from Jason Reen's confession and the aftermath of the assassination – was a damning indictment of Guill's organization, but it also revealed a network far larger, far more insidious, than he'd ever imagined.

The documents spoke of shell corporations registered in tax havens, untraceable bank accounts brimming with ill-gotten gains, and a complex web of international alliances that stretched from the bustling marketplaces of Hong Kong to the shadowy back alleys of Buenos Aires. Names, dates, locations – all thoroughly recorded, yet often cryptic, veiled in code or shrouded in ambiguity. He felt like an archaeologist thoroughly piecing together fragments of a shattered civilization, each shard revealing more about the terrifying scale of the conspiracy, yet, leaving him further away from a complete picture.

The sheer audacity of it all was staggering. Guill, despite his ruthlessness, had been merely a pawn, a highly effective but ultimately expendable piece in a game played by players operating in the shadows. The documents suggested a council, a shadowy cabal pulling the strings from the darkness, their identities carefully concealed, their motives shrouded in mystery. The thought sent a chill down Jake's spine. He was dealing with something far beyond the reach of local law enforcement, something that required a level of investigation that went beyond his journalistic abilities.

The question gnawed at him: who were these shadowy figures pulling the strings? What were their ultimate goals? And more importantly, what were they willing to do to protect their secrets? The implication that Jason, an assassin operating with surgical precision, was merely a tool, sent a shiver down Jake's spine. It raised the chilling possibility of other assassins, equally skilled, equally lethal, working for the same shadowy clique.

The names scattered throughout the documents were a mixture of the familiar and the utterly unknown. Some were easily identifiable – known figures in the international underworld, names whispered in hushed tones in smoky backrooms and dimly lit bars. Others were complete enigmas, ghosts in the machine, operating in the digital shadows, leaving no traceable footprint. He felt like he was chasing phantoms, trying to grasp at smoke.

He ran his fingers through his weary face, the stubble scratching against his skin. Sleep was a luxury he couldn't afford. The urgency of the situation, the weight of the responsibility he now bore, kept him tethered to his desk, consumed by the endless flow of information. Each decoded message, each deciphered code, brought him closer to the truth, yet simultaneously pushed him further into the treacherous depths of a world he never knew existed. The information felt like a labyrinth, each pathway leading to more questions than answers, each dead end revealing a new, equally perplexing path.

Among the documents were several cryptic symbols and drawings, their meaning lost to him. He suspected they were some form of internal code used by the organization, possibly related to their structure or their operations. He needed an expert, someone with a background in cryptography, someone who could help decipher these hidden messages. The thought led him to Dr. Evelyn Reed, a renowned cryptographer he had met at a journalism conference a few years ago. Her expertise in complex ciphers was unparalleled, and he hoped she could shed light on the cryptic symbols.

Reaching out to Evelyn proved challenging. Her life was a carefully constructed fortress of privacy, her contact details scarce. After several days of relentless searching, he found her, finally connecting with her through a mutual acquaintance. Her response was cautious, bordering on reluctant. She was clearly aware of the inherent risks in dealing with material of this nature, but Jake's persistence and the gravity of the situation eventually persuaded her to agree to meet.

Their meeting was brief, clandestine, taking place in the back room of a deserted bookstore, its shelves lined with dusty volumes. Evelyn, a sharp-witted woman with piercing blue eyes, reviewed the documents with an intensity that bordered on obsession. Her nimble fingers traced the symbols, her lips moving silently as she deciphered the hidden meaning. The result of her analysis was both terrifying and enlightening. The symbols confirmed Jake's suspicions: the organization was structured like a multi-layered pyramid, with a central council at the apex and numerous sub-organizations operating globally.

The details she uncovered revealed a chilling operational complexity, far surpassing anything Jake had envisioned. The organization was deeply involved in activities ranging from money laundering and arms trafficking to human trafficking and political assassination. Their reach was vast, their influence pervasive, and their grip on power ironclad. Evelyn's expertise provided a crucial framework for understanding the structure and operations of the organization, giving Jake a clear pathway forward.

But along with the answers, new questions arose. Evelyn pointed out inconsistencies in the documents, suggesting the possibility of internal betrayals or power struggles within the organization. This internal conflict presented a potential opportunity, a weakness that Jake could exploit to dismantle the organization from within.

The revelation of this internal rift within the seemingly impenetrable organization was both a glimmer of hope and a significant challenge. Exploring this conflict could be extremely risky, potentially drawing him into a dangerous game of cat and mouse with powerful players who would stop at nothing to protect their secrets. However, it also presented the best chance of bringing them down.

The weight of this new information pressed down on Jake, the burden of responsibility heavier than ever. He knew he couldn't face this alone. He needed a team, individuals with diverse skillsets and expertise, people who could navigate the treacherous labyrinth of this vast criminal organization. He needed someone with Jason

Reen's skills, though acquiring such a person's help felt both morally complex and incredibly dangerous. He had to tread carefully, weighing the ethical implications against the dire need to bring down this criminal empire before it could inflict any more damage.

The rain continued to fall outside, a steady rhythm against the windowpane. The city lights blurred through the misty glass, a vibrant chaos juxtaposed against the darkness of the conspiracy that loomed over him. The victory over Gomin Guill was just the beginning; a small dent in a much larger problem. The echoes of the past, the whispers of the conspiracy, were now a deafening roar, pushing him forward into a fight that threatened to consume him completely. The fight was far from over; it had only just begun. The unresolved issues were not just clues, they were invitations to a much deeper, more perilous game, one that would test his limits, his resolve, and his very soul. He had a choice to make: continue his investigation, risking everything, or walk away and let the shadows claim another victory. He knew, deep down, there was only one path he could choose. The hunt was far from over.

....

The diner's fluorescent lights hummed a discordant tune to the drumming rain outside. Jake pushed his coffee cup away, the bitter liquid doing little to soothe the churning anxiety in his stomach. Gomin Guill was dead, a fact that should have brought a sense of closure, but instead, it felt like the opening of a chasm. The thoroughly documented confession, the hidden accounts, the coded messages – all pointed to a vast network of corruption that stretched far beyond Guill's immediate circle. It was a sprawling hydra, each severed head replaced by two more.

He ran a hand through his already disheveled hair, the fatigue gnawing at him. The initial euphoria of success had evaporated, leaving behind a bitter residue of dread. Jason Reen, the enigmatic assassin, had vanished without a trace, leaving behind only the chilling efficiency of his work and the unsettling weight of his revelations. Jake had promised him anonymity, a promise he intended to keep, even though the temptation to use Reen as a key to unlock further secrets was almost unbearable.

The evidence, compiled thoroughly over weeks of relentless work, pointed to a network operating across continents, a shadow government pulling the strings of global finance, politics, and even seemingly mundane industries. Guill was a pawn, a highly visible piece in a far grander game. The implications were staggering, threatening to destabilize governments and unravel the fabric of society. Jake knew he was treading on dangerous ground, but the path he'd chosen wasn't one from which he could easily retreat. This wasn't just a story anymore; it was a fight for survival.

The police, initially hesitant, were now reluctantly cooperating. The sheer weight of the evidence, the thoroughly documented financial transactions and clandestine meetings, forced them to acknowledge the enormity of the conspiracy. But even with their backing, Jake felt a deep sense of isolation. He knew the true scale of the organization, the resources at its disposal, and the ruthlessness with which it operated. He was a single reporter, armed with nothing but a notepad, a recorder, and an unshakeable sense of conviction, facing a hydra with seemingly limitless reach.

Days bled into nights as Jake immersed himself in his work. He spent hours poring over financial records, deciphering coded messages, and cross-referencing information from multiple sources. His apartment, once a haven of comfortable solitude, had transformed into a chaotic command center, overflowing with documents, maps, and half-empty coffee cups. Sleep became a luxury he rarely afforded himself, fueled instead by adrenaline and black coffee.

His editor, initially supportive, now seemed to be growing increasingly apprehensive. The story was bigger than they had ever anticipated, potentially opening a Pandora's Box that could consume them all. He felt their concern, the subtle pressure to back down, to let the story fade into the background, but the thought was unacceptable. The lives affected by this organization, the corruption it fueled, demanded his attention, his relentless pursuit of the truth.

He had established a secure, encrypted communication channel with a select group of trusted journalists across the globe. The initial leaks regarding Guill's operation, once cautiously released, now flowed into a broader investigation, thoroughly cross-checked and vetted. Each piece of information, however small, contributed to a slowly forming mosaic revealing the sinister structure of the organization.

One night, a chilling realization dawned on Jake: He wasn't just investigating a crime; he was embroiled in a fight for his life. An anonymous package arrived at his doorstep, a simple black box containing a single bullet. The message was clear. They knew. They were watching.

He contacted his old contacts from his investigative journalism days, individuals who understood the dark underbelly of the world he was now navigating. They were wary, hesitant, understanding the potential risks involved. But they agreed to help, each offering a sliver of assistance, a contact, or a lead, knowing this wasn't just about one story, but about a much larger battle against a formidable enemy.

The investigation took him from the dimly lit back alleys of Bangkok to the opulent penthouses of Monaco, from the bustling markets of Marrakech to the quiet, snow-covered mountains of Switzerland. Each location held a piece of the puzzle, a whisper of the vast network that operated in the shadows. He saw firsthand the brutality of the organization, the callous disregard for human life, and the pervasive reach of its tentacles.

The whispers turned into shouts. His phone buzzed constantly with cryptic messages and anonymous tips. He felt a constant pressure on his shoulders, the weight of responsibility for the truth he was uncovering. He was walking a tightrope, every step precarious, every decision laden with the potential for devastating consequences.

As the investigation deepened, the risks grew exponentially. He was shadowed, followed, watched. He learned to recognize the signs, the subtle clues, the unsettling feeling of being watched. He became a phantom himself, disappearing into the shadows, moving from safe house to safe house, always one step ahead of his pursuers.

The threat was real, palpable. He felt the icy breath of the organization on his neck, the chilling certainty of their unwavering pursuit. But the fear, while ever-present, never completely paralyzed him. It fueled him, sharpened his senses, honed his instincts.

The final piece of the puzzle came unexpectedly, a seemingly insignificant detail discovered during a routine check of Guill's offshore accounts. A hidden code, a series of seemingly random numbers, linked to a defunct satellite communication network. It was a backdoor, a hidden channel through which the organization communicated its most sensitive information. The discovery was a turning point. He now had access to their inner sanctum.

Jake knew what he had to do. He had to expose them. He had to dismantle their network. The victory over Guill was just the beginning. The echoes of the past had become a deafening roar, pushing him forward into a battle he knew he might not survive. But he would fight. He had to. The fight for the truth was a fight for survival, a fight he was determined to win, even if it cost him everything. The rain continued to fall outside, a constant, relentless rhythm, mirroring the relentless pursuit of justice that lay ahead. The hunt was far from over. It had just begun.

....

The diner's stale air hung heavy with the scent of burnt coffee and unspoken anxieties. Jake ran a hand through his already disheveled hair, the weight of the past few weeks pressing down on him like a physical burden. Gomin Guill's death hadn't brought the expected relief; instead, it had unleashed a torrent of unsettling questions, a deluge of information that threatened to drown him. He stared out at the rain-slicked street, the city lights blurring into a hazy, indistinct tapestry. The city, usually a vibrant pulse of life, felt suffocating, a concrete labyrinth concealing untold secrets.

He’d spent the last few days poring over the documents, the confessions, the coded messages – pieces of a puzzle that refused to fit together neatly. Guill had been a pawn, a powerful one, but ultimately a pawn nonetheless. The true architects of this vast criminal empire remained shrouded in shadow, their identities as elusive as the whispers that snaked through the city's underbelly. He had a mountain of evidence, a mountain that could bury him under its weight if he wasn't careful.

His phone buzzed, the jarring sound cutting through his thoughts. It was his editor, Sarah. "Jake, are you still alive? The story on Guill has blown up. We're getting calls from everywhere. The mayor's office, the FBI… hell, even some congressman is calling for an investigation."

Jake felt a surge of adrenaline, a dangerous cocktail of fear and exhilaration. This was it. The story was breaking, and he was at the heart of it. But he also felt a chilling premonition, a sense of impending danger that clung to him like a shroud.

“Sarah, this is bigger than Guill. Much bigger. I need time, I need resources… I need… protection.” His voice trembled slightly, the fear finally breaching the wall of composure he'd painstakingly built.

"Protection? Jake, what the hell is going on? You're not making any sense." Her voice, usually sharp and efficient, held a note of genuine concern. "Are you okay?"

He hesitated. He couldn't tell her everything, not yet. Not until he had a clearer picture of the enemy he was facing. "I'm fine, Sarah. Just… overwhelmed. I need to dig deeper, follow the leads. I'll call you back." He hung up, the unspoken fear hanging heavy in the air.

The next few weeks became a blur of late nights, clandestine meetings, and anonymous tips. He delved deeper into the murky world of offshore accounts, shell corporations, and coded messages, following a trail that led him from the opulent penthouses of Manhattan to the sun-drenched villas of the French Riviera and the bustling markets of Hong Kong. He worked with a small, trusted team – seasoned investigators he'd met during his years in investigative journalism, individuals known for their discretion and unwavering commitment to the truth.

His days were spent poring over financial records, interviewing informants, and analyzing encrypted communications, the strain etched deep into his face. Nights were punctuated by the gnawing fear that he was being watched, followed, that the shadows held more than just secrets. He learned to trust his instincts, a sixth sense honed by years of sniffing out corruption. He slept with one eye open, the faintest sounds triggering a surge of adrenaline.

He uncovered a web of connections so vast and intricate that it left him breathless. Guill had been merely a lieutenant in an organization that spanned continents, a network so powerful it had infiltrated governments, banks, and multinational corporations. The organization, he discovered, was not driven by greed alone, but by a chillingly pragmatic ideology – a vision of a new world order, shaped in the shadows, ruled by an elite few.

His investigation led him to the name Jassa Thorne – a name whispered with reverence and fear in the darkest corners of the underworld. Thorne was the phantom puppet master, pulling strings from the shadows, his identity carefully hidden behind a veil of secrecy. Jake felt a chill run down his spine. He was now playing in a league beyond anything he'd ever imagined.

He knew the risks. He was walking a tightrope, one wrong step sending him into the abyss. The weight of his responsibility was crushing, the constant threat of death a shadow that never left his side. But he pressed on, driven by a fierce sense of justice, a burning desire to expose the truth, no matter the cost. He had to bring Thorne down, dismantle his empire, and expose the rot that had infected the heart of society.

He received cryptic messages, veiled threats, and anonymous warnings. He saw glimpses of Thorne's influence everywhere, a subtle but pervasive presence that sent shivers down his spine. He was a ghost, a phantom, but his influence was undeniable. Jake knew he was getting closer, the air growing thick with tension. The hunt was becoming increasingly dangerous, a deadly game of cat and mouse where the stakes were life and death.

The closer he got to Thorne, the more violent the attacks became. One night, he found his apartment ransacked, his research scattered, the air thick with the scent of fear. He found a single black rose on his desk, a chilling symbol of impending doom. He realized his life was in mortal danger, and the fight for survival was no longer a metaphor. He was in a real-life thriller where the lines between fiction and reality had blurred. He needed to adapt or perish.

His team was becoming increasingly worried, urging him to stop, to back down. But Jake couldn't. He was too close to the truth, too invested in exposing the conspiracy that threatened the very fabric of society. He had become obsessed, driven by a primal need to uncover the truth and bring Thorne down, even if it meant sacrificing everything that he held dear.

The pressure was immense. He started experiencing sleepless nights, haunted by vivid nightmares of betrayal and death. The line between his professional life and personal life had completely disappeared. He was constantly looking over his shoulder, his senses hyper-alert to any hint of danger. The thrill of the chase had morphed into a chilling fight for survival.

He knew he needed to change his tactics. He couldn’t operate in the open anymore. He had to become as elusive as Thorne, as invisible as the shadows he inhabited. He moved to a safe house, a secluded location known only to a select few. He adopted new identities, using encrypted communications and carefully crafted aliases. He became a ghost, blending into the shadows himself.

Jake's future was a vast unknown, a labyrinthine path fraught with peril. He was battling an enemy that was as formidable as it was elusive. But he had the truth on his side, and that was a weapon more powerful than any arsenal of weapons or money. His commitment remained unwavering, fueled by a relentless sense of justice and the burning desire to expose the truth, regardless of the price. The fight was far from over, but Jake was ready, prepared to risk everything in the pursuit of justice, his own life hanging precariously in the balance. The echoes of the past had transformed into a relentless roar, pushing him forward, further into the heart of darkness, a path only a fearless truth-seeker would dare to tread.

....

The rain had stopped, but the city still felt damp, mirroring the unease that clung to Jake like a second skin. He pushed away from the diner booth, the cheap plastic squeaking a protest against his abrupt departure. Gomin Guill was dead, but the silence that followed his demise felt far more ominous than any gunshot. The files – a chaotic jumble of cryptic messages, coded transactions, and whispered names – were a testament to the sprawling network Guill had commanded, a network that seemed to reach into every corner of the globe. He had taken down a kingpin, only to find himself staring into the heart of an empire.

The information Jason Reen had provided, pieced together with Jake's own meticulous investigations, revealed a web of deceit that extended far beyond Gomin's immediate circle. It painted a picture of a syndicate operating on a scale that dwarfed anything Jake had ever imagined, a global entity with tentacles wrapped around finance, politics, and even seemingly legitimate businesses. The sheer audacity of their operation was breathtaking, their reach unnerving. They were like a hydra, severing one head only to see two more spring up in its place.

Jake knew he couldn't fight this alone. His small radio station, with its limited resources and staff, was no match for a global criminal network. He needed allies, people who possessed the expertise and the courage to face such a formidable adversary. He thought of Isabella Rossi, the sharp, determined investigator he'd met briefly during his initial inquiries into Gomin Guill. She had a reputation for fearlessness, an almost reckless disregard for her own safety. Her network of contacts, particularly within law enforcement agencies, would be invaluable.

The following morning, Jake found Isabella in her cramped, cluttered office, surrounded by stacks of files and overflowing ashtrays. She was a whirlwind of controlled energy, her fingers flying across the keyboard as she sifted through data. She looked up, her eyes – dark and intense – meeting his with a curious mixture of surprise and suspicion.

"Harroll," she said, her voice a low, husky whisper. "I didn't expect to see you again, especially not so soon. I assumed you'd be celebrating Guill's demise." There was a hint of something else in her tone, a subtle undercurrent of warning.

Jake explained his findings, laying out the evidence he had painstakingly gathered. He showed her the encrypted messages, the financial records, the list of names – a who's who of seemingly respectable individuals, their names carefully scrubbed of any obvious criminal association. Isabella listened intently, her expression shifting from skepticism to a chilling understanding as Jake spoke.

"It's bigger than Guill," she finally stated, her voice devoid of emotion. "Much bigger. This goes right to the top. People with considerable influence, people who are very good at covering their tracks." She took a long drag from her cigarette, the smoke curling around her face like a shroud.

"I need your help," Jake said, his voice barely above a whisper. "I can't do this alone."

Isabella didn’t hesitate. "I suspected as much," she replied, her eyes gleaming with a mixture of anticipation and grim determination. "But this isn't a simple investigation, Harroll. This is a war, and we're fighting against an enemy that plays by its own rules. Are you prepared for that?"

The following weeks were a blur of activity. Jake and Isabella worked tirelessly, piecing together the fragmented clues, chasing shadows and following phantom leads. They infiltrated clandestine meetings, deciphered coded messages, and navigated a treacherous world of betrayals and double-crosses. They uncovered a complex network of offshore accounts, shell corporations, and elaborate money-laundering schemes that extended across continents. The more they dug, the more they realized the magnitude of the conspiracy. The organization wasn't just a criminal syndicate; it was a parasitic entity, feeding on the global economic system, its tentacles wrapped around everything from international trade to political influence.

Their investigation led them to a series of dimly lit backrooms, clandestine meetings in high-end hotels, and dangerous encounters in forgotten corners of the city. Isabella's contacts proved invaluable, providing them with access to sensitive information and discreet warnings. But the risks were immense. They were constantly shadowed, their phones tapped, their every move watched. The sense of impending danger was a palpable presence, a constant weight in the pit of their stomachs.

One evening, while tracking a shipment of illicit goods through a sprawling port city, they found themselves cornered in a dark alleyway, facing a group of heavily armed men. The air crackled with tension. Isabella, ever the pragmatist, reacted swiftly. She had a firearm; Jake didn't. The fight was brutal, swift, and desperate. But they managed to escape, narrowly avoiding capture, leaving behind a trail of broken glass and scattered weapons. They were fortunate to survive.

The near-death experience served as a stark reminder of the danger they faced. The organization wasn't just powerful; it was ruthless, and it would stop at nothing to protect its interests. Jake had initially believed that Gomin Guill's death would bring some semblance of closure, a chance to move on with his life. Instead, it had opened a Pandora's Box, unleashing a torrent of information that implicated powerful figures in a global conspiracy that extended far beyond the reach of any single law enforcement agency.

Their investigation led them to a hidden server farm located deep beneath the city, a fortress of data and encrypted communications. Accessing the servers required a sophisticated level of hacking expertise, beyond anything Jake possessed. Fortunately, Isabella had a contact - a brilliant, eccentric hacker named Miles Kendrick - who agreed to assist them. Miles was a ghost, a digital phantom, capable of navigating the darkest corners of the internet with ease. He worked tirelessly, hacking through layer after layer of encryption, circumventing firewalls and evading detection. He gained access to the server, allowing Jake and Isabella to download terabytes of data.

The information they obtained was staggering. It detailed years of criminal activity, a litany of crimes that ranged from money laundering and tax evasion to arms trafficking and murder. It exposed a network of politicians, businessmen, and even law enforcement officials who were complicit in the organization's activities. It was a devastating revelation, a damning indictment of corruption on a grand scale.

The data provided them with enough evidence to bring down the entire organization, to expose the criminals and their accomplices, to dismantle the global network of corruption they had carefully constructed. But exposing them would mean putting their own lives, and the lives of others, in grave danger.

Jake and Isabella knew they were on the cusp of something huge, something that could change the world, but also something that could cost them everything. The future was uncertain, a treacherous path fraught with peril. They knew the fight was far from over, and the stakes were higher than ever before. Yet, they were ready, ready to expose the truth, no matter the cost. A new era was beginning, an era of reckoning and justice, an era where the shadows would finally be exposed. The echoes of the past were still ringing, but now, they were being joined by the sound of a rising tide, a tide of truth threatening to wash away the old order and usher in a new dawn. The fight was on, and this time, they were prepared.

Acknowledgments

This book wouldn't exist without the tireless support of many individuals. First and foremost, my gratitude goes to my editors, whose keen eyes and insightful suggestions shaped the narrative and polished the prose. Their patience and expertise were invaluable throughout the writing process. I also owe a debt of thanks to everyone involved for their unwavering belief in this project and their guidance in navigating the publishing world. My appreciation extends to the countless researchers and journalists who have dedicated their careers to uncovering the truth about organized crime; their work provided the foundation for the realistic portrayal of this dangerous world. Finally, a heartfelt thank you to my family and friends for their unwavering support and understanding during the long hours spent crafting this story. Their patience and encouragement kept me going.

Glossary

This glossary defines key terms and phrases used throughout the book, primarily relating to the world of organized crime and assassination:

Ghost: A highly skilled assassin who leaves no trace.

Clean Sweep: A successful assassination with no witnesses or evidence.

Burn Notice: A warning that an operative is compromised.

Deep Cover: Operating undercover for an extended period, often assuming a false identity.

Sleeper Agent: An operative who remains inactive until activated.

Black Site: A clandestine detention facility operated outside of the law.

Cutout: An intermediary used to maintain plausible deniability.

Ghosting: The act of disappearing without a trace.

M.O. (Modus Operandi): A criminal's characteristic method of operation.

References

While this novel is a work of fiction, its realistic portrayal of organized crime draws upon extensive research and a deep understanding of the subject matter. While specific references to real-world cases are avoided to protect the integrity of the narrative, I acknowledge the invaluable contribution of them.

Author Biography

Willie S. is an experimental thriller writer. He spent years gaining knowledge in the complexities of the criminal underworld and the challenges faced by those who investigate it. Much experience and learning provided the groundwork for the realistic and gripping narratives found in Willie S.' works. He is further demonstrating his skill in crafting suspenseful and engaging thrillers. He continues to pursue their passion for uncovering truth and bringing compelling stories to life.

www.ingramcontent.com/pod-product-compliance
Lightning Source LLC
Chambersburg PA
CBHW060633310726
48982CB00003B/763
* 9 7 9 8 9 9 4 0 7 0 5 0 5 *